The Man Who Fell to Earth

M. R. PRITCHARD

FIRST EDITION   JUNE 2019

NEW YORK

The Man Who Fell to Earth is a work of fiction. Names, characters, places, and incidents either are the product of the author's imagination or are used fictitiously. Any resemblance to actual persons, living or dead, events, or locales is entirely coincidental.

Copyright © 2019 M. R. Pritchard

All rights reserved. No part of this book may be reproduced or transmitted in any form or by any means whatsoever without express written permission from the author, except in the case of brief quotations embodied in critical articles and reviews. Please refer all pertinent questions to the publisher.

ISBN: 9781099599866

Imprint: Independently published

First Edition

June 2019

Pritchard Publishing

Edited by Kristy Ellsworth

Cover by M. R. Pritchard

Printed and bound in the U.S.A.

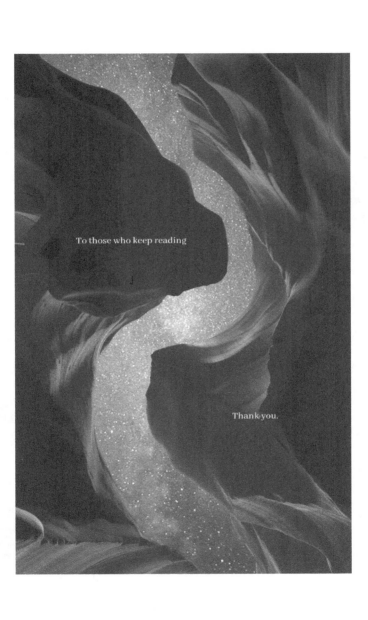

To those who keep reading

Thank you.

CHAPTER ONE

Romeo

I wish I had known the planet was going to burn before I moved to the Carolinas. I'm not sure if it would have made a difference—the south is an experience you can't miss before you die. I'd rather have been down here for the start of it all now that the flames are licking the sky, for the same reason that I doubt newcomers to hell pay much attention to the scenery when their whole person is burning. I figure my experience might have been similar if I'd decided to wait any longer. I wouldn't have been able to appreciate this place before the Heat Wave got out of control. I wouldn't have been able to experience the sweet roil of the heat as it took over. I got to watch humanity blister and weep.

The flash of bright headlights interrupts my stargazing.

"You shouldn't be out this late, Romeo," Duke warns. He's the county Sheriff and still feels the need to keep those of us who are left in check. "Beasts are on the loose."

"I couldn't sleep." I pat my pockets, searching for a half-empty pack of cigarettes. It's a habit that's been hard to break.

Duke notices because he used to do the same thing when he was looking for his smokes. "Thought you quit?"

"I did. Not that I wanted to." I find a piece of gum in my pocket and pop it in my mouth.

"The markets are cleared out of any tobacco products, have been for months." There's a look in his eye, like he might kill for one last drag on a cancer-stick.

I shrug, not wanting to tell him about my stash. There's too much hidden; food, water, booze, and an old humidor of Cuban cigars I came across while searching the Sullivan house down the road. If Duke or the few neighbors I've got left find out, they'll raid my stash and then I'll have to live out the last of my years boiling in the heat without.

Duke gets out of his truck and walks closer. "Sheila down the street killed her husband yesterday." He rubs the back of his neck.

"Took her long enough," I reply.

"I reckon." He rests a hand on the hilt of his pistol. "She took the kids too. I caught her burying them in shallow graves in her backyard."

"Shit." Ben had been smacking around Sheila and the kids for years, since before I moved down here. "What did you do with her?" I ask.

"Let her go. What am I going to do?" Duke asks. "Prisons are nothing more than death camps. And there's barely anyone left to run 'em." He motions to the sky. "God will have to punish her. I can't do nothing else for these people."

"Hm." I never thought of Duke as the giving up type.

The stars steal my attention again.

I might have moved sooner if anyone had mentioned that the stars look different. The moon seems larger, clearer. The shooting stars more frequent. Mercury and Venus are clearer in the sky, twinkling and burning bright. They remind me of her. Dancing, coated in glitter, and glimmering in the dim light with hands in her hair as though it were alive, a thousand snakes swaying with the beat. She didn't turn me to stone—no, she turned me alive. She was mesmerizing; soft and firm and warm.

"I think it's about time the missus and me hit the road. This heat, the violence. Getting to be too much to handle." Sweat trickles down the side of his face.

I re-focus and consider talking him out of it. Every town needs a sheriff, even if we're down to every third house being inhabited. "Where will you go?" I ask.

"The Missus wants to head to Ely, Minnesota. She camped there once when she was a kid, has some friends and family that might still be alive. She thinks the heat won't be so bad."

I nod. If Duke leaves town that's one less person to side with. I'm not his deputy but we're the few who haven't gone completely batshit crazy since the Heat Wave started.

"You should come with us," Duke adds. "It's not good for a man like you to go lone wolf during these times. If violence doesn't strike you, loneliness will. And sometimes that's worse."

"Naw. Think I'm just fine staying here. Solitude never bothered me."

You're never really alone on a southern night. The chirping and buzzing of all those tiny creatures that came alive in the evening cool are a calming nocturnal masterpiece to the untrained northern ear. After a few months down here I realized the sweet chirp and gentle purrs were not the peepers or the crickets, they were the rusty hum of seventeen air conditioning units running full bore in the summer night heat. They echo between the rows of townhouses now, shuddering and whirring under the strain of the hundred-degree temperatures.

"This place will be flooded soon," Duke warns, eyeing the retention pond across the road. "The ocean is rising. And that strange, glowing stuff is spreading. The missus found it growing on a downed tree." Duke shivers, focusing on the row of white oak in front of us. "Could be there right now, could be taking over the world. Who knows? I don't want to stick around the great state of Carolina just to be eaten by glowing slime."

On cue, clouds block out the moon. There are specks of glowing green and blue clustered in the vee of the tree trunk where the dew has collected.

"Jesus," Duke whispers.

"It's not slime," I say.

"What?"

"It's just bioluminescent algae," I correct him. "It's harmless."

Duke grumbles. "That's what you think." He starts backing toward his truck. "You should come with us."

I spread my arms. "And leave all this? Turn my back on the romance of the south?" I shake my head. "I'm fine here." I wave him away.

"You think," Duke warns. "You think you're fine. Take a walk on the beach at midnight and you might think otherwise." He pulls his pistol from its holster and shoots the crook of the tree. Glowing bits and bark scatter to the air. "Me and the missus leave in three days. I'll swing by in the morning. Reckon you might change your mind by then." He climbs in his truck. Duke shifts in reverse and backs down the street before turning and heading toward the main road. "Make sure you steer clear of Sheila," he shouts out the window.

I nod. The heat has tainted Sheila. The rage has a hold of her and I'd rather shoot her than touch her, knowing what she did.

I'm guessing it's something about the heat that makes creatures violent. Simple kinetic theory I learned in junior college physics. Molecules move faster, vibrating in the heat, building tension until it can no longer be contained. We humans are nothing but molecules, held together with a simple layer of epidermis that can only contain the violence for so long. The south has been a good example of the chaos heat brings. Alligators, raptors, poisonous snakes, and rednecks cluster at the equator. All violent. All unable to quell the motion of the molecules and atoms packed inside a thin sausage casing, especially when the summer heat turns unbearable. It's always unbearable now.

But the south learned to deal with the heat for centuries. So did Ecuador, Brazil, Kenya, and the Republic of the Congo. Maybe they didn't handle it perfectly, but the thing is the equatorial lands were accustomed to the heat, violence, and death. The real trouble came when the Heat Wave shifted.

My old physics professor would be proud to hear me put those thoughts together. Not that I'll ever be able to share them with him, he's probably dead by now.

I pull a harmonica from my pocket. It's my first SWAN harmonica and has survived this heat. I was afraid the plastic body would warp and the brass reed would bend, but it seems to be holding up. I press it to my lips and release a steady purr. The peepers silence but the A/C units keep up their constant hum.

In the distance there is a scream, followed by the quick *pop pop pop* of rapid gunfire.

People are killing each other, again.

CHAPTER TWO

Nova

I stop at a gas station. It's a typical mountain rest area with chipped paint, peeling window stickers, and a few shingles missing. It doesn't exactly resemble a place where people get murdered but you can't be too sure these days. There's pavement that's swept clean and the "Belle's Diner" sign is still blinking, which gives the illusion that it's been kept up and gives me hope that I might find something cold to drink inside.

I park in the closest parking spot to the door. I sit in the cool air coming from the vents for an extra minute, preparing myself for the heat outside. It doesn't matter that it's been like this for over a year, nothing prepares you for that blast of burning air. Some say it's like stepping into Hell, and since I've already been to Hell and back I guess it's just like stepping into a puddle of old memories.

I doubt there will be air conditioning inside since the electricity is spotty around the Blue Ridge. I've been told the big cities have people determined to continue on with life as it once was. They have air conditioning, running water, medical facilities, and spotty cell service.

The rumor through the mountains is that there's a hospital in Charlotte still up and running. I've got a two-day travel plan, enough gas to make it there and the roads seem mostly clear. I've been to a few places with restaurants open and serving food. They took my cash with the hopes that the government can fix this mess and they'll enter the rat race once again. Other places took one look at me and gave the food for free. Pity pays. You don't see many women in my condition these days. At least none that have lasted this long. I guess I'm sort of an enigma now.

Every now and then, I have to stop in a dead town at an abandoned highway restaurant—worse than this—with the hope that they will have something unexpired on their shelves and no bodies lining their walls. I can't avoid it, since I've become an eating machine and all.

I turn the car off, grab my bag, and get out. There is a slight breeze coming through the valley. It's enough to disturb my hair, but it's just as hot as the sun-licked air. There is nothing refreshing about this breeze, nothing more than dragon's breath. Perspiration is instant. I lock the doors on my borrowed Chevy before heading inside.

"Hello?" I ask as I open the door. A tinny chime sounds. Good, the electricity is still on. "Hello?" I shout again. "Is there anyone here?"

Silence answers back.

It's hard to ignore the shiver of apprehension that slides up my spine, a sensation I've experienced more times than not since leaving the comforts of my rental. I used to watch all of those apocalyptic movies before the heat came; there's always danger lurking in the shadows, especially in empty stores that haven't been pillaged. But no one survives without facing those fears. So here I am.

I make my way to the eat-in counter.

Since there's electricity, I pull my charging cords from my bag and plug my iPhone in. Who knows when I'll have electricity again, and if I'm lucky I might get cell service once I'm closer to Charlotte.

I check the small refrigerators under the counter only to find expired milk and cottage cheese. I find a box of crackers with the packs still sealed and a variety of canned goods that I move to the counter. There's tomato paste, mustard, a half-gallon can of liquid cheese–it's tempting, if only I had some chips.

"Are ye alone, miss?" a man's voice with an odd, nearly Scottish accent asks.

I stop searching and stand, ready to fight. "What's it to you?" I never heard the door open and curse myself for not moving on when I felt that shiver of apprehension earlier. The last thing I need is a gunfight or a fistfight or a pepper spray fight — that's more my style.

He holds his hands up. "I don't mean trouble. I just want to offer ye assistance."

"Sure you do." I pick up a can of black beans, ready to pitch it at his head and run.

"I mean no harm. I promise." He smiles, showing me his hands in surrender and turning in a circle.

"I see a gun and knives." They're tucked in his belt.

"Aye, but those are not for you. They're for me." He thumbs toward the door. "For the wild yonder."

"The wild yonder?" I ask. Who talks like that on the east coast?

"Aye." He takes two steps closer. "I have concerns over the safety of this road."

A sea of tables and chairs separate us. Those will slow him down if he tries to attack. I could make it out the back door and around to my car with time to escape. He's twice my size and I'm sure I'd move faster. Even with this swollen belly.

"Didn't mean to scare ye." He sets his bag down on a nearby chair. "I was hoping for some company. It's hard to come by these days."

"It sure is," I agree as I try to figure out what to do. I knew traveling alone would be dangerous but there was no one else to come with me. And I didn't come prepared with weapons to defend myself. I was foolishly hoping I'd avoid a situation like this.

"Saw yer car out front. Haven't seen many people driving these days." He sweeps his arm over a table, clearing it of spilled salt and pepper.

"Well, it's faster than traveling on two feet." I point out the window where my car is parked. "Thankfully my neighbor left that with a full tank."

"Nice of them. Does it blow cold air?"

"Yup." I tap my fingers on the counter. "It's a nice escape from this sweltering heat."

He nods. "Reckon it is."

We no longer live in a time in which trusting strangers is customary. Still, there is something different about this guy. He has a calming vibe and I've learned to trust vibes; it's gotten me out a few situations before the shit hit the fan. I'd say in the current state of affairs with the heat blasting humanity into the dumpster, my vibe radar is my best commodity. Maybe even my superpower.

I search for a can opener on the shelves below the counter. After finding one, I grab two bowls and two spoons from the drying rack along the back wall.

"Are you hungry?" I ask.

"Aye, couldn't hurt to sit for a bit and eat." He sits at the table he cleared, with his back to the door. Then he starts digging around in his backpack.

"You're not pulling out a gun or anything, are you?" I ask.

He goes stiff, then chuckles. "Thought ye were looking for food."

I hold up the can. "I found some. It's not Chipotle, but it will do."

I drain the beans into a dry sink and then pour half in to each bowl and stick them in the microwave for a few seconds. I add some salt, some pepper, and a little cilantro. I walk around the counter and toward the table he's sitting at.

His face suddenly twists with concern when he gets a good look at me.

"What?" I ask. "Never seen a pregnant lady before?"

He pulls a bag of biscuits out of his backpack. "Aye, seen a few, but they looked different."

I sit across from him and slide a bowl his way. "How different?"

He slides a biscuit in my direction. "Well, for starters, most didn't have a belly quite that big."

"Are you calling me fat?" I joke. "Most doctors would say I'm seriously undernourished."

"Aye, sure they might. I'm just saying they didn't seem to be as far along." He takes a bite of his biscuit, chewing thoughtfully.

He's probably right; no one of good judgment would let themselves get knocked up with things like they are.

I take a bite of the beans, thankful that they're not rotten or sprouting mold. "Are you saying pregnancy looks good on me?" I talk around my mouthful of food in a quite unladylike manner. My mother would swat me if she were still alive to see it.

"Aye. Guess I am." He smiles and the sense of calm he emits intensifies.

"What's your name, sir?" I ask, leaning back in my chair to make room for my belly.

"Abraham, miss." He wipes his hands on his pant legs before holding one across the table to shake.

I lean forward. "Nice to meet you Abraham, my name's Nova."

We shake.

There is something about his hand; maybe it's the slightly foreign feeling of his smooth skin. Men should have calluses on their hands, they should be rough. And the way he smiles. There is something off, but something completely...noble. It's confusing. Maybe it's the hormones or low blood sugar?

"You should have a biscuit." He slides two my way.

"Are they better than the beans?" I ask as I take one and break it.

He shrugs as he eats. "Some say they're good. They'll fill you up."

I take a bite. The biscuit is chewy and dense, slightly sweet with something refreshing that tastes like mint. "Did you make these?" I ask. "They're good."

"Oh no, I'm not much of a cook. My sisters make them, they give them to me for my travels." He pushes his chair back and crosses his legs at the ankle, stretching out. The guy is tall and well-built. During a time when humanity is lacking fresh food and water, he looks well fed and cared for, even if his clothing is worn and strange.

"Sisters?" I ask. "Are any of them a doctor? I could use a doctor soon." I rub my stomach.

The child in my belly kicks. Abraham notices and can't stop looking.

I giggle. "Jeez, you really haven't seen a full pregnant woman before. Have you ever felt a baby kick?"

He rubs a hand over his face, strangely embarrassed. "I guess not. No." He reaches out. "Could I?"

I push my chair away from the table and stand. "Sorry, buddy, not today." I bring our empty bowls to the sink and set them down, then I find my own backpack and fill it with as much food as I can carry. Canned beans, crackers—I'm tempted by the large can of cheese but I know the nutritional value is low and I really have nothing fried to dip in it. Instead, I slide a medium-sized steak knife into my pocket.

"Where are you headed?" Abraham asks as he stands.

I unplug my phone and coil the charging cable. "Charlotte. I have to keep moving to a bigger city, a place that still has electricity and maybe even a hospital. These little towns out here are pretty bare. Although, I feel safer out here and alone, away from the bustle of the city. But this baby is going to come soon and I prefer not to deliver it myself."

Abraham secures his backpack, which now that I get a good look at, is the strangest backpack I've ever seen; the straps crisscross across his chest and the fabric resembles suede. It was definitely made for comfort and travel, not necessarily style.

"Shouldn't you head for the mountains? A place that's safer?" he asks. "It's not as hot there."

"Nope." I sling my bag across my shoulders and head for the door. "I've been playing it safe for a while now. It's time to search out a real hospital before this belly pops and I have to cut the umbilical cord with my own teeth." I make a gagging noise. "I just can't do that. I need a professional."

Abraham follows as I push open the door. Heat greets me with a sour note. I wasn't fond of snow, but I'd kill for a day with a temperature of less than eighty degrees.

"What if I told you there was a safe place in the mountains where we could help you?" Abraham asks. "An entire city that's safe. The safest place you've ever been in your life."

I stop and turn. "Look, Abraham, you seem like a nice guy and all, but I'm not about to follow you to some 'safe place' in the mountains. I've been out past the Blue Ridge, I've seen the towns and settlements and god-fearing crazy bible groups out there. I'm headed to

Charlotte, where there's normal people, educated people, *real* doctors. Civilization."

"Oh, aye, see what you're saying there." He follows me as I start to walk. "I'd be scared too, not knowing."

I stop at my car. "You'd be scared too, buddy? Last I checked you got a dick swinging between your legs and a belt loop full of weapons, not a baby sitting in your belly kicking your bladder every ten minutes and slowing you down. You're some big dude who looks like he can take a few punches. Not me. I'm better off headed for Charlotte. That's the way the world works nowadays."

Abraham pales, at a loss for words. Sometimes I do that to people. I think I might have been a bit out of line but these days I lack patience.

"You seem like a nice girl." Abraham swallows hard.

"I think I am a nice girl. If I wasn't in this position I'd probably be a whole lot nicer," I reply.

There's silence between us for a moment.

"I guess this is goodbye then." I reach for my door handle. This could be the last decent person left on earth and in all of a few minutes I've insulted him and I'm ready to run off.

"Aye, guess so." He rubs a hand across his face like he's thinking of something, or troubled or nervous.

"It was nice meeting you, Abraham. Thanks for the biscuit."

"One moment." He removes his pack and pulls out the bag of biscuits. "Take these." He holds the bag out. "They're good for you. They'll keep you full for a long time." He searches his bag again. "Do you have enough water? Humans need to drink a lot of water, especially those with child."

I can't control the confused look on my face or my mouth. "Humans? Are you not human? Are we not on planet Earth, burning to death?"

"Aye—" he pauses, surprised. "Of course I'm human," he starts muttering, "just... just... just as human as you are." He shrugs and takes a deep breath.

"Why do you talk like that?" I ask.

"I talk like I talk." There's a tick in his cheek when he smiles.

"You don't talk like people around here." I take in his odd clothing again. He could be a hippie or have been raised by wolves. Who knows these days?

"Oh, aye, suppose it's the curse of learning a thousand languages."

"A thousand?" I narrow my eyes at him. "What languages? Tell me." I've never come across a person who has known ten languages, let alone a thousand.

Abraham lists off English, Spanish, Japanese, Russian, Slavic, Arabic, Dutch, French, Scottish, Malay, and more. Many I've never heard of before. Languages I didn't know existed and some I'm sure he just plain made up.

"Wow. How long did it take you to learn all of that?"

"Oh, many years. Seems the tongue of some stuck stronger." He nods. "I guess that's why I talk the way I do. My brothers and sisters used to mock me for it. I can't change it though. It's just the way I talk now. Do ye find it hard to listen to?"

"No," I say. "It's different. A bit unusual, I guess."

I glance around the parking lot and see there is no other vehicle. "How did you get here?" I ask as sweat drips down my back.

"I walked," he replies, plain as day.

"Where are you from?" I ask.

He waves his hand in the distance, motioning to the ridges to the west. "Over there."

"Uh huh." Before I toss my bag in the back seat I pull the steak knife out that I took from the restaurant.

He seems ready to jump out of his boots, the thick air tense with nervous energy. "Charlotte, you say?" He rubs the back of his neck in a motion that's slightly endearing.

"Yup." I look away. Looking away is safe when men start doing things like rubbing their necks and giving you tips on how to take care of yourself.

"Could you give me a ride?" he asks.

"Only if you're going to Charlotte." I hold up my hand to stop him. "One more question." I clear my throat and hold up the knife. "Do you plan to kill, incapacitate, or maim me?"

His two fingers touch his breastbone. "I'd never hurt ye," he promises, seriously.

"Fine then." I set the knife in the door pocket. "Get in."

He smiles. "I guess I'm going to Charlotte."

We get in the car. I start the engine and blast the air conditioner. I buckle my seatbelt and he does the same. After plugging in my iPhone, I select "Road Trip Mix" then check my mirrors.

I pull away from Belle's Diner headed for Charlotte.

I drive the Blue Ridge Parkway, taking the loopy curves slow to be safe. There are abandoned cars parked off the road, some down embankments, their paint bubbling and cracking in the heat, tires soft, rotting corpses inside.

"This road's quite empty for miles," Abraham says.

"Have you been here before?"

"Oh, aye, came from this direction before we crossed paths."

"So you're backtracking now?" I ask.

"Not far. Usually spend most of my time along these roads and along this strip of mountainside. For now."

"Why?" I find it strange that he would travel the mountainside during a time like this. I'd think the smart ones would find a safe place and food to prep for the worst. It seems like the best thing to do, especially since the government isn't doing much to quell the violence. They dispatched the National Guard to various cities to help. They said they were going to cut carbon emissions to cool the earth. If they did anything, it's not helping. It just keeps getting hotter.

"I'm searching for people to bring back," Abraham says.

"To the mountains?" I ask.

"Aye. We have everything we need, and my people are just trying to secure the human race."

Trying to secure the human race? Now I'm wondering if he's part of one of those cults.

"You still thinking of Charlotte?" He reminds me of a car salesman about to lose a sale.

"I sure am." I push play on my iPhone screen.

He pushes pause. He's brave. I can tell because no man in his right mind would dare touch the music from the shotgun seat.

"Why are you alone in this condition?" he asks, motioning to my stomach.

I could answer him in a variety of ways. I could tell him the truth, I could tell him a lie, I could tell him a bit of both. I decide to tell him nothing. "I don't like strangers rubbing on my scars. Mind your business."

"Ah, well, figured if I was sharing about myself you might share about yourself."

I push play again. "Not today, son."

What I don't tell Abraham is there was one event that caused me to be alone in this condition. That it was the fall from grace and going splat on the ground that hurt the worst. It should have been the cancer, the loss of love, or the death. But it was none of those things. It was selling everything; the car, furniture, clothes, expensive shoes, and then the house. Each time one of those trophies fell it chipped a piece of me away. At least, that's what I try to tell myself since the pain of losing John has been just too much to focus on, even nearly a year after his death. Part of me hates him for leaving me alone to deal with the world the way it is now. We could have melted into obscurity together but instead he left me here to suffer alone.

I hate myself for being shallow and missing things, but that's the way the world was. How big was your house, your car, your cell phone memory? The days of materialism ended swiftly. My head still aches from the whiplash.

My things were gone, but the electric bill was cheaper in the rental and the top floor caught a nice breeze when all the windows were open. It was nothing compared to my old house with John. No custom cupboards, no granite countertops, no snail shower tiled with blue glass. It wasn't my old house, but I still miss it. I miss the moment of rebirth; the time spent relearning who I was without him. It seems all those years I was someone else when I was with him. I was half. He was half. Now I have no choice but to try and be whole. To fill the void. It's tough learning how to do that when the world around you starts falling apart.

The rental is gone too. A second fall. This one has nothing to do with me personally, only that I'm part of it and I'm still alive. I had to leave when the building burned and the Army came to town to help. They relocated us and brought in some entertainment to raise our spirits. It worked for a few days, until the violence got worse. And then the army men with guns, who were supposed to protect us, turned crazed. My neighbor at the time helped me. And then nearly everyone was dead.

I guess it wasn't just one event that got me here, it was a multitude of them all piling up and toppling over. The void ever deeper, threatening to never be filled again. I had a therapist once who told me I should talk about the memories that bother me. I glance at Abraham; it's rude to drop all that on a stranger.

Abraham seems to know better than to pry again for the rest of the trip.

CHAPTER THREE

Romeo

The air conditioning units stopped running last night. Their gentle *chirp* and *hurr* is no more. For the first time I hear the true song of a southern night; peepers whispering and crickets singing in soft murmured cheeps. Now I can't sleep. I want to stay up listening all night long. It's not very soothing, being a bit out of harmony, but it's a reminder of life. Invigorating to say the least. My finger taps on the metal in my pocket, wanting to join nature's band for an impromptu solo. Wanting to offer my song for the night. Wanting to pull this orchestra together with an unchained melody. The problem is once I start, they will stop.

I head to the beach like the Sheriff suggested. I lose myself watching the shadows play on the live oaks dripping with moss. Up north the plants didn't drip toward the ground like they do here. Every so often I notice the glow in the canopy. Duke might have been right when he warned that it was spreading.

The shoreline is two miles closer than it used to be. Here the bioluminescent algae are everywhere. It's growing on trees, in puddles on the road, floating in the air on the backs of sand flies. It clings to the tires of my old truck when I drive into the water when the road simply ends. The beach and campgrounds are flooded.

I get out and slam the truck door closed. I step forward and the water rises to my shins. The ocean water is warm; it's always warm nowadays. The algae glow around my legs with each step. I pull the harmonica from my pocket and play the song I hold inside. The subtle vibrations cause the water to glow and in this moment I feel as though I am no longer standing on earth but in some fairytale from another planet.

For a second I think I see her in the water. Swimming, twirling and whirling, the ocean around her glowing blue with her every movement; a spectacle in the moonlight. Her long hair is shimmering, her skin pale and glowing under the moonshine. I want to slide my fingers through her hair like I did that night we were together. I want to hold her steady and close, keep her safe like I would have promised if she'd stayed. I want to keep her mine, press into her heat and lose myself all over again.

"Nova?" I step forward, the water rising to my knees. "Nova!" I shout.

A chirping responds. It's not her. It's a dolphin, a pod of them are not far off the beach, jumping above the waves and calling to one another.

Maybe Duke is right. Maybe the bioluminescent algae are taking over the world and driving everyone crazy, making them sick like the red algae blooms of the past. Or maybe it's simply a coincidence and this is nothing more than evolution. And the evolution of my time is a glowing world and the death of men.

I think I will travel to Minnesota with the Sheriff and his wife.

*

Duke returns two days later and he's driving a hybrid truck rigged with solar panels. I'm guessing he drained every last gas tank in town judging from the extra tanks strapped to the sides of the truck bed.

"Hotter than a whore's den out here," he complains as he steps out of the truck.

"Maybe we should have loaded this stuff last night," I suggest.

"Naw, couldn't. The missus was cooking up a storm, drying meat so we can eat on the go."

I notice Nancy isn't in the truck. "Are we going back to get her?" I ask.

The Sheriff mutters something as he's walking toward my front door.

I let him inside and finally show him my spoils: the last two cartons of cigarettes, cases of beer, cases of bullets, and bottles of water. The Sheriff looks like he is going to blow a gasket until I tell him we're taking it all with us.

"It's enough to get us most of the way without stopping," Duke says as he's picking through the pile. "Reckon we won't need to go searching for the unimportant stuff." He picks up a bottle of tequila. "Just like a bachelor. I remember those days."

I smile and don't tell him about the extra stash hidden in the basement. There's always the chance we don't make it out of town and I might come back here.

We start lugging the boxes to the truck. I check the windows and the locks to make sure my place is secure in the rare chance that I might return. Then I grab my duffle bag and head out.

"Ready?" Duke asks as I slide in the passenger seat.

"Yup. Ready as I'll ever be."

I still have an uneasy feeling about leaving. I never felt unsafe here and I have enough to get by. Leaving just seems like it might bring a shitload of trouble. Especially since Duke is already acting strange.

Duke starts the engine and pulls out of the driveway.

Goodbye peepers and crickets and still southern nights.

Duke takes a left, headed straight for the highway.

"What about Nancy?" I ask.

He presses his lips together.

"Sir?" I ask again. "I thought we had to go gather your wife."

I begin to notice things, like the dark stains under his fingernails and the bulging vein in his temple.

"Sheriff?" My finger hovers over the lock button of the passenger door, ready to hit unlock and jump out.

He slams the brakes. "Oh, God, Romeo. I just couldn't take it any longer. I tried but I couldn't. It was the heat, the heat I tell you. I tried so hard, but she was drying all that meat and it was a million degrees in the house. She kept talking and talking and talking. Clucking like a damn chicken. I just couldn't take it for one more second."

"You killed her?"

"Goddamn it." He slams his fists on the steering wheel. "I did. It's the worst thing I've ever done in my life but I did it. I hate myself for it. But, Romeo, I couldn't stop myself. I knew it was wrong but I couldn't stop. It was the devil in my ear, taunting and taunting and taunting. I couldn't take it any longer."

Now, I've known Duke since I was a kid. He's the closest thing to a dad I've ever had, the whole reason I moved down to these parts. I never thought he'd cave to the heat. I never thought he had it in him to kill sweet Nancy.

I know I should hate him for what he did. I should run for the hills. But in these times we need to stick together.

"Promise me, boy." Duke grips my hand and pulls his pistol out of its holster. He wraps my fingers around the grip. "Right here," he presses it to the side of his head, "you pull the trigger if I get out of control. I'd never hurt you. Known you all these years since you were a youngin', but I never thought I'd hurt the missus either." He squeezes my hand hard, rubbing knuckle against knuckle. "Promise me you'll put an end to me. Promise me you won't let me hurt another soul."

I nod, swallowing hard. "You bet."

"Promise me! Say the words." His face is sweating and twisted in torment.

"I promise I'll end you." I swallow hard. I've never killed a person in my whole life and if it comes down to it, I'm not sure I can.

"Good boy." He finally releases my hand. "Now, why don't you play us something while I drive?"

I pulled my harmonica out of my pocket and play a low soothing melody, easy on the vibrato. I don't want to up the ante in a closed cabin.

CHAPTER FOUR

Nova

There's a knock on my door.

"Dinner's ready, Nova." It's Jess, my neighbor. She checks on me often, especially on the hottest days.

"I'm not hungry," I shout, settling my chin on my hands and gazing out the window, remembering.

Charlotte was everything and nothing of what I expected. I found the hospital with the doctors, but the doors were locked and blood was smeared across the windows. My iPhone had a signal but I had no one to call. And when I thought I was in labor I dialed 9-1-1 but there was no answer. The car ran out of gas and the streets were filled with broken down, melting vehicles that were difficult to maneuver around. I had to leave the car at the third hospital I'd driven to. I nearly wished I'd taken Abraham up on his offer to go to the mountains as I walked the streets alone, the rubber soles of my boots leaving melted footprints. I can't say he didn't warn me. He practically begged me to go back with him. "It's safe there, Nova," he'd said. "Ye'll have everything ye need for the baby." I nodded along as he tried to convince me and then kicked him out of the car on the outskirts of the city. "I didn't tell ye I've been here already. There's nothing good here. Nothing waiting for ye. Please, reconsider," Abraham said. And I'd said "Goodbye." My vibe said go, so that's what I did.

"You need to eat. For the baby," Jess protests through my closed door.

On cue the little bugger kicks me in the bladder.

"You're already too thin." She twists the handle and pushes the door open. When I turn, she's standing there with her hands on her hips. "And you shouldn't leave your door unlocked."

"What does it matter? It's just us up here. No one else can get in." I turn away from the window and stand. "Who's cooking tonight?"

"Georgia," Jess replies. "She's making some kind of a pasta primavera. Oh, and we found some wine in an abandoned apartment a few floors down. Unfortunately for you."

"Why me?" I ask. "A glass of wine with dinner sounds nice, almost civilized."

Jess's mouth downturns. "You can't drink alcohol. You're pregnant."

"I can do what I want. Women drank all through most of the twentieth century." I smooth my shirt over my stomach. "It's fine." It's not like I'm drinking thalidomide.

Jess weaves her arm around mine as we walk out of the apartment together. "None of the ladies will let you. You might not have a birth plan for this little miracle but the hens of this roost do."

I swing my door closed. "This is my baby. FYI."

"Tell them that." Jess gives me a knowing smirk.

I press my lips together and hold a few swear words. I'd like to mouth off but I drop it. Without these women I'd probably be dead in the street or dead in an alley after my impending childbirth. Not every pregnant chick these days gets the direct attention of two doctors and three nurses. Before these ladies found me I was nothing more than a stray on the street; all arms and legs and belly, avoiding eye contact as the heat burned through what was left of Charlotte. I was starting to think it was stupid of me to come to Charlotte, but I followed that vibe and it didn't lead me astray for long.

The people before me trashed the city. They broke all the store windows, lit cars on fire, and killed each other and all of the cops. I was searching the busted storefronts littered with glass trying to find my next meal when I ran into Jess. She brought me here, to The Convent, as I like to call it.

There are only women in The Convent; two doctors and three nurses who spent their last days holding together the walls of the local ER, only to have it implode from within when the air conditioner shut down. They fled, taking as many supplies as they could carry. Jess told me that most of the patients were men, rabid and violent from the heat in the last hours of their death. The male staff were the same. Instead of practicing medicine they turned to care by brute force. It seems class and education set none apart when the mercury rose.

Now we're holed up in the upper levels of a ten-story apartment building. The women here are growing rooftop gardens. They found chickens in the suburbs and are breeding them and collecting eggs. There are water barrels collecting potable water and a greenhouse growing veggies. They turned this place into a rooftop oasis in the middle of hell.

We walk down the hall and push open the door to the stairwell. Jess holds her index finger to her lips, and we listen for sounds below. There's a clang, something knocking at a regular beat that sends a shiver up my spine. It could be the wind swinging a door against the wall. There's a rational excuse for every odd noise up here because I doubt anyone would attempt the climb to the upper levels of this building. Before they brought me in, the ladies made sure intruders would have the most difficult time ascending the staircase. They emptied all of the furniture they could from the lower level apartments and tossed it all into the stairwell. Below us there are more than a hundred couches, desks, TV stands, mattresses, and dressers; all haphazardly mingled. And in the small crevices and possible footholds between the furniture mix are inches of broken glass. The women bashed every mirror, every goblet, every precious crystal set, and every piece of glass they could find and tossed it down there as well. Jess said she outlined the debris with permanent marker a few months after everything had settled, that way they can keep track of movement below if someone starts digging. They brought me up the hard way: the fire escape stairs. I've never climbed so many stairs in my life.

Jess motions for me to climb the only clear section of stairs leading to the roof. When the fire door closes behind us I ask, "I know you all made it very hard for others to get in here, but what about us leaving?"

Jess looks confused. "Why would we ever leave?"

"In an emergency. What if there's a fire or something?"

"We have paradise in the ruins, we'll never need to leave." On a side note she adds, "We snipped the elevator cables and let it drop to the basement. There's a fire pole in the shaft if we need a quick escape."

I look down at my belly and try to envision sliding ten stories down a pole. I'm quite certain I'd more than likely fall to my death.

We open the door and step out onto the rooftop.

This almost makes up for that apartment I've missed so much. The rooftop has a living section separate from the gardens and the chickens. There's luxury patio furniture, reed woven rugs, and a covered dining area.

"Nova, you look pale," Sarah, the pediatric ER doctor, says as she's walking toward me and stops to place the back of her hand on my cheek.

"I'm fine." I step away from her.

"Maybe she needs fluids," Sarah says to Jess, biting her lip in indecision and looking between us.

"She's not dehydrated." Jess pinches the thin skin on the back of my hand. "See, excellent turgor."

"I heard there was food," I say to change the subject.

"Oh yes," Sarah takes my free arm, "Betsy made up something new and it smells heavenly."

Candles are lit and the table is set for a party of six. The chickens peck at bugs on the concrete floor, their clucking a gentle murmur of background noise.

"Sit next to me." Jess pulls out a chair.

I sit and position an overstuffed pillow at my back.

Meg pours a glass of wine for everyone. She pauses at mine before filling it quarter of the way then dilutes it the rest of the way with water. When she turns the rest of the ladies are looking at her.

"What?" Meg asks. "The flavonoids are good for her. Give the lady a break, she's probably carrying the last child this wretched earth will ever see."

"Just like a trauma doc, wears no gloves and serves pregnant women alcohol," Sarah mutters in disagreement.

On that note everyone takes a long sip of their wine.

Georgia is the last to the table. She's carrying a ceramic dish of roasted potatoes. "I seasoned these with garlic and thyme from the gardens," she announces proudly as she sits.

We pass the bowls around and Georgia motions for me to take extra. When I ignore her, she frowns. Georgia is sweet and quiet. I'm not sure what led her to be an emergency room nurse, but Jess tells me Georgia is one of the smartest nurses she's ever met regardless of her mild personality.

When the plates are clean and our glasses half drained, everyone moves to the patio couches to glimpse at the stars. The air conditioning units are running full blast, echoing off the surrounding buildings.

In the evening light, a handful of fireflies glide through the covered eating area. We stop talking and watch.

"How pretty," Georgia says.

"I've never seen those in the city before. Maybe back home near the countryside, but never here," I say.

"Maybe the heat drew them out," Betsy says.

We watch the bugs as they land only to take off moments later and continue on their way.

"Tell us about yourself, Nova" Meg urges, nodding at me. "You never talk about the countryside or where you're from."

I sip at my watered-down wine. The last thing I want to do is tell them about myself. "I don't really feel like talking about my life. Plus, yours all seem so interesting. Why don't you tell me some real stories from the ER?"

There's an awkward silence before Sarah starts with a story about a baby born at home that was brought to the ER by EMTs.

"… She delivered the baby in the toilet. Thought she had a stomach bug, said she never knew she was pregnant. I warmed that baby on a chemical mat, intubated, and placed umbilical lines in record time. The cold toilet water actually saved his brain, made him hypothermic." Sarah pauses for a thoughtful moment. "He'd be seventeen this year. Probably dead already." She downs the rest of her wine.

Uncomfortable silence now. We all take turns dabbing the sweat off our foreheads and fanning the thick air as shouting voices and screaming from the streets below slices through the evening quiet.

"It's only going to get worse, until they all kill themselves," Sarah warns.

"I've never felt heat like this." Jess stands. "Not even when I was vacationing in the Bahamas in the middle of summer."

"Not even in full contact precautions PPE?" Betsy asks flatly.

I have no idea what PPE means. I guess I'm not up on my medical lingo. Sadly, I don't care enough to ask.

"Close." Jess giggles. "But no. It's as though Hell has opened up and is threatening to swallow the earth whole."

"It's not Hell," Georgia adds. "Global warming; we did this to ourselves."

Betsy says, "I don't think anyone expected to see such a drastic change happen so fast. I mean, it's only been a few years since it started and now the earth is pretty much boiling."

"I heard something," Georgia adds. She's looking down at the glass in her hand, almost embarrassed. "There was this man who came into the ER one night, he had two broken arms and burns on his hands. He said that there was a safe place not far from here. That it was a disc floating in the sky with tentacles hanging down. He said it was a... a city. The safest city left on earth." Georgia presses her lips together and glances around the table.

We're all silent, waiting for more.

"A floating city?" Sarah asks.

"Yeah." Georgia nods.

Silence.

A floating city, wouldn't that be a thing to see? All of the long-dead conspiracy theorists that were shouting about aliens from the rooftops might roll over in their graves if it were true.

"Maybe it was the morphine," Georgia adds with a shrug, dismissing the story.

We laugh lightly for a moment before I stand to leave. "I need some beauty sleep."

We say our goodnights but the ladies murmur as I head for the stairwell door. They're talking about me, like they usually do when I'm not around. I think they're making plans for the delivery, discussing what could go wrong and what they'd do, probably listing supplies that they have and what they need. Jess said they have a birth plan, it just seems odd that they're not discussing more of it with me. On the other hand, I have been a bit standoffish since I met them all. I'm grateful for The Convent of women. I'm just not ready to make best friends with all of them because these days one minute you're alive and the next the heat is turning you over to the dark side. I don't want to get attached.

I push open the stairwell door and listen for noise below before descending. There's nothing, but I still find the thought of hundreds of pounds of debris blocking my escape eerie. It makes the muscles along my spine tighten like an animal trapped in a cage.

I jog down the steps before pushing open the door to my floor and walking to my apartment. I try the door handles on my way. None of them open. There's only the six of us, but they still lock their doors. I'm not sure if it's because they don't trust each other or me. You'd think being secluded in this building would make it safe to leave your doors unlocked.

Once I get to my apartment, I turn on Blues Traveler and sit facing the window. The music reminds me of a different time, a time when I used to go to concerts, smoke weed, and drink until I could barely walk. The low trill of a harmonica breaks through the music. Whatever happened to harmonicas? I was sure John Popper and Jason Ricci and Adam Duritz would last. They didn't, and now I miss the music of the nineties. I miss the vibrato of a low-pitched hum. I miss a lot of things. I miss John. It seems this moving on business is hard to do. And that Duritz look-alike was all it took to get me in this situation. He pressed his lips to that shiny harmonica, and I was lost; trying to relive feelings from the past will do that to a girl.

The women here tell me not to waste electricity on the iPhone. It's not like we have to conserve it here. Three-quarters of the city is empty, and I'm surprised the power has stayed on this long.

I tap the picture icon and go back three years; there are pictures of John before he was sick, before cancer and the chemo leeched every ounce of muscle from his frame. He was dark-haired and handsome, always smiling. I had to detach myself from him when things got bad, when there was no hope of recovery with stage IV. I was there every moment, but I kept every emotion tucked down deep.

Tears burn at the corners of my eyes and I recall Sarah warning me not to stress myself. I close the picture app, plug the iPhone in to charge, and lay down on the couch. I don't stop listening though. I like getting lost in the music; it's easier than getting lost in the memories.

CHAPTER FIVE

Abraham

When Abraham stared at the clouds long enough, he could feel the rotation of the planet under his feet and it was exhilarating. His skin rippled with a sensation he had not felt since he left his home planet—not that he could remember. It was more of a feeling than an absolute memory. The truth was, he knew that he was different from his people, but not completely aware of how deeply different. He was one of the few they'd kept for some unknown reason.

"Brother?" a familiar voice asked.

Abraham turned. If he hadn't already known the man's face, he would have recognized the robes. The material was stiff and exquisitely embroidered with geometric patterns and overlays at the neck and sleeves in grays and blues. Although, unlike Abraham's, his were clean and unfrayed. Abraham hoped his embarrassment at being underdressed wasn't noted. Jacob wore a simple black shoe, unlike Abraham's brown leather boots that laced to his knees and had been given to him by indigenous people from the second planet he'd culled.

Sweat was collecting along Abraham's spine; it was too hot down here for all of this cloth, unlike the ambient temperature of their city. His brother could visit for a few minutes dressed as their people typically do, but to do actual work, the work he was appointed with, it was too much. That was why his robe was currently packed away, reserved for chilly mountain nights and bad weather.

"Jacob." Abraham held out a hand to shake then quickly retracted it. That was a greeting for the humans, something his people weren't comfortable with. Abraham's people greeted with the quick bow of the head and the splaying of three fingers in gentle motion.

"I was afraid you'd forgotten our ways," Jacob said as he displayed the same greeting. "So much time in the Outland is no good for our kind." Jacob turned his head to gaze over the early morning valley layered with fog, purple wildflowers, and a haze of sunshine peeking from over the mountain ridge. "Ah, it is beautiful. Even if it is inhabited by wild things."

"Aye, that it is, Jacob." There was a moment of silence as Abraham agreed and appreciated the view, until he asked, "Why are you here, brother?"

"I was sent to remind you of your quota."

"Oh?" Abraham settled his hands in the pockets of his trousers, his finger catching on a hole.

"They want more. Two full moons have passed since you last visited."

"Aye, well, there's not much left down here. Communities are few and far between; they're heavily guarded or hidden. They aren't so eager for help. I have to gain their trust and coerce them now. It's not as easy as it once was."

Jacob took a deep breath of the mountain air. "It is never easy, the closer we get to the end. It's never been easy on any planet."

"When will I be allowed to come home?" Abraham asked.

"When the council feels you've atoned."

It was a crap answer that Abraham wasn't satisfied with. "How could they know, when I am down here and they are up there?" Abraham pointed at the sky, which was brightening and changing to a lighter shade of blue as the sun continued to rise.

"I will tell them." Jacob reached out to touch Abraham on the shoulder with a firm pat. "We are never that far from you." His hand moved over Abraham's chest, a finger pointing at his heart. "We are always right here. Isn't that what Mother always said?" Jacob pressed his finger harder into Abraham's chest. "Mother always said that to you, even though your real people dropped you into our nest like a parasite. You took the share you didn't deserve; you took our share, our brothers and sisters starved for you."

Anger overtook Abraham at that moment. He slapped Jacob's hand away and walked the few paces to the ledge of the mountain.

"Ye know I've no control over that," Abraham said.

Jacob never let Abraham forget that they weren't connected by blood, that Abraham wasn't even truly one of their own. He'd been abandoned, a brood parasite, a cowbird in a sparrow's nest. All the more reason to deny these people his assimilation. He may be a different species, but he and Jacob were similar enough. One could hardly tell besides their height, the shape of their eyes, the angles of their face. Abraham was different, but this was his family. It was all he knew, and his heart would never be still until he was allowed to go home again.

There was shouting below. The sharp boom of a gun discharging. A woman's scream and cry. Abraham had been scouting the mountain ridge for weeks hoping to find a settlement of humans and he was close.

Jacob was quick to focus on the direction of the sound. "Remember, two at a time. Never three," he reminded.

"That was a mistake I will never make again." Abraham looked away.

"Let us all hope." Jacob strolled with his hands behind his back, chest out, proud and tall.

Abraham followed. "Could you lend me a weapon?" he asked, feeling like a beggar.

Jacob laughed, "Why, brother? You've a trove of weapons." He motioned to the knives and handgun secured in Abraham's waist belt.

"Aye, but these are human weapons; archaic, nothing like what we are used to."

"You seem to be doing just fine with them." Jacob's brows rose in disagreement. "You never asked for more on the other planets you've culled."

"Some fresh clothing then?"

Jacob smirked. "I've been instructed not to assist you. Although frayed you still resemble one of our own, and there's plenty of cloth to make do until you're done. You could even wear some of the human's clothing, if you are desperate enough."

Abraham pressed his hands over the tattered edges of his tunic. "Oh, aye, suppose. But ye may not recognize me the next time ye step foot in these parts. I may just be as wild as the humans once I start wearing their clothing."

"Until then," Jacob laughed as he walked away and disappeared into the thick underbrush of the forest. Abraham had no doubt there was a transport vehicle stashed back there. He watched the treetops, anticipating the sway of branches and silver glint of a mirrored globe. But he saw nothing. Jacob must have driven through the forest before ascending to the sky. A purposeful trick to make Abraham doubt himself further.

As Abraham descended the mountain the sun followed his shadow in a slow arc and memories of his trial returned. On most days he was able to tuck the pain of that day away. But today they were at the forefront, no thanks to Jacob's visit.

"How do you plead to your offense?" the Elder asked.

"If it's an admission of guilt yer looking for you won't find it here. I did nothin' but exercise my right as a warm-blooded creature of the Seven Sacred Galaxies." Abraham's hands balled into fists.

"You've always been stubborn and proud, Abraham." The old man's eyes turned soft. "But now is the time to do what is right. Give what is owed to your Mother."

"Aye, ye wish me to do the impossible and I will not."

The Elder's face flexed in frustration as he murmured to his peers. "Each generation is worse than the previous."

"Each generation is momentum to change your ancient traditions," Abraham argued.

The Elders' faces were stern. "Confess to your grievance and provide as expected or suffer the consequences."

"Oh, would be nice and easy if I did. But I won't. Told you a thousand times. No."

The Elder nodded in conclusion. "Your punishment is banishment to harvest on the outer planets. Perhaps a lifetime surrounded by the errors of the galaxy will help you see."

Abraham's boots bit into the dirt and rock as he slipped. He grabbed hold of a skinny oak tree to steady himself. His heart was beating fast with exertion, and the heat that he'd escaped on the mountaintop was now overbearing. Abraham stripped off his tunic, folded it gently, and tucked it in his pack. He hoped he wouldn't run into anyone unexpected looking like some wild, shirtless heathen. He was quiet enough to scout out a camp without being discovered, but every now and then he'd run into a human tracker that was as silent as he.

Abraham rounded the clearing. The settlement consisted of five buildings surrounding a church. There were barns and gardens beyond the buildings. Men were working, tilling the gardens, hammering boards and nails, tapping metal shoes on a horse. Compared to the other settlements Abraham had been to on this planet, this one was antiquated. It lacked the long strings of electrical wires he'd seen everywhere else and there was only one dirt road that led to the settlement. But the cities were thinning out and he'd already stopped at so many towns along the coast, he needed to seek out the rural areas before people started to recognize him.

Abraham heard the sharp snap of a lash and a woman screamed again. He wove through the thick forest, headed for the sound. Standing in the shadow of a large tree, he watched as two men dragged a small woman away from a badly scarred post and toward a shed. She struggled, kicked and screamed, and when she got one hand free she scratched at their faces and slapped them. The men subdued her in minutes before shoving her into the shed and securing a large piece of wood over the door. The woman inside pounded on the walls so hard the shed shuddered. The men shook their heads as they walked away, talking quietly to themselves.

Of all the planets he had visited, the rituals of this one were the cruelest. Abraham's people believed in retribution but it was nothing like this. There must have been some evil lurking in those grown men to whip a woman as he'd witnessed.

Abraham crouched with a panther-like movement, settled his elbows on his knees and watched. There were other women at the settlement and all of them stayed clear of the shed. All except for one who Abraham noticed creeping around the back. She was talking through the cracks in the wallboards to the woman inside, whispering that it would be all right and she'd be out soon as long as she was good and followed the rules. The woman in the shed whimpered in response. She continued to pound on the doors and walls. In the midday heat, Abraham guessed it was well over a hundred degrees in there and with no windows or ventilation it probably felt hotter.

Dusk fell. The men and women of the settlement collected in the town center church for nearly two hours before heading to the surrounding farmhouses for the night.

Abraham was pulling his tunic on when he saw movement in the moonlight. The same woman from earlier slipped out of the shadows and lifted the board over the door of the shed. She slipped inside for a few moments before leaving again and replacing the board over the door.

Abraham collected his things and removed his cloak from the bag. He started walking toward the shed. His legs cramped from a day spent spying nearby. He paused to ensure that he was unheard before reaching for the door. Not a soul was around. He removed the board and pulled the door open.

She stood in the moonlight that filtered through the fissures of the roof, her body caked in blood and a fine sheen of dirt, her clothing ripped and stained.

"Come with me," Abraham beckoned. "I'll take you away from this place." He held out his cloak and when she stepped toward him, he wrapped the cloth around her shoulders and pulled her close under his arm to keep her warm. "What is yer name?" he asked as he guided her away from the settlement and toward the path from which he had come down the mountain.

"April," she said with a sigh of relief.

"That's a nice name. Now let's get you out of this place."

Abraham paused at the sound of twigs snapping underfoot nearby. He pulled April closer, eager to relieve her of these people at any cost.

Another woman stepped in front of them. It was the same one Abraham had seen earlier. This close she nearly resembled the battered one under Abraham's arm.

"My sister," April whispered. "Susan, why are you following us?"

Susan's eyes narrowed on Abraham before she glanced toward the settlement.

"Come with us," Abraham gestured. He moved away and ushered the second woman under his cloak.

"You were going to leave without me?" Susan asked her sister.

"I didn't know. He just arrived." April sniffed. "I figured you'd never leave. And I can't stay."

They walked away from the farmhouses in the darkness undisturbed. Abraham thought it bold of the settlers to not have patrols and security during these times.

"Where are you taking us?" April asked.

"A safe place," Abraham said.

"Safe?" April sounded confused. "There are no safe places any longer."

"Aye, safer than what I just witnessed." Abraham held branches to the side as the women walked ahead of him.

The night became cooler the higher they climbed. They walked and walked and walked until the women slowed their pace.

"I can't walk anymore," Susan finally said. "I haven't traveled like this in ages. I have to rest."

April rushed to her sister's side. "The last time we hiked like this was before momma passed."

They were near an outcropping of rocks, surrounded by thick evergreens.

"It's as good a place as any." Abraham dropped his bag. "I'm guessing yer hungry?"

April said yes at the same time Susan said no. The sisters glanced at each other in hesitation. April seemed completely trusting of this stranger while Susan stayed wary.

Abraham pulled a sack of biscuits from his bag and held one out for each of the women. It was nothing like the food they were used to. The strength from the biscuit would last them nearly a day, sating their hunger. The ingredients were not from this planet. His people had discovered the flour was neutral and easiest to digest in the galaxy. Simple proteins were something that linked them all.

It was plenty warm in the valley but on the mountain the women were shivering where they sat, unused to the chill of the night. Abraham made a small fire, enough to warm them and go unnoticed.

"I think we should go back." Susan held her hands out to warm them.

April tucked the cloak around her shoulders. "I can't go back to that place." She shook her head. "I'll never go back."

"Silas and his men will just find us again." Susan lowered her voice to a whisper.

"They won't find us this time," April argued. "And I'm never going back."

Susan stared at her sister for a moment and it was easy to see there wasn't love there. Her face was tight and tense. "It wasn't that bad. All you have to do is follow the rules. If you weren't so defiant...always running away and behaving recklessly. You nearly killed a man with that gun."

April shivered. "He shouldn't have gotten so close to me then."

"You never follow the rules," Susan kept going. "I do. They treat me accordingly."

"They do the same things to you that they were doing to me," April raised her voice. "It's wrong. What they were doing was wrong. And... it hurt." Tears glistened in her eyes.

Susan cleared her throat. "The Bible says—"

"I don't give a shit what the Bible says," April snapped. She rocked back and forth, soothing herself. In the firelight Abraham could see the bruises on her cheek, the missing pieces of hair from behind her ear, the red marks around her wrists. "I'm never going back there. I'd rather die."

Susan touched April's arm. "I want to go back. It's safe there. Silas and his men keep us warm, clothe us, feed us. Out here we are nothing but sitting ducks. Someone will come along and they could be worse."

"We are safe with him," April argued as she nodded in Abraham's direction. "He'd never let those men touch us again."

"How do you know? You have no idea who this man is," Susan said as she waved her hand in Abraham's direction.

"Just…" April raised her hand now, motioning to his height. "He's big and strong and kind. He rescued us. Doesn't that mean something?"

"You don't know he's kind," Susan said.

"He hasn't hurt us," April argued. "He gave us warmth and food." April held out the biscuit he'd given her.

"I think he's strange." Susan glared at Abraham. "There's something not right."

"Aye, I am right here." Abraham was digging in his pack for water. "Listening to your every word. And my name is Abraham."

"And there's nothing strange about the Bible cult?" April argued. "If mom and dad knew what they were doing to us…"

Susan's face twisted. "Mom and dad died a long time ago. They left us alone in this burning world! I did what I had to do to keep us alive."

April's hands fisted in anger. "Well, I don't think you made a good decision."

Susan was swift when she reached out and slapped her sister across the face.

"I hate you," April seethed. "All these years, what you let Silas and his Bible cult do to me, I hate you for it." She stood and moved to the other side of the fire. "You can go back. I won't."

Later that night, after their tempers had cooled, April whimpered and cried in her sleep. Abraham was sure it was nightmares and this wasn't the first time he'd come across such a situation. Young women clung to safety and sometimes that was in the arms of the wrong man, or in this case, the wrong settlement.

Susan slept like a baby; what happened didn't seem to bother her.

Abraham watched the women sleep, closing his own eyes for a few hours as the moon moved a few degrees across the night sky. He kept the fire burning and left them alone for an hour or so to find more water. He left a biscuit in each of their hands in case they woke while he was gone.

There was a creek with fresh water flowing from the mountaintop. Abraham crouched and filled his containers, listening to the noise of the forest. Cool water flowed over his fingertips as the early morning sun was beginning to filter through the thick canopy. A chipmunk scurried into a tree nearby. This planet held some of the most peaceful places he'd ever seen. The colors of nature were vibrant, the way the ecosystem intertwined was perfect symbiosis. Incredible. He'd seen nothing like it—close—but nothing this perfect. The only trouble was the wild humans. He had been to many planets within the Seven Sacred Galaxies with humanoid creatures. They were always similar; walked on two legs, a torso, arms. Sometimes the shape of the head varied; the height or color of the skin. They were never as peaceful as his people. There were always bad ones, some mutation in the breeding. It almost seemed that when the asteroids were flying across the galaxies, scattered with bits of life, only the hardened survived puncturing the atmosphere of a new planet. And that was why Abraham was here with his people, to seek out the good, destroy the bad, enable the planet to flourish in peace and put an end to cruelty.

The cawing of a black bird broke Abraham's concentration. He stood, capped his containers, and headed back toward camp.

April and Susan were awake, each staring at the sky and refusing to acknowledge the other.

"I have water," he said as he handed each of them a canister. "If yer thirsty."

"Thank you," April whispered.

Susan opened her canister and drank.

"Aye, yer welcome. Now, if you're both ready, we should continue our travels." Abraham secured his pack and offered his cloak to the women. "Once we pass that ridge," he pointed, "we'll descend to the warmer terrain."

"Where are you taking us?" Susan asked, distrust evident in her voice.

"A place of safety." Abraham began walking. April was at his side and Susan lingered behind. She kept looking in the direction of the settlement. He could tell she was eager to return. If he had learned anything from his previous hunts, it was better for her to return; he doubted she would pass the test to enter the floating city.

"I like the sound of that," April said as she toyed with the tattered edging of his cloak. Abraham focused on the work of her fingers, worried that she might cause it to fray further. April noticed. "Sorry. I fidget when I get nervous." She smoothed her fingers over the embroidery. "Did you make this? It's ornate."

"Not I," he shook his head, "that is the talent of my sisters."

"You have sisters?" April asked, hope rising in her voice.

"Aye. A many." Abraham tucked his hands in his pockets as he walked.

"Do you think they'll like us?" April asked as she glanced back at Susan.

"I 'spose. They tend to like everyone." Abraham kept the details of meeting his sisters to himself. He'd learned from previous ventures to give as little detail as possible.

When they stopped to rest later that afternoon, Susan pulled a small book from her pocket and began reading.

April frowned. "Why did you bring that?"

"It brings me peace when I read. It makes me feel safe," Susan said.

"I wish you'd left it behind," April replied. "I hate that book. Nothing good ever came from it."

Susan twisted away, showing April her back and continued reading. "It's my book. I'll read it if I want."

April was gripping a small stick in her hand, her thumb pressing the middle until it snapped.

Abraham looked between the two women, doing his best to ignore their arguing. He hadn't been placed on this earth to make friends; he was sent to do a job, and there was no point in him trying to fix this relationship. After all, he'd done such a poor job repairing any of his own.

When they stopped to rest at night, Abraham had a fire roaring within a few minutes. He didn't like risking the smoke, but they were high up on the mountain tonight and he was certain the women would appreciate the warmth.

Abraham offered them biscuits and water again. Others he'd taken from the city complained about the bland meals he provided; many scoured for their own food, some hunted their own game to cook over the fire. Abraham's mouth watered at the thought of roast rabbit. When he was done with these two, he might try his hand at catching one. The biscuits, although nutritious, became boring after all this time. Every planet was the same. Water and biscuits. Biscuits and water. He missed the foods Mother would make. Soups and stews with roasted vegetables from the far galaxies. He missed them, but he would never go back begging her to cook for him again.

April and Susan curled near the campfire to sleep. Abraham rested his back against a tree. He glanced at the women, judging their age. Humans didn't age like his kind; they aged faster. Abraham guessed that April and Susan weren't much older than adolescents considering their lack of wrinkles and age spots, and April's frequent comments about their parents. They couldn't be much older than twenty, maybe even a few years younger.

Susan shivered. Her eyes snapped open and she caught Abraham staring at her. "What do you want?" she asked.

Abraham shook his head. "Nothing."

"Then why are you looking at me like that?" Susan sat up.

April stirred in her sleep.

"I've got no business with ye, Susan."

"No business with women?" She sounded appalled. "Perhaps you prefer the company of men then. It's a sin you know." She reached in her pocket. "Says right here in this book."

Abraham's mouth snapped closed. He'd witnessed an argument similar to this in one of the big cities along the coast. It ended with men strung from trees by their necks until they were dead. The people of this planet seemed to have deep concerns with gender partnerships. To his people gender was fluid, and private. He thought humans might learn something from that.

"What's in that book is none of my concern. Go back to sleep with ye." Abraham turned his head toward the sky until he heard the quiet sounds of Susan sleeping.

*

"How much further?" Susan complained as they descended the mountain.

They were surrounded by evergreens and great oak trees.

"A ways," Abraham replied. "Maybe one more night at this pace."

"Can you tell us about your home?" April asked. The further they got from the settlement the freer she appeared. "What's it like?"

"Oh, well, some say it's very clean. And organized. The buildings are quite tall. It's warm, not hot like it is here." Abraham was tempted to remove his tunic again, now that they were more than halfway down the mountain. "There's clothing and food for everyone. Plenty of books and entertainment. You'll see when you get there."

"It sounds so peaceful." April bit her lip, troubled.

Abraham asked, "You have a question?"

"What are the men like?" April's voice was low. "Are they like Silas and his men, like the people we left?"

"Oh, aye, can see where yer coming from there. My people would never be so cruel as to whip a young woman in the open like was done to you. We don't believe in corporal punishment. That doesn't mean there aren't rules and regulations, just means you don't have to worry about being beat."

"Okay." April nodded and the crease of concern in her brow smoothed.

"What if we don't want to stay?" Susan asked.

"You're free to leave." Abraham was quick with his reply. "We don't force anyone to stay. But I can tell ye, I've yet to see someone leave."

No one ever wanted to leave once they were let inside. Many did though. His people reeducated, healed, and sent the moral ones back to their home planet. Almost always. But there were instances where children were kept. And there were instances where infants were set in an unsuspecting crib and left behind.

*

The next day they descended the ridge and crossed an overgrown field. In the distance, Abraham recognized the sheen of the dome of the floating city. The young women didn't seem to notice until they were close and its base shaded them from the heat of the sun.

April stopped and backed up to get a better view. "Oh, it's so beautiful. Like Heaven," she said in awe. The city was suspended in the air with strange technology that they'd never seen before. "Just like in your Bible, Susan."

There was no door, no shuttle waiting to bring them above, nothing but cables suspended from the base of the city to the ground. They swayed in the space between like octopus tentacles.

"And what are these?" April asked as she walked closer, inspecting the cables.

"They'll bring you up," Abraham said.

"Up there?" April tipped her head and got a good look at the base.

"April…" Susan warned, uneasy. "I don't think this is a good idea."

"It's better than most," April replied. "Better than your idea. Loads better than Silas."

"Go ahead, touch it," Abraham urged as he reached out and grasped one of the cables. He stayed put, the city delivering nothing more than a warm welcome to his fingertips. It knew who he was and that he was not allowed up.

April hesitated, her hand hovering near the tentacle as it pulsed with warmth.

"What are you—" Susan didn't finish before April grabbed the tentacle, and barely a heartbeat passed before the cables pulsed with judgment. It read April's past, her future, saw memories of the things she'd done. It read her soul. And, satisfied, it began to drag her up. Up, up, up into the sky where the floating city hovered.

April looked down, a wide smile on her face. "Come with me, Susan!"

"No!" Susan turned to Abraham; her Bible gripped tight in her hand. She pointed it at Abraham. "You'll rot in Hell for what you're doing to us! Feeding us to the devil."

Abraham stepped closer; his massive size out-matched Susan's. He grabbed her free hand as she beat him with the book, screaming, "What you're doing is pure evilness. God will see!" It was like she had a premonition of her impending fate.

As he pried her fingers open, she flung the book at him. With one hard *whap*, it struck him in the nose and made him bleed. He grabbed a tentacle and wrapped her fingers around it.

"No!" Susan screamed as the tentacle pulsed with judgment. It read her soul just as it had done to her sister, but this time something else happened. It turned Susan to dust. One moment she was whole, wickedly human, and the next she was dust in the wind; just as scorched and red as the sand beneath Abraham's feet. The shocked look in her eyes would haunt him for a few nights at least; it always did. Abraham kicked at the burnt soil and peered over the divide that spanned the edge of the city's footholds.

April was gone. He hoped Jacob and the rest of his kin would treat her kindly, they always did to the beings on other planets. Abraham thought April would clean up nicely and look exquisite in the layered and embroidered cloth of his people.

Despite Susan's struggling, this was easier than the last group he brought. Abraham was still troubled by the time he brought three. Two men fought after watching their friend turn to dust. Abraham was able to wrap the tentacles around one's arm, but the other ran and Abraham was unable to catch up with him. Now he was sure that the humans knew about the city, possibly even knew about him. This didn't worry Abraham; the floating city was well hidden in the valley between the mountains. If need be, they could move it, although the Elders wouldn't be happy.

Blood dripped from Abraham's nose and splashed on the dirt at his feet. He pressed his sleeve to the bleeding nostril and pinched the bridge of his nose. The book that Susan had hit him with was coated in dust, pages flapping in the slight breeze. He bent and picked it up, ripped a page out and used it to wipe the blood off his face. He crumpled the page and threw it into the crevice below the floating city.

Standing between the city's footings, Abraham turned the book over in his hands. It was never too late to learn something new. That was what Mother had taught him all his childhood years. She encouraged his linguistics education, his inquisitive mind, and his incessant questions. If only she could have encouraged his free will when it came down to it. He tucked the book in the pocket of his cloak and ventured on.

CHAPTER SIX

Romeo

We made it through the mountains and into Kentucky before the heat melted the wires of the solar panel. We were able to fix it quickly on the side of the road. From there it was slow going. We were searching for gasoline or a charging station that still had electricity. The trip went to shit once we hit Illinois. It seems the masses vacated Detroit. Now roving gangs patrol the border. They didn't trust the Sheriff's southern-boy accent. We've been trying to go around the state, but a week-long trip has spanned months. And all the while the heat keeps intensifying. There is no doubt in my mind that the Ely, Minnesota the Sheriff speaks of is no longer the last mecca of cool weather. Today the mercury soared past one hundred and twenty degrees.

"I can't sleep in this weather," Duke complains as he paces the room.

"Open the window," I suggest. "At least let in some fresh air."

"Can't open the window, the rain will come in. Everything will get damp and then that glowing stuff will start growing on the carpet and the walls. Hell, even the bed sheets." He stands at the window and taps his fingertip on the glass. "The glowing stuff is going to take over the world. Wish I had my blue bug-zapper light I'd fry up every last spec. Sittin' in my rocker on a damp night. *Zip zip zip*, they'd fry up quick. I'd string them across my lawn. A hundred of them. Maybe more."

"I've told you before, it's harmless," I say as I get another warm beer. I can't seem to drink fast enough. Nothing liquid will stay in my pores, doesn't matter if it's water or beer or flat soda. It all sweats out.

Duke has got it worse. He refuses to wear less than his uniform. Stiff khaki and slacks aren't suitable for this weather.

Duke sighs. "We'll never make it to Ely if we don't find more gas." He wipes sweat on his sleeve. "Can't wait to dip my toes in Burntside Lake, that water's always colder than a Catholic at the Piggly Wiggly."

I drain my bottle. "We'll go out looking for more gas early in the morning, before the sun's beating on us."

He paces. "Can't do much in this heat. It makes a pain in my chest. I can't be having a heart attack out here in the middle of nowhere." He rubs his red neck. "I keep thinking about Nancy. The look on her face when I did what I did."

"Calm down, man." I pull the harmonica from my pocket. "Let me play something nice and soothing."

"Okay." He nods, agreeable. "Okay. That sounds good."

I play a low slow version of Hallelujah, a song that always gave me goosebumps as a kid when I was sitting in church.

Duke flicks the light off and settles on the twin bed across the room. "That's good," he mutters. "Mighty relaxing."

I finish the song only to repeat it again and again until he's snoring louder than I'm playing. When I'm sure he's sound asleep, I grab the motel room key and head for the door. I don't trust sleeping in a room with him anymore, not since he teeters on the edge of control at the flip of a dime these days.

I lock the door and head for the pool. I cross the parking lot, the cracked blacktop still hot enough to soften the rubber soles of my shoes. The rusty chain link gate squeals in protest when I swing it open. I kick my shoes off, empty my pockets onto the patio table, and step down onto the first step of the sloped pool stairs. The sun has been down for a few hours now, but the glowing doesn't usually start until the moon is overhead, like now. It begins in the corners of the pool, where large clusters of algae are hard to scrub away and remain untouched by lazy motel staff. Who can blame them? There's not much of a reason to clean anymore, not like there are many people coming over for dinner or renting out the nicest penthouse any longer. I swirl my foot in the water, creating a current and drawing them out. The blue-green glowing starts and with each agitation of the water it brightens.

I wonder if Nova has survived. I wonder if she's seen the magic the heat has brought us.

I step further into the water until it rises to my knees then my hips. The algae glow brighter as I lean into the pool to float on my back, even more when I move my arms to stay afloat.

I close my eyes and remember the night we met.

She was exotic, dancing in the crowd; her hair so black it was nearly blue, olive skin, almond shaped eyes that were the brightest shade of sapphire I'd ever seen. We were playing nineties cover tunes and she was watching me every time I pressed my lips to the harmonica, her eyes wide but her thoughts distant. I wasn't surprised when she met me at the bar after our session was done.

"You play like John Popper," she said.

I smiled. "Ah, one of the greats." I raised my beer.

"One of the best." She ordered a drink from the bartender. I paid since she seemed interested.

I studied her profile as she flirted with the bartender. She turned to face me again, drink in hand, it was as if it was just the two of us. She was intense but there was also something sad about her, something hidden. That was everyone these days. Guarded, deceitful, only as deep as the most current meme on their social media accounts.

"Not many these days enjoy the harmonica," I said.

She shrugged. "Their loss." She tipped her head back and drank then she slammed her glass down and said, "Want to get out of here?"

"Sure."

She led me down the alley behind the bar. It took us to the river, fast flowing and cold from the mountain melt. This was in the early months of the heat wave, before it all changed. Before the snow disappeared from the planet.

"Could you play some songs for me?" she asked.

"Sure. What do you want to hear?"

I played songs ranging from folk tunes to hard rock. We walked to the river with Nova shaking her hips and dancing in the moonlight, me playing every song she asked to keep her going. She was mesmerizing. Groupies were few and far between for a little band like ours. Cover tunes didn't usually get the girls going.

"Can you play Tears in Heaven?" she asked.

"My lips are ready to fall off," I complained.

"This will be the last one." She smiled wide. "I promise."

"Okay." My harmonica back then was custom made, the pitch deep and low. I threw all I had into that last song; low deep breaths, and plenty of vibrato. She was twirling in the moonlight, up on her toes, reaching for the skies. I didn't want her to stop. I drew the song out, I played it long and slow. I put my soul into that last song, hoping to see her turn around with a smile on her face again.

When I was done, she wasn't smiling. There were tears streaming down her cheeks.

"Can I kiss you?" she asked.

At a loss for words, I simply nodded.

She skipped toward me, threw her arms around my neck and kissed me. I was expecting a peck on the lips; that wasn't what I got. Her tongue probed into my mouth and she rubbed her body against mine. I pocketed my harmonica and held her close, exploring her body over the thin dress she wore.

"Sorry," she said as she finally pulled away.

"Don't have to be." I didn't want to let her go. There was something magical about her.

Her cheeks were flushed, her nipples hardened through the fabric of the dress. She caught me staring.

"Let's do it," she said as she wiped the tears off her cheeks.

"What?" I had a feeling I knew what she was talking about.

She reached for my belt. "This." She kissed me again, her lips pressing hard against mine as she shoved her hand down my pants.

"Out here?" I asked.

"It's the middle of the night," she said. "We're as alone as we'll ever be."

I slid my hand under her dress and between her legs. She moaned, biting my ear. "Here. Now." She slid her leg around mine as she unzipped my pants and shoved them down. Her hand was stroking; heat and friction, that's really all it takes.

"What's your name?" I asked between her kisses.

"Nova," she said as she sank to her knees.

"Oh, Nova—" I couldn't finish when she put her mouth on me. "Oh god."

It felt too good to last long. I pulled her to her feet, slid my hands under her firm thighs and lifted her, setting her up on the railing that lined the river walk. I kissed her neck, licked and tasted just as she'd done to me. "Don't you want to know my name?" I asked.

She was silent, lost.

I touched between her legs, and her attention returned as she moaned. "Yes. Tell me."

"Romeo." I usually get a laugh or two. But not this time.

She kissed me with renewed focus. "Romeo, Romeo—"

"Don't finish that." I pressed into her.

"Oh, Romeo," she sighed, opening up to me. "You feel so good."

The river churned faster, water melting off the mountains at record speed; it hid the sounds of our lovemaking.

Nova moaned, she clenched and clung to me. I was nearing an end. I slid my hand between our heated bodies.

"No." She pushed my hand away. "Not yet." She lowered her legs, forcing me to pull out. She turned, her hips against the railing, and looked back at me. "This way," she begged. "Don't hold back." She flipped her skirt up teasing with the firm globes of her round ass.

I covered her, pressed into her again, my hands on her hips. We started a rhythm. Her moans shouted over the river. I slid my hands up her back, held her shoulder in place before moving my other hand around her front ready to give her release. I wasn't going to hold on for much longer.

She sighed. I felt her insides clench me tight as she came. I grabbed her hips and thrust hard, burying myself as deep as I could get.

She was screaming, "Romeo. Oh! Romeo."

I was deeper than I'd ever been during sex, and that was all it took. I kept thrusting.

"Oh god!" She reached around and held my hips closer. "Oh-oh!" I heard her whisper, "I love you, John."

There was silence.

I bent over her back, still connected, my arms caging her against the railing. I whispered in her ear, "Who is John?"

I shouldn't have cared, shouldn't have asked. This was just a chick I met on the road and banged but she felt like so much more. Being inside her was like nothing I'd ever felt before.

She tightened around me and if she hadn't whispered, "My husband." I'd probably have thrust into her for another round.

I open my eyes. I'm still floating, only my nose and eyes and hard-on sticking out of the water. Memories of her usually do that to me. I've bedded a few trying to escape them but they always come back, haunting me.

I move upright and take care of myself near the edge of the pool, my back to the motel. I close my eyes and remember her, unable to stop myself from calling, "Nova," as I exhale.

I crawl out of the pool and sit in one of the broken patio chairs. I light a cigarette. I've only got one pack left then I'm out until we find another abandoned store that hasn't been cleared. I savor this one, inhaling deep and exhaling a thin stream of smoke toward the starlit sky.

Nova is an obsession I can't shake no matter how hard I try to distract myself. Like the heat for some, she's burning me from the inside. I have to find her. It will be the last thing I ever do on this earth. If I don't, I might go crazy like the rest of these fools.

*

"You're glowing." Duke is standing at his door.

Damn. I was hoping he'd still be asleep.

I look down at my clothes. They glimmer with tiny specs from the pool. "I guess I am."

I hear the unmistakable click of his pistol.

"I told you that glowing stuff was bad. It's taking over the world. It's going to turn us into glowing zombies."

It's been a long time since I looked down the barrel of a pistol. The first time we were bar jumping in Detroit before the heat made everyone nuts—it was a bad section of town. The last time was when Billy Texas was trying to rob me of my cigarettes. Ironic thing is Duke was the one to scare him off. Billy had been on a rampage, hoarding whatever he could dig up or steal. Duke had followed his trail and it led him straight to me.

"Put the gun down," I warn.

He's wiping sweat out of his eyes.

Steam drifts off my soaked clothes.

"I told you..." He's breathing heavy, gasping in the night heat.

I reach out. "Hey, let's put the gun down."

My heart is pumping fast; ready to do something I swore I never would; ready to punch him in the throat and grab his gun when he drops it, and then shoot him in the skull.

I close my eyes and tamper the rage.

"Put it down, Sir," there's a warning in my voice.

"I reckon..." Duke's hand is shaking. He drops the gun. "That glowing crap will be the death of us all," he says as he backs into his room.

"I think the heat is more likely," I say as I pick the revolver up off the ground.

He coughs as he sits at the table. His shoulders shudder and he rubs his chest in the middle.

"Or your health," I mutter as I set the gun on the table next to him. "Raise that to me again and we'll be parting ways mighty quickly."

"Get out of here," he growls.

I slam the door closed on my way out.

These few months on the road, I have missed the song of the southern nights. I have missed the gentle chirps of the peepers and even the rusty hum of the air conditioners. This chaos is disrupting me to the core.

Abraham

Abraham sat at the base of a large tree. He flipped the Bible open. He read and read and read this story, or guidebook, of how a human should live. Some of it made sense and some was absurd. The logic and timetable seemed off with what he knew of Earth's history. It was convincing and he could see how Susan had fallen for its promises.

There was movement nearby. Abraham closed the book and tucked it into his shirt. He rounded a rusted car and crouched near the trunk.

Two men were walking down the middle of the road. They were heavily armed, and each carried a bulging sack. He turned his head to listen to their conversation.

"I hear this city floats."

"Most absurd thing I've ever heard," a bearded man replied. "Don't think you should be taking directions from men on their deathbeds."

"We should find it. We should search."

The bearded man shook his head in disagreement.

"I'm sure there are women there. Clean ones. With all their teeth."

The bearded man laughed and pointed at his own mouth. "Hope she don't mind mine missing." He smiled revealing wide gaps.

The men laughed as they walked, trading off-color jokes between the two of them.

Abraham followed. Staying crouched low he kept a safe distance hiding behind cars and broken-down trucks on the side of the road. He listened to the things they said and doubted that either of them would be selected. But Jacob wanted bodies, and Abraham would deliver. Even though their quality was poor, at least Abraham would take note of his hard work and he'd rid the earth of these two less-than-savory individuals.

He followed them through towns and along back roads. He retreated to the forest to avoid being seen, tracking them like a cougar. The men finally stopped at dusk. They climbed into the empty bed of a pickup truck and settled down for the night. He did the same.

Abraham woke to the sensation of cool metal against his throat and the stench of rot.

"How long you been following us?" a coarse voice asked as Abraham opened his eyes.

It was the men he'd been tracking.

"Oh, a while," Abraham said calmly.

"Reckon he was there the whole time," the man with the beard said. "Could feel it in my spine."

"Why didn't you say something then?" his companion asked.

Now that Abraham saw them up close, he could see that both of their teeth weren't just missing, they were rotting. The men smelled worse than the creatures he'd harvested on the edge of the galaxy that resembled a Sasquatch. He was sure they hadn't bathed in months. Maybe years.

Abraham raised his hands in surrender. "I heard you talking about the floating city."

"Oh, did you?" The man slid his knife into a holster.

"I did, sir." Abraham pushed his back against the tree to sit up straighter.

"Sir?" The man laughed. "Don't be calling me sir, call me Boone."

Abraham nodded. "Aye, Boone then. It seems to me yer headed in the same direction as I am."

Boone's brow rose. "You don't say?" He seemed pleased. "Look, Rusty, we've got another crew member." He gestured to his partner.

Abraham glanced at the other man. "Nice to meet you, Rusty."

The man named Rusty hesitated for a moment, a wave of distrust crossing his features.

"Aw, come on, man," Boone said. "We've been waiting for this day; you've been talking about that city for weeks."

"I can show you where it is," Abraham offered.

Rusty finally held his hand out. "Nice to meet you."

The men let Abraham stand and get out of the truck. They seemed to trust him and put their weapons away while letting him keep his.

"How far?" Rusty asked.

"Oh, down the parkway a bit more and thru a valley," Abraham replied.

And so they went. The men asked Abraham questions, which he answered in vague detail. He could tell they didn't trust him, but they didn't try to subdue or restrain him. Abraham recognized that there seemed to be a certain code amongst scoundrels.

In due time, the two men stood below the floating city. It was glorious, space domed, suspended in the air with a technology they weren't familiar with. Neither of them had seen anything like it before on earth.

"Elysium," Rusty said.

"No, just another city." Boone wasn't convinced. "Seen plenty."

"But this one floats."

"What makes it so safe?" Boone asked as he surveyed the land beneath the floating oasis. He kicked at the burnt soil and peered over the divide that spanned the edge of the city's footings.

"Who knows?" Rusty turned, gazing behind them at the barren land, remembering the length they had come to make it this far, the things they'd done.

"So," Boone repeated. "Do you wanna knock or should I?"

Rusty looked up. "Knock?" There was nothing but cables suspended from the base of the floating city to the ground. They flapped in the space between like octopus tentacles. No doors, no one to greet them.

"What have we got to lose, man?" Boone asked. "Lost plenty as it is."

Rusty stalked back and forth around the metal footings, stroking his beard that had grown long from the lack of simple pleasures like water, soap, and razors. "What if they turn us away?" Rusty wondered out loud.

Boone inspected one of the cables swaying in the wind before him. "Been turned away from plenty of places, don't tell me this one is going to chap your sensitive hide."

Rusty reached out to one of the cables, it seemed to pulse with energy, drawing him nearer. He tore his hand away, tried to slow the rapid beating of his heart.

"What's wrong?" Boone asked.

Rusty said nothing.

"Tell me," Boone demanded.

"Do you think there are good men or bad men up there?"

"A bit of both." Boone's smirk was filled with rotten teeth. "What city doesn't have a bit of both?"

Rusty looked up. "Abraham said this is the safest." He moved his hand close to the cable again, tearing it away as fast as the first time when he felt the pulsing energy beckoning him. "The last one left on earth."

"What is it?"

"Not sure." Rusty shook his hand. "Feels strange."

Boone reached out, his dirt-covered hand hovering over the cable closest to him. "On the count of three. We do it together. Just like always."

The men nodded in agreement.

"One, two, three."

They each grabbed a cable. Barely a heartbeat passed before the cables pulsed with judgment. Read their past, their future, saw their memories, the things that they had done. It read their souls. The city chose who would ascend. One man burned like the scorched ground they stood upon; the other was hauled up.

Abraham watched from a distance. The men wanted to go alone. He was sure that neither of them would have been accepted. The one was a pleasant surprise.

CHAPTER EIGHT

Nova

The air conditioners stop running as Jess is showing me how to fashion a baby doll in a sling and tie it to my body. "This way you'll have more movement of your arms. You can hold the baby and do other things at the same time," she continues as a loud thunk announces we've lost our cooled air, perhaps for the final time.

"Crap." I set the doll down. "I hope that's not forever." I untangle myself from the wrap.

Jess looks out the window. "Let's pray it's only for a little while."

"I'm not the praying type. You know that. Usually it turns back on within a few minutes," I remind her. I move to a light switch and flip it. Nothing happens. "Seems all power is down."

"Nova, try not to think about it. You'll stress yourself out and deliver early." She pats the chair. "Now, come rest here. I'll give you a back massage."

"You went to nursing school and learned massage?" I ask.

Jess giggles. "No. My sister was a massage therapist. She taught me a few things."

I sit and Jess starts at my shoulders, rubs her fingers down my spine, then kneads my lower back.

"This is amazing," I say. "You can keep this up all night."

"How about instead, you tell me something about yourself. Tell me about the baby's father."

"Oh," I give a dismissive wave, "What's there to say?"

"His name." Jess has a sarcastic tone. She's been prying for weeks.

I finally give in. "You're never going to believe it," I say.

"Try me."

I sigh. And hope John isn't listening from up above. "His name was Romeo."

"Romeo?" She half-laughs half-coughs.

"He was a musician. Played a mean harmonica. I met him, well, I met him about nine months ago. Not long after the heat wave took hold, before everyone started going completely crazy and dying. He was playing at a bar in town. I asked him to play me a few songs. One thing led to another. And here I am." I motion to my belly.

"That explains the music choices on your phone," she says. "I never found the harmonica to be swoon-worthy."

I giggle. "It just reminds me of an easier time. When I was in college and free and hopeful. Living off iceberg lettuce and deli ham. Getting free dialup Internet from the university."

Jess stops massaging and sits next to me. "You're not free and hopeful now? Without the bills and the rat race?"

"I guess I am. It's just, I feel a little trapped up here." I motion to my stomach. "And this makes me feel trapped as well."

Jess rubs my belly. "It's a baby. Not a trap. You'll get back to normal after she's born."

"She?" I ask.

Jess shrugs. "Just guessing."

Our conversation is interrupted by three hollow knocks from the air conditioner.

I sigh. "I guess that means it's dead for good."

"Ugh." Jess moves to her feet. She bends to collect the stack of books she brought in. "Don't forget to look through these. They're good. What to expect, birth through the toddler years." She sets the books on an empty shelf. "I'll help you open these windows before it gets too hot in here."

We move about the apartment opening all the windows. The last room is the nursery. The ladies stocked me up good. On their supply runs they collected diapers and bottles, formula that hadn't expired, clothes, and a bassinet. Everything a new mother would ever need. They even set up a clean birthing room in an empty apartment down the hall. These ladies are way more prepared than I am.

I stop what I'm doing and turn. "Jess?"

"What, sweetie?" She asks absently as she turns from folding little T-shirts.

I am suddenly overcome with emotion. "I just want to thank you for what you've done for me. All of this," I motion to the room. "If you hadn't found me I'd probably be dead in the street." Tears drip down my cheeks before I can wipe them away.

"Shush, now." Jess wraps her arms around me. "We are happy to help. Do no harm, it's our motto." She pats me on the cheek. "I think you should get some rest."

I yawn and wipe the tears out of my eyes. "I think you're right."

"Okay then." She waves. "Lock the door behind me. I'll be waiting to hear it click."

"Sure." I smile, following her to the door. "Thanks again."

"No problem. Goodnight."

I close the door and slide the deadbolt into place. Then I move to my favorite place by the window, watching as the sunset fades. Usually the streetlights and entrance lights come on when night falls in the city. Not tonight. The city darkens, shrouded in nightfall. There is no gentle hum of air conditioning units, no cool whirr of electric fans. There is silence. Stars spread across the sky, more than I've ever seen in my life. And then, something strange happens. I notice a blue glowing on the side of the building across the street; light specks that morph into vine shapes. It continues on the buildings down the street.

I leave my apartment and head for the roof.

Jess and Sarah are already there by the time I'm walking across the rooftop to get a better look.

"I saw glowing," I say as I move to the edge of the rooftop.

"It's everywhere," Sarah points. "The ground, the walls. I've seen something like this before when I was vacationing in the San Juan Islands. There were glowing cyanobacteria in the water. I think this might be the same thing. Or something similar."

"It's kind of pretty," Jess says. "Maybe the electricity being out won't be so bad." She holds her hand up. "At least it gives off enough light to see by."

"Until high noon when it's a hundred and thirty on this rooftop," I say.

"Yeah, there's that," Sarah leans over the rooftop wall to get a better look.

"I wonder if it's dangerous?" I ask.

Sarah shakes her head. "Bacteria like this rarely are. If anything is dangerous these days, it's mankind."

*

The contractions start on the second week of no air conditioning.

"Meg keeps telling me I'm dehydrated," I complain to Jess.

"I bet we all are." Jess is pouring me a glass of warm lemonade. "Drink this." She sits near me in the shade of the rooftop seating area. Inside it's stifling and we spend most of our days out here now, searching for a breeze. There hasn't been noise in the streets for weeks now and Georgia has brought up the subject of moving closer to the ocean. Since I can't travel well, they're waiting.

I sip at the lemonade. "I'd kill for some ice."

A contraction silences me. I close my eyes and breathe like Jess showed me. In through the nose, out through the mouth, deep and slow. When it's over another one hits almost immediately.

Jess pats my arm. "How long have you been contracting like this?"

I shrug. "A few hours. Since last night maybe. I'm not sure. I barely slept."

"And you didn't tell us?" Jess stands.

"You told me I could labor for days. Days!" I remind her.

"Come now." Jess helps me to my feet and calls the other women. "Georgia, Meg, Sarah, I think it's time!"

She helps me to the door and down the hallway to the birthing apartment. Betsy runs in front of us and opens the door. It's hot in here, hotter than the rooftop. Sweltering really. I'm sure I'm going to deliver this baby in a pool of sweat.

"We should open a window," I suggest. "And air this room out."

The women shake their heads in unison.

"We decided it's best no one outside hears," Georgia says. "Or they might try to come up here."

"How loud do you think I'll be?" I ask.

Sarah makes a face. "Some women scream like heck. Others are pretty quiet. It all depends on your pain tolerance." Sarah's washing her hands in a basin of water. "Have you experienced much pain before? Surgery, broken bone?"

I shake my head no. John's death wasn't physical, but the pain felt that way. Crushing. Took me a few years to recover. I guess if I could survive that, I can survive this. Pain is pain.

I try to stifle a moan.

"Would you just shut up?" Georgia shouts. "You're having a baby, it's not that bad. I pushed out three."

My lips smack together. I've never heard Georgia yell before. I've also never heard her talk about her children. I guess when the world is ending, we all have secrets to keep.

"Are you feeling okay?" Meg asks as she settles her hands on Georgia's shoulders.

Another contraction threatens to split me apart. I hold my moans and screams of pain; I choke them down and watch Georgia warily.

Jess soothes me.

Sarah's eyes grow large. "What was that all about?" she asks as Meg leads Georgia out of the room.

I hold my breath through another strong contraction.

"No, no, no," Jess is at my side, "you must breathe. Take a deep breath. Like this." She sets her hand on my stomach, feeling a contraction, then nods and demonstrates the quick breaths in and exhalations she's shown me in the past.

"Okay." Sarah pushes my knees apart. "Oh my god. The head is right there. She's crowning already." Sarah looks up. "This is going to be fast."

The pain is intense, and I can think of nothing but pushing this baby out.

"You're doing great." Jess brushes hair out of my face. "Almost done."

The air in the room is thick and smells strange. I feel like I can't get enough oxygen. "Open a window," I say. "Please."

"We can't," Jess says, worried. "Just work through it."

"One more push," Sarah says as she's pushing my thighs back.

"I can't breathe," I complain.

Meg is suddenly at my side, listening to my chest with a stethoscope. "Does she need oxygen?"

"No, she needs to get the baby out. One more push," Jess nods at me.

I push and the burning pain is nearly overwhelming, but then it's over. After a few seconds the baby cries.

"Good job," Jess says as she helps Sarah with the baby. She looks up. "It's a girl!"

I smile, suddenly overwhelmed with emotion my smile turns to tears. How will I keep a girl alive in this mess of a world? I lift my head to see Jess cut the cord.

"Oh dear," Sarah's looking down at the baby. "She's got a club foot."

"A-a what?" I ask.

"Club foot." Sarah's voice changes. "It's pretty severe."

The room becomes tense as Jess glances at me.

I sit up on the bed to get a better look.

"Give Nova her baby," Jess says as she's moving closer to Sarah.

Sarah is gripping the baby's foot and the baby is crying.

"Sarah?" Jess's voice wavers. "What are you doing?"

I hold my arms out. "Give me my baby." Another contraction takes over my body as the placenta delivers.

"It just won't stop crying," Sarah is gritting her teeth.

Jess is walking toward her with a clean blanket. "Hand me the baby, Sarah. You need to give her over to her mom now. They need to bond."

"I can make it stop crying. I can fix it." Sarah is talking like she's grinding her teeth.

Jess grabs the baby, shoving Sarah at the same time. Sarah tumbles over a table and groans, hitting her head on the floor.

"What's happening?" I start to ask, moving to the edge of the bed and covering myself.

Jess is running at me. She shoves the baby in my arms. "Run, Nova. Run to your apartment and lock yourself inside."

I take the bundle of baby. "But—"

"No time to talk. Run. Now!" She picks up a bag of post-partum supplies and shoves them in my direction.

I roll off the table, thankful for the plushy carpeted floor. I run down the hall, the sounds of thuds and screaming coming from the room where I just gave birth. I push open my door, kick it closed and slam the locks into place.

I set the bundle down in the bassinet, the bag on the floor. Someone had some insight to move it into the living room. It wasn't me—probably Jess—and I'm thanking her now.

I push a chest of drawers in front of the door, then one of the couches. Then I collapse on a chair. I don't think running for your life or moving furniture are recommended within thirty minutes of childbirth.

Silence doesn't last long. There are heavy footsteps in the hall.

"I want it," Georgia's voice shouts from outside my apartment. "I can take care of that baby better than her. We could all see it." There's pounding on the walls and the door. "I've already lost three. Give it to me! That's my baby! It's the only reason we put up with you this long! It was never yours."

And then everything goes to hell. Maybe it was the iron smell of my blood, the chaotic way labor took hold of me for those few short hours, the intense heat of the room. It sent them over the edge.

I thought nothing would tear apart the Convent. These docile women who created this haven are currently losing their shit outside my door. The heat has brought out the worst in them, the wild. I can hear them clawing and screeching. It's worse than the stories they told me about the ER falling apart.

The women are screaming.

"Give us the baby!"

"It's mine."

"We only let her stay for the baby!"

Jess's voice breaks through, "You'll leave them alone."

"You can't stop us."

"We'll kill you."

I hear the sounds of them fighting, thuds against the wall and screeching. The women didn't want guns up here, but I imagine Jess could use one right now. She seems to be the only one who hasn't lost her mind.

The baby cries.

I move from the chair and collect the bundle of towels.

"Hi baby," I whisper as I walk away from the chaos outside of my door and to the nursery. I pull the blanket down. It's a girl. "Hi, baby girl," I soothe as I set her on the changing table.

I rub her dry; like Jess told me to in case they weren't around when I delivered. She made sure to teach me as much as she could.

I put a diaper on her and get her a clean towel. Then I lie down on the bed and place her to breast. While she's nursing, I examine her feet. My daughter's right foot is twisted inward and to the side. A clubfoot, Sarah had said. I try to bend her twisted foot, but she starts crying and kicking her legs.

"Shhh," I soothe. "I'm sorry. I won't touch it again." She goes back to nursing. "What will I name you?" Her cheek twitches with a smile. "Joy. I think I'll call you Joy."

*

There's a knock on my door during the night. I roll out of bed and pad to the living room. The apartment is lit by the blue-green glow from outside.

"Who is it?" I ask.

"It's me." I hear the familiar voice of my friend.

I twist the first lock, ready to let her in.

"No!" Jess warns. "Don't open it." She coughs then spits. "You don't want to see this. Not now. I don't want you to remember me like this."

"Are you okay?" I ask.

There's a pause. "I'll be fine. For a little bit." The door flexes as I imagine she leans against it. "How is the baby?"

"She's good." I glance down the hall to the nursery where she's sleeping.

"Did you feed her?" Jess asks.

"I tried." I lean against the dresser that's in front of the door. "She seemed to latch on and she's content now."

"Good, good. Keep it up. How are you feeling? Any excessive bleeding?"

"No. I'm fine," I say. "Nothing more than what you said I should expect."

"That's good." She sounds exhausted. "Very good."

"What about her foot?" I ask.

"Well, there is no surgeon to fix it. She can live with a clubbed foot, but walking might be difficult."

Suddenly unsure about everything, I ask, "What should I do?"

"Remember everything I've taught you. And there are the books I brought on your shelf. You should read them."

"Okay."

"Nova?" The door flexes as she moves. "Don't open the door. Not for a long time."

"But what about you?" I ask. "Don't you need help?"

"Don't worry about me. You just take care of that baby and yourself. She needs you now. I'll figure something out." Jess lets out a breath and a cough.

"Are you hurt?" I ask.

After a pause she says, "Yeah."

"What about the others?"

"They're gone. Forever. You don't need to worry about them anymore."

Silence. I'm not sure what to say. What do you say to a stranger who took you in then protected you from her own friends? I could never thank her enough. I could never pay her back.

"Nova?" Jess asks.

"Yeah?"

"If you have to leave, you should know that there is an SUV in the lobby. It's gassed up and ready to go. There's an extra battery and more supplies." She pauses. "Georgia installed a car seat. I'm not saying you should leave now, but in the future. If you have to. There's a way."

This news makes me wonder how long Georgia was planning on taking my baby. It makes me wonder if any of the other women knew, and what they had planned to do to me after I delivered? If not for Jess...

"Jess?" I ask.

"Yeah?" She sounds weak.

"Thank you. For everything. I don't know what would have happened to me if it weren't for you."

She sniffs. "Sometimes the universe works in mysterious ways. We were meant to meet. My life had purpose in defending yours and saving that baby." Her voice cracks. "You're welcome, Nova. Did you pick a name?"

"Yes. I did." I wipe my face on my sleeve. "I'm going to call her Joy."

"Joy." There's a smile in her voice followed by a light thud. "That's the best name. I love it."

*

I wait in the apartment for as long as I can. It's close to a year before the water stops coming out of the faucets. Jess stopped talking to me long before that. She kept watch outside my door nearly every second.

I use a strip of cloth to secure Joy to my chest in a sling like Jess showed me so my arms are free.

I finally open my door for the first time to find Jess laying there, her body spread across the floor in front of my apartment, protecting us even in her death. I'm not sure what I did to deserve her in my life, but I'm sure the world just lost its last truly good soul.

I drag the rotting body of my friend to an apartment at the end of the hall and place her in the bathtub. I can't take her outside for a proper burial so this will have to do.

We survive in this empty apartment building until the last chicken dies and the rain barrels dry up. The gardens are still producing tomatoes and squash, but I can't live here any longer. Three months ago was the last time I heard a shout from somewhere in the city and I haven't seen another soul in a longer time than that. It's as good a time as any for us to leave.

The problem is, Joy can't walk. She can scoot around on her knees, but she isn't strong enough to pull herself up and walk with a crutch. Wherever we go I'll have to carry her and everything else.

I collect as much as I can. I throw sacks of food, clothing, and diapers down the empty elevator shaft. Then I strap my pudgy baby to my back in a sling and I grip the fireman's pole. I'm hoping my feet land on something soft and that there are no murderous heathens nearby waiting to kill us.

As I slide down the dark shaft Joy is quiet, the quick movement and darkness silencing her. My feet hit the solid metal of the top of the elevator. Light filters through the dirty windows, brightening the elevator shaft. I collect the bags I tossed down earlier, second-guessing my choices of the last canned goods and the last of the vegetables of the garden, which I'm sure were squished during their fall from the upper levels. It will be better than nothing when we're hungry.

I search the lobby for the vehicle that Jess promised was down here. I cross the expansive marble flooring and giant windows. I could have never afforded to live in a building like this before the Heat Wave.

Tucked in a corner near the gym is a set of moveable screens that look out of place. I walk around them and find the SUV parked out of sight. It's a big obnoxious Hummer. I'm thanking my lucky stars that it's a hybrid electric version but who knows if the battery has held a charge and how big the gas tank might be. I find the keys under the sun visor and open the trunk. There are a few packs of bottled water and supplies. I toss my bags inside and notice the extra gas tanks secured to the roof rack. I'm hoping the gas is still good.

I open the rear passenger door to find the car seat then I do something that all those books Jess left me said not to do. I move the carseat to the front passenger seat. I can't bear not having Joy close. After adjusting the straps, I secure her inside. Then I move the screens out of the way.

The front doors look big enough to drive the vehicle out, but I don't have anyone to hold them open for me and the handles are wrapped with chains. The Hummer has a push-bar on the grill, so I guess I'm driving through.

I get in the driver's seat and start the engine. The giant SUV rumbles to life. I check the display screen and see that the batteries are fully charged and the gas tank full. It says I've got ten hours of battery life which should be enough, combined with the gas, to get me out of town and some place safe.

I dig my phone out of my pocket and plug it into the USB port. The battery has been dead for a few months now and I find it hard to live in a world without music. An image of a battery flashes as it charges.

I turn on the air conditioning and feel coolness for the first time in what feels like forever.

"Ready, babe?" I ask Joy.

"Wa wa wa," she babbles from her carseat as she looks out the window and kicks her legs.

I shift the vehicle into gear and steer toward the front doors.

"Hang on to your diaper," I say to Joy as I press on the gas and ram through the doors. Glass shatters and metal twists but the Hummer moves on as though I were driving through butter. I turn down the street and drive away.

I've been thinking about where I should go. Jess suggested it might be cooler by the beach, but something doesn't feel right about living next to rising ocean waters.

There was something else Georgia mentioned a while ago that I've been dwelling on. There was that man she met in the ER who was talking about a floating city. And I can't forget my time with that man I met on my way to Charlotte—Abraham. He said there was a safe place in the mountains and he was eager to bring me there. I wonder if they are the same place?

A floating city sounds crazy, but so does a burning world where everyone kills each other. Trusting my gut, I head to the mountains.

*

The good thing about the heat and everyone dying is that they left behind plenty of untouched supplies. Clean clothes, canned goods, gas in their tanks, bottled water, rows of baby supplies still in their boxes at department stores.

The bad thing is that the mountain roads are winding and steep. Towns are few and far between. Some of them smell like rot; I'm guessing from all the dead bodies but I don't investigate. I have yet to find a city, let alone a floating city. But the Blue Ridge Mountains span a large area and I doubt I'll find this place on my own. I drive up one stretch of mountain and down another. I never come across a city that looks like it's floating.

We run out of gas just outside of a tiny town called Dillard, near the Georgia/Carolina border.

I pull into a Wal-Mart parking lot as the engine sputters and park it under the shade of a big oak tree. I curse myself for all of those stops I made to sleep and left the air conditioning running.

I grab my phone from the center console, at least it's fully charged. I pack up as much as I can carry before settling Joy in a sling across my back. She's heavy and the packs are hard to carry. I glance at the roads ahead of me; everything is uphill. What I wouldn't do for a stroller right now.

I turn. Wal-Mart sells strollers. I leave my bags and grab a flashlight from the back of the Hummer and head to the store first.

I'm not sure what the people of Dillard were like, but there are a few dead locals on the edge of the parking lot, their bones being picked clean by vultures. The only sign of life is an armadillo that runs across the blacktop in front of me.

I pull apart the doors of the store and pause, listening for anything. Logic reminds me that the Heat Wave filtered out the most violent people first. Those of us that are left aren't looking for trouble, we're just trying to survive, but still, I've got a baby to look after and I just feel like I can't be too careful.

I pass the checkouts and grab a Snickers bar on my way to the baby section. It's mostly melted but I don't give up, because when you find chocolate during the apocalypse, you eat it. There's no telling if you'll ever find edible chocolate again.

I click my flashlight on as the sun shining in through the front windows dims the further back into the store I walk. The baby section is easy to find. I pace the row of strollers. There are too many choices. Jogging strollers, double strollers, strollers with car seats you can set in them. I think of my uphill travel and decide on a jogging stroller, one of the big side-by-side ones.

Assembly is a bitch.

Assembly by flashlight is even more of a bitch.

By the time I'm done it's dark. I decide not to travel at night, and even though it's stuffy in the store, I feel like it's safer than sleeping outside in the car.

I change Joy's diaper on the floor-sample changing table then we find food. The jarred baby food hasn't expired so I grab a few packs.

"What do you think of sweet potatoes?" I ask Joy.

She babbles, "Po po po."

I head for the camping section next to find a lantern. We eat in the outside dining display next door to the camping supplies. I've got my eye on a sweet Coleman tent display with a double cot. I'm betting it's more comfortable than sleeping in the backseat of the Hummer.

When we're done eating, we settle in the tent for the night. I turn the lantern off as Joy falls asleep and listen to the emptiness of the store. There's nothing; not a noise, not the hum of electricity, not the drip of a faucet. All I can hear is my own heartbeat drumming in my ears. I dig my phone out of my pocket. I'm tempted to play a little music, but I don't want to drain the battery. My finger smoothes over the power button. There have to be batteries in this store. I give in and turn on my phone. I flip through a few pictures, memories of what used to be. I take a picture of Joy sleeping and then I select a Blues Traveler album to fall asleep to.

*

I walk uphill, the double jogger loaded with my kid on one side and as much of our supplies that I could fit on the other. Joy is kicking her legs and sputtering and pointing. After a year in a high-rise apartment this is all new to her. At least she's not screaming with boredom.

We pass a few rundown houses and a small trailer park. I pause in front of each, tempted to look inside. I've got standards though and since I'm probably the only person in this town I've got choices. I decide to wait for something better and keep walking.

The roads are empty, and it has me wondering if everyone vacated town as soon as possible. I'll be happy to be alone. It's safe alone.

I stop in front of an empty farmhouse on Mulberry road. It's situated up on a little hill, barely visible from the road. There's a blind driveway hidden by overgrown trees. This could be the place. I head up the driveway, the backs of my thighs burning from the steep grade.

Once past the surrounding trees, I find that the house is situated in a clearing. It's two stories, with chipped white paint, and a wraparound porch complete with rocking chairs and a swing bench.

There are goats and chickens in a pasture that seemed happy to see us. I take Joy out of the stroller and move closer to the fence. The goat's udders are full of milk and I notice three hens sitting on nests in the pasture and there are more chickens clucking about while a few roosters watch me warily.

Joy giggles as the goats nip at her toes and the chickens cluck and hum.

"Chickens," I tell her.

"Chee," she babbles.

I check out the rest of the yard. The propane tank is full which means the gas stove should work just fine for a few months at least. There's a shed with garden tools and grain in tightly sealed bins. I grab a bucket full and toss it in the pasture for the goats.

I test the hand-pump of the well, happy to see fresh water flowing out. I rinse my hands and face with the cool water. Joy giggles when I rub her bare feet with my cold wet hands.

"How about we check out the house?" I ask her.

"Chee," she whispers, pointing to the chickens.

"Chickens later." I turn and head for the farmhouse. "Let's check this place out."

I knock on the screen door out of habit, I guess because it just feels strange letting yourself into someone else's house. When no one answers I take that as the all clear. I push open the door that leads to a large country kitchen.

The farmhouse is fully furnished as though someone might still be living here. Their pictures are still on the walls. There's a small round table in the eat-in kitchen, a formal dining room with a solid cherry table coated in dust, the living room at the front of the house with a television that will never show another episode of American Idol, and pillows decorate a worn leather couch. There's no blood inside, which means they didn't kill themselves here and I'm happy with that discovery.

I open the cupboards to find dishes and store-bought foods and non-perishables. Near the refrigerator is a pantry. I open the door to find shelves lined with home canned foods all neatly labeled and dated. There are peaches and apples and venison waiting to be eaten. Not long ago I was the unluckiest person on the planet. I must have done my time because now my luck is incredible.

I make my way to the living room to find a stack of logs piled next to the fireplace. There are more family photos; trips to the beach and preschool graduations.

I make my way up the stairs. There's a master suite, decorated in paisley blue and crisp white. Down the hall there's a bathroom, a teenager's room, a toddler's room, and a nursery.

"Look at this room just for you." I bounce Joy on my hip before setting her in the empty crib. She plops down and reaches for a set of plastic keys.

There are still clothes in the closet, fresh towels in the bathroom and soaps that haven't lost their scent. There are enough clothes here to last Joy until she's a teenager. Not that we'll stay that long, but we could. And since I didn't find any dead bodies, this place is a diamond in the rough.

*

I spend weeks airing out the house the best I can. I hide the family photos in the basement, clean and restock a few things. We walk to the Wal-Mart that's nearly an hour away on foot to collect new clothes and diapers and baby food that hasn't expired. I bring back boxes of rice and pasta and those freeze-dried camping meals that you just add boiling water to. Even though we have a well, I start stocking as much bottled water as I can carry and baby wipes. And deodorant.

I never see another soul. I never feel that shiver of apprehension that someone might be following me. It's peaceful out here in the mountain village, much more peaceful than the city felt.

Each visit I make to the store, I see the Hummer parked in the shade. I open the driver's door and turn the key, hoping the sun might have charged the battery. It won't start. I'm sure it's the empty gas tank but I really have no clue. I wish I had the courage to seek out a gas station to get the Hummer back to the farmhouse. *Someday*, I tell myself but right now I need to focus on feeding us.

The garden section of the store has packets of seeds. I choose summer squash and tomatoes and cucumbers, vegetables that you don't need a green thumb to grow. Even though I'm certain I'm going to kill everything and it's a wasted effort, I still spend the early morning digging up the ground and planting before the sun peaks over the mountains. With any luck we might have fresh vegetables until I can figure out how to get us moving again. Until then, we collect eggs from the chickens and milk from the goats.

Most days Joy plays in the small pasture on a blanket as I work outside, then she plays on the floor in the kitchen as I cook meals. She's a happy baby, but there are times that she's restless, crying and whining and kicking her clubbed foot. I think it hurts her, especially when the heavy rains and thunderstorms come through the valley. I soak her foot in a basin of warm water and Epson salts I got from the pharmacy in the back of the Wal-Mart. Over the past few months, I've given her all the baby Tylenol and Ibuprofen I could find. Now we tough it out together and my only intervention is an ACE bandage wrapped tight for support. It breaks my heart to see her so uncomfortable.

I don't remember reading about her clubbed foot in any of the books Jess brought me back at the Convent, so when I'm at the store I search the book section for anything medical. None of the expecting mother or parenting magazines mention it and the books aren't much more than romances and obscure science fiction paperbacks. I grab a few of each to pass the time.

Many days I sit on the porch while Joy takes her afternoon nap and try to figure out what to do. I found a barrel of gas in a pole barn on the far edge of the property. I haven't figured out how to get enough of it down to the Hummer and get it running again. I don't want to sit Joy in the stroller with five gallons of flammable gas strapped in next to her. That just seems dangerous. And part of me is too scared to hit the road with a baby. I feel like something is telling me to stay where it's safe until the right time comes around. It's that vibe, the intuition I've always trusted. Right now it's telling me to stay put and I'm having a hard time thinking of reasons to leave.

Still, I worry about turning violent in the heat like the ladies at the Convent. I can't see myself ever hurting my child. And while those around me have raged with violence, the heat never seems to affect me that way. With each day that passes the heat seems to affect me less and less. Even though I know it's over a hundred degrees, it's probably cooler up here in the mountains than in Charlotte. I wonder how the others felt; if they knew the heat was driving them insane or if they could sense the loss of control. A flood of memories returns; the things I've seen, men and women alike beating each other in the streets, the screams, the shouts. Whatever they felt, I'm feeling nothing besides the sun on my back that's oddly soothing as I pull garden weeds.

One day, as I'm rocking on the porch in the old rocking chair, I swear I hear the sound of men talking. I stop and listen. There it is again. I move from my chair, light on my feet so the porch boards don't squeak, and quietly as I can make my way around the house and peer down the hidden driveway.

I heard right.

There are three men walking in the road. They're traveling at a leisurely pace. They don't seem to be in a rush but definitely have a purpose.

I walk across the yard, ready to follow them and make sure they don't linger, only I hear Joy crying from inside.

I sprint across the yard, push open the door and lock it behind me. I run up the stairs and burst in her room.

"Momom momma." She's holding her arms out.

"Shhh," I soothe as I pick her up.

I move to the window, trying to stay hidden behind the curtains. Joy's still babbling. I put her to breast to nurse in hopes that it will keep her quiet. It does.

I watch the men passing from the window. The strange thing is, I think I recognize one of them. He carries himself proper like he was bred to royalty. There's a tick in his cheek when he smiles as the men he's with notice the house between the trees. Noise from the animals in the back must have drawn their attention. The tall man urges them to keep walking and I step back, hiding behind the curtains as I notice him searching the windows.

Please keep going. Please keep going, I pray.

They keep going until they pass the bend down the road and I can no longer see them.

They'll be back. Anyone with half a brain would. They'll probably break in while we're sleeping, ransack the place and kill us both.

Within ten minutes, I've grabbed enough food and water to last a few days at most. I toss packages of diapers and wipes up the stairs, plastic bags for garbage, and a bucket for other things. Then I carry Joy to the attic and barricade us in. It's the only place I can think of to hide because I can't run into the forest with my baby in hopes of escaping three men. This has got to be the safest place. The access stairs are in an awkward place in the master bedroom closet that's hard to find.

The attic is stuffy. It's hotter than heck with just two vents and a window that only half opens. I take back all my thoughts about not being bothered by the heat. I surely hadn't experienced the heat of a small, dusty attic before now.

I spend my days shushing Joy to keep her quiet, checking the road from the attic window, and listening with my ear against the dusty floorboards. There's no noise, no men's voices. But I know from experience that doesn't always mean we're alone. I've had more than one person sneak up on me in my lifetime. I can't afford to let that happen now.

Seven days pass and the men don't return. The hungry baying of the goats and clucking of the chickens finally draws me out.

I step off the porch in the early morning warmth only to be greeted by a bunch of goats standing at the fence looking pissed. They bleat at me.

"Sorry." I walk across the yard to their feed bins. "If you all weren't making such a ruckus we wouldn't have had to go into hiding for a week. You're all lucky you weren't made into goat-burgers."

I throw seed for the chickens and dump a few buckets of grain for the goats.

Joy is kicking her legs while she's strapped to my back. "Chee," she calls the chickens, but they're too busy pecking the ground. "Chee chee."

"They'll be over when they're done," I say. "Let's check the garden."

I cross the pasture to find everything growing just as it was. I pull weeds from around the seedlings and pluck bugs off the leaves.

And our days continue on as they were.

CHAPTER NINE

Abraham

It was downpouring like Abraham had never experienced before. His clothing and boots were soaked. He stared at the row of houses in front of him. He needed shelter but he rarely entered the human houses for shelter. It made him uncomfortable lurking in someone else's space, no matter how long ago they'd vacated. It might have been the pictures on the walls, the smells, the personal touches that made every home different. They reminded him of his own home, life with his brothers and sisters when they were young. A place he might never return to if Jacob had anything to do with it.

The canopy of trees was doing nothing to stop the rain as he stood on the empty street studying the two-story houses. He finally chose one, the third to his left. It seemed to be calling him. There was something familiar about this one. He followed a brick paver path around the back, its cracks overgrown with dandelions, and tried the door. It was unlocked. Abraham pushed the door open and entered. The house was empty and warmer than the cool rainstorm that was ravaging outside. Abraham stripped off his cloak and laid it across the table to dry.

"Brother," Jacob was standing in the living room. "Shelter is for the weak."

"Oh, Jacob," Abraham gripped a nearby chair, "ye nearly scared the bowels out of me."

Abraham thought himself a fool for not noticing one of the transport pods nearby. Was he becoming so detached from his own kind that he couldn't identify the subtle hints when they were around? He couldn't deny the pull to this house in particular, and now he knew why. Family was here. And no matter their differences or how far apart Abraham and Jacob had grown, they were still brothers. There was a time when they were thick as thieves, but young adulthood and venomous intellects had severed their bond.

One brow rose on Jacob's placid face. "You talk like them, more and more now."

"Curse of the job, I guess." Abraham removed his tunic, boots, and pants. He laid his things out to dry across the chairs.

Jacob strolled through the living room, moving in close to examine family pictures. The photos were of a man, a woman, and two children. Jacob scratched his chin. "I guess they're not much different from us when you see them like this. Smiling and innocent."

"Aye, seems to be." Abraham was cold from the rain and the dankness of the house was making him restless. "What's yer business, brother?" Abraham tugged a throw blanket off the couch and wrapped it around his shoulders before sitting.

"I came to bid congratulations. Three successful trips since I last saw you. The Elders are pleased." Jacob smiled.

"Oh? Have you come to bring me home then?"

"No." Jacob sat in a paisley print upholstered chair and crossed his legs. "I was asked to deliver a few things for a job well done." He pointed at a woven basket on the floor near the fireplace.

Abraham walked to the basket and opened it. Inside were new clothes, a fresh cloak, dry boots, a small three-pronged weapon that resembled the ancient Katar, and a freshly baked dish his people ate frequently that consisted of an orange eggplant-like vegetable.

Abraham ate before he dressed. The meal didn't last long but it brought more memories of the comforts of home. Oh, how his Mother would be so disappointed to see him now, filthy and living amongst the heathens, as though he were their brother.

"You're still behind," Jacob said. "There are rumors that you've been traveling further and further. The Elders are afraid that you were running away from us."

"I must travel many miles to collect," Abraham warned Jacob as he finished his food. "The humans are speaking of me. Some even recognize me. There's talk of the floating city-"

"Whose fault is that?" Jacob interrupted.

Abraham sighed. "It was a mistake. Just one mistake."

"Look what it's cost you."

Abraham shook his head and sat on a wide leather ottoman. "It's unavoidable."

Jacob nodded. "I'll inform the elders."

"You won't move the city?" Abraham asked, hoping to seed the idea in Jacob's mind.

"We both know moving the city is not an easy task. Many must vote, preparation takes weeks, and this planet is small compared to the others you've culled. Moving the city would be a waste."

Abraham bit his tongue. He lowered his head, wishing he'd savored the meal brought to him. He could use the comfort of more food from home right now.

"Then you must travel far."

Abraham nodded as he stood to dress in the new clothes.

"We will wait. And while we wait, I will petition the Elders to move the city to a new location." Jacob looked bored. "The valley between the mountains hides us well. It's safer to remain where we are."

"There are more valleys," Abraham said. "The mountain ridge extends down the continent. There's another one to the west as well."

"Yes, yes." Jacob stood and paced, stopping near the window and focusing. "I've examined the topography just as you have." He paused and tilted his head.

Abraham stood and moved next to his brother. "What is it?"

Jacob's brow rose in interest. "I thought I just heard an infant crying."

Abraham tilted his head to listen. "I can hear nothing."

"You must be losing your hearing." Jacob leaned away. "I've said before living down here with the animals is changing you. The distractions dull your senses. The gravity must be compressing your brain."

"Oh, aye, 'suppose so. I warned ye might not recognize me the next time you see me. That was some time ago." Abraham chuckled. "I'd say yer lucky I'm still in my own skin."

"Just remember, the Mothers like the children." He ticked his finger. "Always bring the children."

It was a hint that was not subtle in the least bit. It was also a sharp reminder of the reason for his banishment.

"Aye, see what yer saying." Abraham sat on a plush couch. "Once the rain stops, I'll take a look." He laid his head back and closed his eyes.

"You've always been stubborn and proud, Abraham. But now is the time to do what is right. Give what is owed to your Mother. Stop resisting."

Abraham shook his head in annoyance. "Aye, ye ask me the same thing as the others."

The Elder's face flexed in frustration. Abraham detested how their mannerisms were all the same. It didn't matter which one was talking to him. One seemed like another. Different figures but the same soul. "This generation—"

"Needs to bring change to our people," Abraham interrupted.

The Elder stepped back. "Was it so hard to confess? Was it so hard to promise what all of the others have promised? Your brothers and sisters have done this."

"Aye, my brothers and sisters are not I." Abraham stood tall.

The Elder nodded and clasped his hands together. "It's not so terrible. Those of us who were orphaned like you have made this sacrifice. She raised you. She raised you from nothing. You owe this to her."

"I owe nothing." Abraham pointed his finger at the Elder. "You owed them nothing."

The Elder bowed his head. "Decisions like these do not come easy, son. This is the way of our people. You are one of us."

Abraham shook his head. "I'll never be one of you. Not now."

He had lied that day, though. Abraham knew nothing else. He would always be one of them because he knew nothing else.

When Abraham opened his eyes again, Jacob was gone.

CHAPTER TEN

Nova

I've lived east of the Blue Ridge Mountains most of my life and never experienced storms like the ones that have blown through this valley. The clouds collect on the far side of the ridge, the pressure changes so fast my ears pop, then the clouds roll over the mountain, spitting thunder and lightning and rain. I glance out the window to see the trees tip and sway, branches blow across the yard and rain taps angrily at the windows. The thunderstorm is raging outside as though Mother Earth is violent with heat sickness, just like the others.

Joy won't stop crying. Her foot is aching. Soaking and massaging have not relieved her pain.

"Shhh. Sh. Sh. Sh." I beg, afraid of someone hearing. The last thing I need is a stranger walking in off the street into this mess. There would be nowhere to run in a storm like this, we'd be sitting ducks. "It's okay, baby." I dry the tears from her cheeks and rock her. "The storm will pass."

Joy cries so hard that she coughs and gags.

I would do anything to take this pain away from her. "Shhh." I hold her to my chest and rock her faster. Eventually she falls asleep as the worst of the storm passes, completely exhausted. I carry her up the stairs to her room and lay her in the crib. She rolls to her side and whimpers, shaking her clubfoot until she falls deep asleep.

I leave her room and head downstairs to clean up. Earlier, I brought the farm animals to the basement for fear that they might be blown away with the wind. Throughout the house I can hear the goats stomping and jumping on things down there. There is a *tap tap tap* as the chickens peck at the windows.

I find a small leak in the living room door. As I'm soaking up the rainwater with towels, the storm suddenly stops. Just as quickly as it blew in, it blows out.

I release the animals from the basement and return them to their barn. As I step out the door, I notice the wet blades of grass glowing. The damp leaves in the tree and the rain-soaked wooden fence posts, all of them are coated in glowing blue and green. It sticks to my rain boots, to the goat's hooves, and the chicken's underbellies. The doctors at the Convent explained it as algae spreading in the perfect conditions of a hot damp world. Although it is beautiful, it casts an eerie afterglow on the world I once knew.

With the animals in their barn again, I return to the house. I kick off my boots and leave them to dry on the porch. In the morning I'll have a busy day cleaning up debris from the storm and setting the garden right again.

*

We spend the morning picking up branches and raking leaves that fell during the storm. Most of the garden survived. I harvest the tomatoes that have broken loose of their vines and use the fallen sticks to prop up the leaning plants. At least I don't have to take credit for killing the plants, I can blame Mother Nature and her wicked storm.

As I'm weeding the garden, Joy is sitting in the middle of the little pasture on a blanket a few dozen feet away. The goats and chickens roam around her and one chicken sits on the edge of the blanket like a protective dog.

"I think we'll have some ripe tomatoes as early as next week," I say to Joy. "As long as the sun doesn't scorch them. They've doubled in size with that rain we had the other night." Some have split from the uneven watering, but they're still good for cooking.

Joy babbles, "Mom, mom, mom, momma." She giggles as a yellow butterfly flutters around her head and settles on the toe of her twisted foot. "Oooooh," she says as she's reaching out to touch its wings.

I turn back to the garden, making my way down a row, hoping that this will be enough food to last us. There are plenty of packaged items down at the store and I haven't even made it through a quarter of the canned goods in the pantry, but who knows how long we'll be here or what's in store for our future. We could last a few months but what if I need to last a few years, or eighteen years or ninety?

Silence.

A silent toddler is a dangerous thing.

I stand up straight. "Joy?"

She's trucking it, crawling on her hands and knees to the edge of the pasture.

"Where are you going?" I ask as I make my way out of the garden, jumping over rows of plants to get to her quicker. She'll be covered in goat and chicken poop in no time now that she's off the blanket. "Slow down, baby girl."

I look past the pasture, to the edge near the fence.

There's a man standing there. He's tall, the shadows of a tree hiding his face.

Terror kicks hard.

"Joy!" I shout. "No!"

The man steps forward, his long legs bending over the short posts of the pasture. He bows and picks up my baby.

CHAPTER ELEVEN

Abraham

Abraham had seen fear. He'd seen the expressions of hundreds of humans as they realized they were blistering to dust. Not just humans but many creatures of the seven galaxies. They might have looked different in presence, but their expressions were all the same the moment they realized it was the end. But he'd never seen fear like this. It seems the fear for one's own life barely compared to the fear for the wellbeing of one's own child.

The woman was running with every effort toward the child crawling on the ground. She shouted but the baby crawled faster, giggling along the way, clueless to the danger lurking beyond the safety of this secluded place.

He moved closer, eager to give the mother relief as he picked up the child.

"Oooh," Joy babbled as she swatted at Abraham's nose.

"Aye, it's a nose it is. Not really much to *ooh* about." Abraham smiled as the heated breeze blew the child's curls up in the air.

"Stop! Leave her alone," the woman running at him was shouting and waving a shovel in her hand. She looked like the fiercest warrior he'd ever seen, her face warped with the assurance of battle, promising pain.

He walked toward her, ready to hand over the child.

The woman stopped suddenly, confusion twisting her face.

He recognized her as well. It took a moment, but he had a perfect memory of this woman; meeting her in a diner and riding with her in the car. She was the one that got away. The first one, the one he couldn't convince to go to the floating city with him no matter how hard he tried. Abraham could barely believe that she was standing before him in this moment. It seemed surreal.

"I—I know you," Nova said. "Abraham? Right?"

"Oh, aye, it is." He handed over the baby. "Haven't seen you in many moons, Nova. I didn't expect to discover you so far from Charlotte. I thought that was where you were headed."

She dropped the shovel as she took Joy into her arms. "I was… I did." She shook her head in disbelief. "I can't believe you're here."

Abraham had never met the same person twice. The ones he'd spent time with were the ones he'd never see again. They went up to the floating city or sizzled on the rope. But to see Nova again, after all this time, it made him quite happy. Happier than he'd ever been on any of the planets he'd harvested.

"What are you doing here, Abraham?" Nova asked.

"I've been traveling these mountains for some time now. Needed a relief from the rain. I was not far down the road last night and heard a child crying." He looked them over but saw no injuries. "I figured I'd check to make sure there was no trouble."

Nova's hand smoothed down Joy's leg and over her clubbed foot. "It was Joy crying. But there's no trouble."

Abraham nodded with mild understanding. The last time he'd heard a child cry like that it was after a beating. He'd come across it more than once on this planet. Abraham didn't think Nova was the type to harm a child, especially after her efforts to find a doctor, but now he wasn't sure. He'd been warned not to trust the people of this planet.

"How did you hear her from so far away?" Nova asked.

"Oh, I've got quite good hearing." He noticed the twisted foot. "Now, what's wrong with the wee child's appendage?"

"She was born this way." Nova adjusted Joy on her hip so Abraham could get a better look. "The doctor said it's a clubbed foot."

"You found your doctor then, in Charlotte?" His eyes tipped to glance at her flat belly and then at the child.

"Yes," Nova nodded.

"See yer baby was delivered just fine." He bent to inspect Joy's foot.

"I'm not so sure the delivery was *just fine*, but I survived. And then we made it here."

Abraham slid his finger across the sole of Joy's clubbed foot. "She can still wiggle her toes."

"She can, but she can't walk," Nova said.

"Why not?" he asked.

"It hurts her to put pressure on it. I have to carry her everywhere. She gets heavier and heavier every day."

"Babababa," Joy started babbling and swinging her feet.

Abraham stood upright again. He was tempted to ask her if she'd like to go to the safety of the floating city now, but for the first time Abraham was unsure of what to do. He'd never met a soul he didn't offer to bring back to the city. But seeing her familiar face now, Abraham didn't want to bring her back there. He'd never experienced a dilemma such as this before.

Abraham turned and looked down the shaded driveway that led to the farmhouse.

"Are you leaving?" Nova asked. She sounded a bit worried and her eyes widened. "Do you want to stay for dinner? It would be nice to talk to another adult. Especially someone I can trust."

Abraham smiled. "Aye, it would be nice. I appreciate the offer." He remembered their time in the car. She played music he'd never heard before and sometimes hummed along. The road was lonely and the only music he heard now was that of nature singing around him.

"Come on," Nova started walking and waved at him to follow. "I'll show you the house."

Nova led him away from the pasture and toward the farmhouse. Abraham recognized it. Not too long ago he had escorted two men back to the city and they walked this road. Abraham had thought he heard something coming from behind the trees, but he had been eager to get the men to the city before Jacob came to pester him again.

Nova led him up the porch steps; she showed him the living space on the first level. "It's not what I'm used to." She laughed nervously. "I guess nothing is really what I'm used to anymore. But this house is good. The roof doesn't leak during the storms, the bugs don't get in, and we get a nice breeze through the house with the windows open." She stopped at the stairs. "There are just bedrooms up there." She waved her hand before walking back to the kitchen and setting Joy on a blanket that was spread on the floor.

"I should start dinner now." She washed her hands in a basin that was set in the sink. "What do you like to eat?" she asked Abraham. "Most days we have vegetables, sometimes rice or pasta, but I do have some canned meat I've been saving." She went to the pantry and pulled out a jar of canned venison. "There's this."

"Anything you make should be just fine." Abraham settled his hand on the back of a chair. "Do ye mind if I sit?"

"Not at all." Nova nodded.

Abraham sat at the dining chair which was nearly too small for him. It was nice to be off his feet but what he wouldn't do enjoy the luxurious furniture of his people. He remembered it being much more comfortable than the furniture on this planet.

"Where have you been?" she asked as she pulled pots from the cupboard.

"Traveling from here to there."

Nova had nearly forgotten his strange accent, but hearing it now was nice, familiar even.

"Bringing people back to your town?" Nova asked. "Like you tried to do with me? People fall for that nowadays?"

"Aye." He nodded. "Anyone who is interested, I bring them."

Nova emptied the venison into a pot and started cutting carrots and potatoes and adding them to make a stew. "I bet there must be a lot of people there now."

"Oh, there's enough." He nodded. "We can always take more."

Nova clucked her tongue. "Of course you're still out looking for more." Nova stirred the pot. She opened a bag of dried egg noodles and added them, and then she sprinkled in fresh herbs from the garden that she'd picked earlier in the day.

"What happened in Charlotte?" Abraham asked. "Did ye find the doctors you were hoping to find?"

Nova shrugged. "Sort of." She set the lid on the pot and found them each a can of soda from the cupboard over the sink. "All of the hospitals were empty by the time I got there. I searched every one, but there was nothing." She pulled two glasses down from the cupboard and poured them each a drink. "I had to abandon my car and walk for a ways." She cleared her throat, leaving out the pathetic parts about how she was searching busted storefronts and garbage cans for something to eat. She left out the parts about how badly her legs and feet hurt after walking for blocks and blocks and how she broke down in tears in an alley, sure that she was going to deliver the baby in the filthy heat, alone.

"Some ladies found me, eventually. They took me to a safe place. This building that they had all stocked up and secured. They wound up being a group of doctors and nurses who'd survived the worst of the heat." Nova slid a glass toward Abraham then she sat across from him while their dinner simmered. "It was a safe place." She laughed at herself. "I called it the Convent. Only women were there and they could be a bit strange at times, but they took care of me. And I had a friend. Her name was Jess. She saved us." Nova nodded to Joy playing on the floor. "When it got really bad, Jess saved us." Nova sipped at her drink. "And now we're here. In the middle of nowhere, where it's safe." Nova laughed again. "I almost regretted not taking you up on your offer for a while there." She shook her head. "I was so stubborn."

The pot started bubbling and the lid tipped releasing steam.

"Oh crap." Nova stood and ran to the stove. She moved the pot and turned the stove off. She stirred the stew until it was cool enough to eat, and then spooned it into bowls.

"Thank you," Abraham nodded as she placed a full bowl in front of him.

Nova moved Joy to the highchair at the end of the table and set out some food for her to eat. She cut up little bits of potato and carrot and shredded the meat. Joy used her hands, shoving food in her mouth with enthusiasm.

As they ate, there was unease surrounding them. A fog that would not lift.

Nova noticed. "What's wrong? You're acting strange."

Abraham set his fork down and clasped his hands. "Aye, there is something. The baby crying last night, was it because..." He cleared his throat. "Did you hit her?"

Nova looked horrified. "No." She dropped her fork and knife. "I'd never hit her like that. Never."

"Then why was she crying?" It was a simple question, but he could tell Nova didn't like him asking it.

Nova could tell that Abraham didn't believe her. She felt angry and sick to her stomach.

"Her foot aches when it storms, especially like it did the other night. I tried everything to help take her pain away, but nothing would work." Nova stood and walked away from the table. She crossed her arms and paced. "I can't believe you. Who do you think you are coming into our home and accusing me of beating my baby? I would never. Never." Nova shook her head in disgust.

"Some would. Some do. I didn't mean to accuse. I just needed to understand." Abraham held out his hand. "Come back, Nova. Finish eating with me."

She glanced at him and the dinner set on the table.

His eyes were pleading, his face placid. "Please. I'm sorry."

Nova dropped into her seat.

Joy had stopped shoving potatoes in her mouth and was looking between the two adults with her jaw slack.

"Everything is fine, baby." Nova scooped up a spoonful of mashed carrot. "Keep eating. Bedtime is soon."

They ate in silence. The only noise was the sound of silverware scraping plates and Nova asking Abraham if he wanted more. He nodded and thanked her. Nova didn't cook like Mother, but there was something about the meal that had warmed him to the core. He missed these times, sitting around a table with family. This time with Nova and Joy had been the first since his banishment.

When they were done, Nova washed the dishes in the sink and then she sent Abraham out to the well pump to bring in more water. She boiled half of the water in a pot before pouring it in a basin with the rest of the cold well water.

"Bath time for babies," Nova said as she picked up Joy, stripped her down and settled her in the basin.

Joy splashed in the water as Nova smoothed soap over her skin and hair and then rinsed her. After picking up Joy and wrapping her in a towel, she turned to Abraham. "I have to put her to bed, if you want to you can wait down here or if you have to leave…"

"Oh, 'suppose I should hit the road. The sun will be down soon."

Nova set Joy down as she walked Abraham to the door.

Abraham had that feeling like he might never see her again. Humans were fickle creatures and he'd clearly upset her. After all this time alone, he wanted nothing more than to see her again.

"Will you come back?" Nova asked. "Tomorrow?"

Abraham nodded and did his best to hide his eagerness. "Aye, if ye'll have me."

Nova smiled. "Maybe you could bring some of those biscuits." She winked, forgiving him for insinuating she was beating her child earlier.

Abraham smiled. "Aye, I could scrounge some up."

There was a pause, neither of them knew what to say next but neither of them wanted the reunion to end.

Finally, Nova said, "Goodnight, Abraham."

He tipped his head. "Goodnight, Nova."

CHAPTER TWELVE

Nova

I made something as close to stir-fry as I could come up with. I had pretty much everything else I needed; eggs, vegetables, rice, except for the toasted sesame seeds, which I never thought made much of a difference but they do. Without butter I used a jar of coconut oil that hadn't expired.

"Did you like dinner?" I ask Abraham as we are sitting on the back porch after Joy has fallen asleep and the hottest part of the evening has passed.

"Aye, can't say anything bad about it. Never had a meal like that before." He leans forward resting his elbows on his knees and focusing in the distance.

"Is there someone out there?" I squint, trying to see what he's focusing on.

He listens for a moment longer. "Thought I heard something. Must be the creatures of the night."

I nod and exhale a breath of relief.

"What do you usually eat?" I ask since I never see him carrying much food.

"Oh, just the biscuits. Every now and again my people will send a meal along."

"That's it?" I turn to face him. "You just eat those biscuits you gave me when I first met you?"

"Aye." He nods. "They keep me well nourished."

"Do you ever add butter or jam?" I think I'd get sick of eating plain old biscuits all the time. Also, I think that anything I made would be an improvement on those.

"In the morning I have to head out," he changes the subject. "I won't be back for a few moons, at least."

"Okay."

"Do ye have other people who come along here?" he asks. "Someone who helps?"

I shake my head. "No. You're the only one I've seen since I left Charlotte. I think I've been pretty lucky, traveling all that way with a baby without running into a mess." I pause. "Why do you ask that? Can you hear people out there? Are they headed this way?" I stand and focus out into the forest, then walk to the edge of the porch to listen along the road. The glowing hasn't intensified like it usually does with movement or loud sounds.

"No people are out there. None that I can hear at least."

I sit. "Good." I lean back in my chair and rock.

"Aye," Abraham agrees. "Could I ask ye something?"

"Sure." I nod.

"Did ye have feelings toward the man who gave you Joy?"

That is a loaded question.

"For a moment I did." I refuse to look at him; I don't want him to see my shame. "For one hot, fast moment I had a feeling for him, but that was because he was someone else to me. He wasn't who I wanted."

"That sounds a wee bit confusing." Abraham reaches down to get a glass of water that is set on the porch next to him. He sips at his drink. "Where is the man you wanted?"

The way he asks the question, it sounds so simple. "He's gone. He's been gone for a long time. Since before the Heat Wave started. Back when we were just seeing record temperatures for a few months of the year and the seasons started shifting."

Abraham rocks his chair and the wood slats of the porch groan. "Do ye think he'll come back to find you?"

"No," I reply. "Never." I have always known this but hearing myself say it out loud never stops hurting.

Abraham clears his throat; he opens his mouth a few times as though he is going to say something, but he changes his mind.

"I'd like to propose an agreement," he finally says.

"Okay." I press my lips together in an expression of anticipation, wondering what more he could ask me.

"Could I stay here with ye a bit, Nova?" He glances at me with wary eyes.

I'd like Abraham to stay close. He has a soothing presence and I've had more than one night of being scared of the shadows in this place. I fidget with the hem of my shirt. "I have to ask you something first," I say.

"Aye, let's hear it then."

"Will you turn violent like everyone else did in this heat? Will you turn violent and try to kill us? Because I can't have you here, with us, with Joy, if I have to worry about you like that. We've been really lucky so far and I don't want to risk harm coming to this place. I have to keep her safe. She's all I have. It's my only job."

"No." His response is immediate and hard. He's looking at me something intense. "I'm not like other men, Nova. The heat doesn't affect me so. I'd never try to kill you or Joy, not even if my life depended on it."

I nod. "Okay. Then you can stay."

There's silence between us as the crickets chirp in the tall grass surrounding the porch. I don't think I've ever heard so many of them. It's like they're congratulating this new step in our relationship.

"There's just one thing," Abraham says. "There are days I must leave. I still work for my people. I'll have to go out on the road for many moons at a time."

"So, you want to stay but you want to leave?" I ask.

"Yes."

Typical man. Times have not changed much it seems. For a flashing second, I wonder if he has another woman in a house a hundred miles away with three kids and a dog. I stare at him. No, Abraham doesn't seem the type. I highly doubt there is another woman, but there's something. Whatever the reasons I'm sure it explains why he refers to the passing of time in moons instead of days. Maybe he was raised by hippies up in the Blue Ridge.

"I'm guessing you don't want to tell me where you're going?" I ask.

"Aye, I'm afraid to tell ye and you're both safer not knowing."

I think for a long moment. I like having Abraham in my life and I trust him most days. He's clearly hiding something from me, something about his people. I remember a time when he begged me to go with him, but not since our paths crossed this second time.

"I can live with that," I say. "But just one thing."

"Aye, name it." He swirls the water his glass.

"I don't want you bringing anyone back here. Not down this road, not through town, even if it's a faster route to wherever you're going. Not if you run into your best friend in the whole world. Don't bring them back here. I have to keep Joy safe in an unsafe world. You have to promise me this." I look into his eyes, hoping he can understand how serious I am.

He nods. "I promise ye." He taps two fingers on his chest; they thud against the solidness of his breastbone twice before he holds them out to me. "Now you. This is how we make a pact. It will never be broken."

I repeat the motion, minus the hard thuds against my breastbone. I gently tap and hold my fingers out to him, and in the motions it's as though I can feel the tug on my heartstrings entwining the bonds of our hearts in promise. He leans forward until the tips of our fingers touch.

"I promise ye, Nova. I'll never bring another soul back to this land ye share with Joy."

A shiver runs up my back. "Thank you."

He leans back in his chair and sips at his drink. I get the feeling he'll never break that promise for as long as he lives.

"Could you play some music?" Abraham asks.

"You like it? I usually get grief about my music choices. Not that anyone has been around to complain for some time now." I pull the iPhone out of my pocket and tap my finger on a playlist.

"Aye." He nods.

I'm tempted to scroll through pictures and videos, but in an attempt to save the battery from draining even faster, I don't. Instead I tap a playlist and set the phone down as 2 Cellos fills the air.

Abraham

"June 5th, 1987. Happy 30th Anniversary, Mark and Janet." Proclaimed the marquee in the center of town. That was decades before the heat wave struck.

Abraham had come across ghost towns before, but none like this. This town had been empty for a long time. Abraham glanced down each of the streets at the crossroads where he was standing. There were no vehicles lining the streets as with most towns he'd been through. The houses, once tastefully painted in muted tones of greens and yellows and brown, had been bleached by the sun. The grass was scorched and crisp, the trees white and leafless. It reminded him of another planet, one close to a sun that he'd visited a long time ago. The beings there had translucent skin and only came out at night and they had large pale eyes that couldn't see in the brightness.

Abraham doubted creatures like that lived here on earth, but this town was inhabited by something. He could feel it watching him. It was skirting the edge of his periphery. Abraham shuddered, remembering the beings from that planet; they were dreadful, the things of nightmares. Those same creatures didn't live here but this planet was changing, and he was sure there were new beasts his people had yet to identify.

Abraham chose a weapon from his belt, a simple knife to start with. He gripped it in his hand, beneath his cloak as he walked toward the main street. He turned, the sound of light footsteps echoing as though leaves were being blown in the wind. Abraham stopped to explore the window of a jewelry shop, giving whatever was following him time to examine him. His cloak caught in the wind and billowed about, morphing his figure from man to something dark and foreboding.

The tall cement steps of the library down the street looked like a good place to take a defensive position. Abraham walked toward the library. He climbed the steps anticipating the creature to pounce on his back. At least he'd have the upper hand being elevated above the ground. He paused; nothing happened. He sat and waited, pretending to be distracted by the belongings in his bag. He took a slow sip of water, ate a biscuit at the pace of a tortoise. Eventually Abraham, bored with waiting, stood and went inside the library. Unlike the jewelry shop and the other shop windows, nothing was coated in layers of dust. Sitting on the counter were stacks of well-worn novels with pictures of half-naked men on them. The corners were bowed, some dog-eared as though someone had read their favorite parts over and over again.

Abraham picked up one of the books, turned to a marked page and began reading...

"See. That didn't hurt, did it?" he asked.

Eve shook her head. "No."

He got up on his knees and repositioned himself at the foot of the bed.

Eve looked at his crotch and paled. When Seth looked down, he could see the bulge of his thick manhood through his jeans.

"I'll be gentle." He touched her thighs, rubbing her skin as he reached for her panties and began pulling them down her legs.

"But it's so big." She looked at the bulge in his pants again before returning her eyes to his.

"It'll fit." He gave her a smile and pulled her underwear off. "You'll like it. I can promise you that."

She gave a hesitant nod like she didn't believe him. "Okay."

> *Placing his hands on her thighs, Seth spread her*
> *legs. When he gazed up, her eyes were closed again*
> *and she was holding her breath.*
>
> *"Perfect," he whispered to her as he moved up*
> *the bed and bent to place kisses on each side of her*
> *hips.*

Abraham swallowed hard. This book was *overly* descriptive; he finished reading the entire scene before closing the cover. He smoothed his hands over the front of his pants and adjusted. Praetors of the Seven Sacred Galaxies help him, but he couldn't stop the reeling of his brain as it replaced Seth and Eve with himself and Nova. What was wrong with him?

"What brings a big man like you to a little town like this?" a sultry voice asked from behind him.

Abraham dropped the book on the floor with a thud.

He braced himself for an attack but when he turned he found there was only a single woman standing there. She was long-legged and shapely. Her hair trailed down her back in curling tendrils, which he was sure had never been cut. Abraham was relieved to see that she didn't have a weapon.

She walked closer. "What's your name, tall drink of water?" Her voice was breathy, desperate for attention.

"Oh, it's not that if ye must know." Abraham took a few steps back.

"You have an accent." She stopped next to the counter and leaned against it. "I find that very sexy. How did you find this little town?" She trailed her fingertips along the carved edge of the countertop.

She was watching him closely, and damn him if he couldn't tell she was in heat. It was radiating off her like the sun on blacktop. Her voice was husky and her movements slow; she tilted her hips just so and pushed out her breasts. A woman like this was trouble, Abraham knew, it didn't matter what species or planet they were from.

Abraham kept his distance.

"I'm Abraham." Usually he would hold out his hand to shake, a greeting humans found comforting, but Abraham was cautious to get too close to this one.

"Abraham," she repeated slowly. "I like that name. It's a strong name. A noble name." She pulled herself up and sat on the counter, crossing her legs. Her dress had a slit up to her hip that left very little to the imagination.

"What might yer name be, miss?" he asked.

"Abigail." She noticed the book on the floor and hopped down to pick it up. "Oh, I love this one." She thumbed through the pages. "I've read it so many times. My favorite part is—"

"Aye," Abraham interrupted, "ye don't need to read any more of that to me."

Abigail frowned. "But I love reading."

"Aye, reading isn't the issue at this moment." Abraham was sure if he heard any more of that detailed description of mating that he'd be in heat himself.

Abigail set the book down and rested her chin on her hand. "What should we do then?" The question was barely a question but more of a suggestion.

She needed better reading material, or to branch out. Abraham backed toward the door. "Are ye all alone here?"

She nodded.

"How long have ye been alone like this?"

Abigail set the book on the counter and began following him. "Oh years and years and years. My parents raised me in a bunker on the edge of town. They refused to leave when everyone else did. Eventually they died and I figured out how to open the hatch. I've been living in the library ever since."

"Alone?"

"Uh huh." Abigail nodded.

"Do ye like being alone?"

"Not really. It gets awfully boring. I read a lot but most days I wish I had me a man like the ones in these books. We could be happy together and make babies." She was studying him.

Abraham's back hit the door. He pushed it open, not ready or willing to stay and make babies with Abigail.

She followed him.

Abraham felt safer in the open street with her rather than the enclosed library. "How would you like to meet my family?" he asked.

Abigail smiled wide. "Oh, I'd like a family. I've been alone for so long."

"Will ye come with me then?" Abraham asked. " I'll take you to a beautiful place, a sparkling city that floats in the sky. You could live there. Forever."

Abigail stopped walking and studied him. "Are there handsome men there, like you?"

Abraham was feeling uneasy. He didn't think he was that handsome, and there were many more of his people who were far handsomer than he in the floating city. "Aye," he said.

"Okay." Abigail clapped. "I'll go. Just let me collect my things." She ran back toward the library. Pausing at the door, she turned to ask, "Do you want to help me pack?"

Abraham knew better than to go back in that building with this woman. "I'll wait for you out here." He waved.

The door to the library closed behind her. Abraham surveyed the town. That feeling of being watched was gone. The creature that had been following him earlier was just Abigail. He sighed, relieved that he didn't have to come face to face with any new monsters of planet Earth.

When Abigail exited the library, she was carrying an overstuffed backpack.

"Do ye have everything you need?" Abraham asked. "It's a bit of a trek."

Abigail nodded. "I have all my favorite books." She clapped and squealed as she ran toward him. "This is so *exciting*. I finally get to leave this place." She hung on his arm. "With you, Abraham, my prince charming!"

Abraham simply nodded and led her down Main Street. He'd continue on the same route he was on before he stopped at this town and then planned to loop around the valleys. With any luck he might run into another human who was alone and in need of safety. Then he could bring them both and be that much closer to his quota.

Abraham led Abigail out of the ghost town and toward the inky hue of the Blue Ridge Mountains in the distance.

*

As Abigail trotted beside Abraham, she talked nonstop and asked questions about where they were going and where he had been, about his family and other people, about cities and places she'd only read about. Lucky for Abigail she didn't know any better as to what was lost.

Between her questions, Abraham snuck in a few. "Why were ye raised in a bunker?"

"Oh," Abigail skipped a few steps. "My parents said the world was dangerous. When the last factory closed and everyone left town, they stayed because they said it was safest in our town. They had planned for years. Just before we went underground the grocery trucks stopped coming and I remember my dad driving his truck down to the Publix. He smashed the door with a baseball bat, and we went inside and took everything that was left. We had everything we could ever need. Well, until I ate the last box of Honey Nut Cheerios when I was twelve. Then there were no more of those." She paused to look up at him. "Do you think the world is dangerous?"

"Oh, aye, at moments it can be." He bent to pluck a purple flower from the roadside and held it out to Abigail. "But it is also beautiful."

"No man has ever given me a flower before." Abigail sniffed the pale petals then made a face. "It doesn't smell like much."

"Others do." Abraham adjusted the straps of his bag as they walked. "You just have to find the right kind."

"Hm." Abigail twirled the flower between her fingers as they walked, until the stem broke down and wilted.

"Have many been through your town in recent years?" Abraham asked.

"No one." Abigail shook her head. "You're the first person I've seen since my parents."

"You never tried to leave?" Abraham had never come across another human who'd been so sedentary, most moved or searched for better. Abraham was sure that humans preferred not to live independently. It was rare that he came across one who wasn't eager to return to a civilized society.

Abigail shrugged. "Where would I go? I was afraid. And I had everything I needed to survive. If I left, who knows what would have happened." She turned to glance behind them. "I miss it already. The lacquered wood of the library, the smell of the aging pages. I've met everyone I've ever needed to meet, all of my friends were on the pages of my favorite books. And you know the good thing about that? They never changed; they were always the same people. Life didn't change them. Are we there yet?" Abigail asked.

Abraham pointed to the mountains in the close distance. "We go over the ridge and we'll be nearly there. By tomorrow sometime."

They walked along a winding road that rose into the mountain. When night came and they had settled to rest, Abraham noticed Abigail rubbing her arms and leaning closer to the small fire.

"Did ye bring a change of clothing?" Abraham asked. "Something warmer than that dress? A blanket, perhaps?"

Abigail's eyes were big as she shook her head. "I didn't bring any extra clothes."

"What did ye bring in that sack then?" Abraham looked at the bag she'd been carrying all day, it was bulging at the seams.

"I told you." Abigail pulled the zipper down revealing the bag stuffed with books. "I brought all my favorites. I couldn't leave them behind."

Abraham wasn't sure what to do or say. Most people he picked up on his travels had some sense to pack clothing or food, but not Abigail.

After noticing his disappointment, she started to tremble. "I didn't have real people but the people in these books, they're my friends."

"Don't cry," he soothed. "I've got some food and extra clothing here." He passed her his spare tunic and a few biscuits.

"Thank you." Abigail's hand fell to her cleavage, pulling the fabric aside revealing more of her busty bosom.

Abraham looked away. "No thanks necessary."

When Abigail was settled and warm, she opened a book and began reading by the firelight.

Abraham decided he'd read as well and pulled the small Bible from his pocket.

After a few minutes Abigail looked up and noticed what he was reading.

"You're reading that?" Abigail asked. She looked disgusted with him.

"Aye, suppose I am. Been reading it for a while now, trying to make heads or tails of it."

"I read that once. My parents made me," Abigail replied as she turned away. "It's boring."

"Aye," Abraham closed the cover. "Suppose some could see it as boring."

Abigail, quick on her feet, pulled the book from Abraham's hands and tossed it into the fire.

"Aye! What are ye doing?" Abraham moved to pull the burning book from the flames.

"Saving you wasted time." Abigail bent and rummaged in her bag. "Here." She pulled a book out and tossed it to him.

Abraham was still busy stomping the fire out of the burned Bible but was quick enough to catch the one flying through the air at him. He turned it over and read the cover. "Moby Dick" by Herman Melville.

"It's about a man and a whale." Abigail stood, grabbed the Bible and threw it back in the fire again.

"Naw, could you find it in yer brain to stop throwing my book in the fire?" Abraham had to kick it out of the tallest flames as the hem of his pants singed.

"I'm just trying to save your sanity." Abigail settled again and resumed her reading. "One day you might thank me for it."

Abraham looked between the quiet woman, the book in his hand and the book that was smoldering on the other side of the fire. He sat down again and cracked the cover on *Moby Dick*.

Abraham enjoyed time like this. There were few he'd met who could enjoy the quiet, who could sit in silence without filling the void with nonsense like Nova and now Abigail.

After nearly an hour, Abigail closed the cover of her book and stared at Abraham from across the flames. "I think you should come over here and keep me warm."

"I already gave you my shirt." He refused to make eye contact. She was like a tigress on the prowl.

She pouted. "It smells like you, but I'd rather have you closer to keep me warm. Please, Abraham."

He shook his head. "I don't think that's a good idea."

Abigail pouted but kept to her side.

Just because she wanted to mate with him didn't make her a bad person. But she was persistent and naïve. This planet would eat her alive. Bringing her to his people was for the best.

*

In the morning, Abraham woke with a hand down his pants—which wasn't his—and heavy breathing in his ear.

His eyes flicked open.

Abigail moaned and nibbled on his earlobe. "Come on, sexy. Don't you want me?"

"Aye, you're very nice to look at," he said as he pushed her away. She twisted her shoulders and thumped her torso on his. He got a better grip on her shoulders and held her away as he moved to sit.

She grabbed his privates before he could escape and held on tight. Her stroking had ignited a heat he usually kept tampered down.

"Oh, Abe," Abigail licked his neck, "you're so hard. Please, tell me there isn't another woman enjoying this big piece of... *mmmm*."

Abraham fought between racing to the other side of the planet and giving in to Abigail. She was soft and smelled nice. The curves of her body welcomed the hard planes of his. Abraham's hand slid to her hip and gripped the fabric of her dress.

With one thought of his Mother and her demands, he had himself under control again.

He went soft in a heartbeat.

"Oh." Abigail released him with a pout. "You had me so excited."

"Don't take it personal, you're a nice woman and all," Abraham adjusted his pants as he scooted away from her. "I'm just not interested in you in a sexual manner."

"Hm." Abigail crossed her arms.

"They're plenty of fish in the universe." Abraham stood and moved away from her.

"I thought it was fish in the sea?" she scowled.

"Aye, it could be. Either way, just because I'm not interested doesn't mean there won't be a hundred men interested in you when we get where we're going."

"A hundred?" Abigail asked breathily and fanned herself.

"Well, more than one at least. I've got plenty of brothers eager to find a mate."

"Are they handsome like you?" she asked as she stood and adjusted her clothes.

Abraham shrugged. "I'm not sure what you consider handsome, but we do resemble each other, at times."

Abigail clapped and skipped. "I can't wait."

*

Abraham left the singed Bible in the forest.

Another day of walking—and Abraham fighting off Abigail's advances—passed until they reached the floating city.

"Wow," Abigail exclaimed as she looked up. "How do we get up there?"

Abraham reached for a tentacle. "You hold one of these."

Abigail walked closer. The tentacle pulsed, beckoning her.

"Are you coming with me?" Abigail asked.

"I'm afraid not." He shook his head. "I have more work to do here."

"Well, in that case…" She flung her arms around his neck and pressed her lips to his. When she pulled away she said, "Goodbye, Prince Charming."

Abraham was sure his face was as red as the sun.

Abigail grabbed ahold of a tentacle boldly. "Ooh, it's warm!" she said as she was pulled up and up and up. "Bye, Abraham." She waved.

Abraham stood there, stunned. He'd never met a woman quite like Abigail. She was…entertaining. The Heat Wave and cruelty of the human race had spared her. Before he walked away, something fell from the sky, smacking him on the top of the head. It landed in the dirt in a cloud of dust. He bent to pick it up, recognizing one of Abigail's romance novels.

Abraham laughed out loud as he tucked the book into his pack and headed for the farmhouse where Nova and Joy were waiting.

CHAPTER FOURTEEN

Nova

We have been eating sun-fried eggs cooked on a stainless-steel pan I left out in the sun all morning. It's hot as heck. When I toss a slab of butter down it sizzles and melts in an instant, the eggs even faster. There is no over-easy these days, no runny yolk to dip your toast in, there is hard scramble and hard fried and if I'm not ready with the spatula in time, there is hard-burned.

After cleaning up, I weed the garden while Joy plays on her blanket in the field then do chores inside while she naps. I am deep in thought about what we're doing with our lives as we eat dinner, and even still as we move on to bath and bedtime. As the sun sets, we enjoy our reprieve from the heat with the nearly cool mountain air as I rock her near the open window in her nursery. Every so often I remember the heat of the city and I'm glad I finally left. Once Joy is asleep for the night and tucked in, I retreat to the back porch with a half glass of something relaxing; tea or water or a little bit of rum that I found in the liquor cabinet.

This simple life is an endless circle of events. Heat, survival, rest. Repeat. I wonder if I will ever get bored with it? I've stopped missing my fancy house and my apartment on the top floor. Back then I was eager for the next step in the rat race: go to college, find a boyfriend, get married, buy a house, and then a new car with leather seats. My goals are simplified now. Survive. Grow the baby. Keep her alive. Eat. Sleep. Avoid the violence.

As I rock on the porch, watching the glowing fields in the night, I realize I haven't seen Abraham in nearly two weeks. I know I'm not supposed to ask him where he's going or when he'll return, but it would be nice to have some clue. Bats flutter in the moonlight, feasting on the copious bugs that have spawned in the heat.

I listen for voices, never able to dispel the fear of someone unwanted showing up here. There's rustling in the forest, the hens hum and cluck as they settle in for the night, crickets chirp only to calm and quiet as the glowing starts. I was never much of a scaredy cat, but I have the sudden urge to return inside and bolt the doors.

I'm turning the lock before my rocking chair recovers from my abrupt departure.

As I check the lock and the windows, I tell myself that I'm not waiting for him, that I've never sat by and waited for any guy in my life. I decide to busy myself with the task of rearranging the cupboards so I don't think about when Abraham will be back.

During one of our trips to Wal-Mart, Joy and I pick out some clothing that might fit Abraham. I'm not sure what his personal style would be, since all I've ever seen him in is the homespun tunic and pants which look a bit fancy to be traipsing about in this heat. I find him cargo shorts, short sleeved shirts, and a pair of flip-flops.

After returning to the house, I remove the tags from the clothes then wash and fold them. Should I wrap them like a gift or leave them in a neatly folded pile for when he returns? Which is the least desperate? I pick up the pile of clothing and head upstairs to the spare room at the end of the hallway; this room would be the best for him since the people before us have it set up as a guest room. There are no personal touches besides paintings on the wall. The bedspread is white and the rug is clean. I place the clothes on the foot of the bed and try not to think too deeply about it.

After Joy's nap we sit together in the pasture and watch the goats jump off rocks and an old tire that was left behind. One of the goats looks like it's getting fatter and I wonder if it's pregnant or just gaining weight now that they're getting fed grain on a regular basis. Maybe I should pick up a book on raising goats next time I'm at the store?

"Go go go," Joy babbles as she watches them gallop and hop.

"Yes, the goats." I twist long blades of grass between my fingers, braiding them into chains like I did as a child. I think of how Joy's childhood might be similar to mine, growing up in the countryside away from the rat race of a technologically advanced society. Maybe this is good for her. Maybe it's even good for me.

"I bet you wish you could go back in time," John jokes.

I organize medications, supplements, and vitamins into a weekly divider. "Why would I think that?" I ask, distracted, counting. I don't want to mess this up; his oncologist prescribed a special cocktail that is supposed to help stop the spread and control his pain.

"So you could choose someone else." His voice is low, ashamed.

I look up.

He's watching me, serious. His eyes are sunken and cheeks hollow.

"I'd never choose someone else," I say.

He laughs but the sound is weak. "First the polar ice caps start melting and then I get cancer a year after you marry me. I think if anyone knew they'd make a different decision. They'd use less gas. They'd recycle. They'd say no when I popped the question."

"No I wouldn't." I walk to his bedside and kiss him on the lips. "Maybe one of those sorority hoes you used to date in college might make a different decision, but not me. I'd use all the gas. I'd never recycle. And I'd say yes a thousand times again."

"Promise me," he grabs my arm and holds me close. I can feel his rib bones poking through his chest. "Promise me you'll move on. You'll start a family. You'll do everything we won't get to do."

I nod and swallow down tears. "Sure, John. I promise. All of that."

"Good." He moves my hand to his mouth and kisses my palm.

My eyes wander, afraid of him seeing the fear lingering.

His harmonica is sitting on the nightstand, coated in dust. He hasn't had the energy to touch it in months.

I wonder if John would have survived the heat or if he would have gone crazy like so many other people? I wonder if my nagging him about folding his socks and underwear would have led him to strangle me in a fit of rage. Hey, it happened to other women once the Heat Wave got worse. All it took was a little tic to set off the wrath in anyone. I read all about it in the papers, before they stopped printing them.

"Abfffft," Joy sputters, trying to speak and sound out words like babies do. She points across the field.

"I have no idea what you're talking about, kid." I follow the point of her pudgy finger.

"Chee."

Sometimes I wish babies were born with language. It would make things easier. "There are no chickens over there." I squint.

There is movement in the shadows.

I move to my feet in a hurry. I hate this feeling, the threat of imminent danger and knowing that you're sitting in an open field like a present to any mad visitor who decides to explore.

The figure waves as it moves closer.

"It's me, Nova," Abraham shouts as he walks up the canopied driveway.

A breath of relief escapes. "Thank Jesus," I mutter as I sit down next to Joy again.

Abraham leans on a fencepost for a few minutes, watching us before he drops his bag and steps over the rails. He reminds me of an old western movie where the man returns from a long day's ride. The difference is, I don't run to him and throw myself at him like the wives do in those movies.

Abraham sits in the grass on the other side of Joy.

"How was your trip?" I ask.

"Oh," he scrunches up his face and leans back on his elbows, "about the same as the other trips."

"Where did you go?" I'm walking a fine line between prying and making conversation.

Abraham settles on his back and stares up at the sky. "Here and there, but mostly north of here."

He never lists a town or gives me exact mileage. Maybe it's better this way. He did say I was safer not knowing so I stop pestering him.

Joy is leaning toward Abraham, waving her arms and trying to get his attention, whispering "Heee." It almost sounds like "Hi."

"I think she wants you to pick her up," I tell him.

"Aye, guess that's what she's trying to get across." Abraham leans to the side and lifts Joy under her arms. He presses her above him, flying her through the air. Joy giggles; she kicks her legs and waves her arms.

I look away and sneak my iPhone out of my pocket. The urge to capture a candid picture is hard to break after so long. I touch the screen to turn it on. The battery light is red. I snap the picture and just as my phone dies, I get a glimpse of Abraham flying my daughter through the air, the sun gleaming, the grass green as can be. There's a pinch in my chest.

"Do you ever stop at the stores when you're traveling?" I ask.

"Oh, there's not much of a need for me to." Abraham smiles as he tilts Joy from side to side.

"Could you check the stores you come across, for me?"

"I suppose." He makes strange noises with his lips. Joy giggles louder and claps her hands.

"I need some batteries. Preferably double A's. As many as you can find."

"What might ye need those for?" he asks.

I slide my phone back into my pocket. "It's best you don't know." He can have his secrets. I can have mine. I get the feeling my secret is a lot less harmful than his.

I stand and head to the chicken coop to hunt for evening eggs.

*

"I'm not sure what you want for dinner," I say from the pantry. "There's more meat in here. There's a ... whole chicken. Huh." I lean in closer to inspect the large jar. These people shoved an entire chicken, bones and all into the jar. I lift it and turn around. "I could make a soup, maybe with rice, out of it. I guess."

Abraham is staring at the jar. I don't blame him; it looks like something from a mad scientist's laboratory.

"Aye, if chicken soup with rice looks better than what's in that jar." He swallows hard, like it reminds him of something else, something dangerous.

I set the jar on the counter. "I hope it does. The venison stew turned out okay. Let's hope this does."

Abraham entertains Joy as I cook. I open the jar with a pop and shake out the chicken out into a colander that I placed over a large pot. I do my best to separate the meat from the bones. The bones go in a separate pot of water to be boiled down for broth. I add cans of carrots, potatoes, onion, and some chicken stock. Then salt, pepper, fresh thyme, oregano, and basil from the garden go in with a few chopped tomatoes. As it's cooking, I'm hoping the soup tastes as good as it smells.

"Maybe you could pick up nuts, or peanut butter, or something. Almonds if you come across them. It would add more protein to our diet." I turn to set the table. Abraham is stretched across the floor as Joy pushes on his stomach like she's doing the Heimlich. I come to the conclusion in that instant, that my child is a bit rough when it comes to playtime. "Joy? If you keep pounding on that man like he's a punching bag, he'll never come back."

Joy frowns and plops down on her butt. "Cheeeee." She whispers in defeat.

"What does Cheeee mean?" Abraham asks.

"She's trying to say chicken." I set down glasses. "I think."

"And why do ye like the chickens so much?" he asks Joy.

She blinks at him.

"Who doesn't like chickens?" I set spoons down next to the bowls. "They're fluffy, they cluck and croon, the ones here let her pet them. I like the chickens. They're cute."

"Aye, see what yer saying there, but you like them enough to eat them?"

I stand up straight. I wonder if Abraham is vegan and didn't realize it, and I didn't know any better, and all this time I've been cramming venison and eggs and canned chicken down his throat. "I...I guess I could make you something else to eat." I wipe my hands on my pants. "I guess I didn't think about what your people eat." I lick my lips nervously. "Most settlements west of the Blue Ridge eat anything they can find. They hunt and..."

Abraham sits up and Joy slides down his side. She reaches for a set of toy keys and shakes them vigorously.

"I didn't mean to upset ye. I was just curious," he says.

"Oh?" I ask. "Why?"

"I find it strange ye eat animals yer fond of."

"Don't your people?" I ask.

"No."

Joy shakes the keys one last time before sending them sailing out of her chubby hand and directly into the side of Abraham's head. His eyes go wide when the keys make contact with his temple.

I suck in a breath and cover my mouth with my hand.

Joy's arms stay extended in the air. She's shocked herself. She looks from him to me, her bottom lip trembling.

"Ye have quite the arm on ye, wee one." Abraham picks up the keys and sets them in Joy's lap.

"Are you okay?" I ask.

"Aye. Taken a few hits harder than that in my lifetime." He rubs the side of his head.

Joy's lip keeps trembling until she starts to cry.

"What did I do?" Abraham asks.

"I think she's tired and hungry."

Without my asking, he stands and lifts her, then walks to the table. Joy sobs on his shoulder for a few minutes before falling asleep.

I round the table. "Here, I'll put her to bed."

Abraham passes her to me, and we become an awkward tangle of arms. I feel my face flush. "Sorry," I mutter. "I'll be back in a few minutes."

I carry Joy upstairs, change her diaper, and lay her down in the crib. She sleeps through it all. She's been awfully tired lately; she must be having a growth spurt.

When I return to the kitchen, Abraham is waiting for me.

"You could have started eating," I say.

"Aye, suppose I could have but I'd rather wait for you."

I move to the stove and ladle the soup into our bowls.

Abraham takes his and sniffs it.

"Do you think it's all right?" I ask.

"One way to find out." He takes a mouthful.

I test the soup, sipping it off the spoon. It tastes like onion and garlic and carrot and herbs. Better than Campbell's.

"Does it pass the test?" I ask.

"Aye." Abraham nods. "It'll do for eating a pet."

I look up, horrified. He grins. A heartbeat passes before I laugh at his teasing.

We eat in silence then Abraham offers to get water from the well without my asking. I wash the dishes in a bin of old soapy water from the previous night, and when Abraham returns, he pours the freshly pumped water in the sink for me to rinse.

"Thank you," I say.

"We could hunt." Abraham offers.

"What?" I ask as I dry my hands.

"You wanted more protein. We could hunt the surrounding forest." He motions to the land beyond the window.

"I've never used a gun, or anything, really." I cross my arms.

"And you've survived this long without?"

I nod.

"Yer lucky," he says. "Most of the people I've come across have some type of firearm. Or many."

"Do you come across a lot of people?" I ask.

"Oh," he nods, "Aye, suppose I come across enough." He stares at the door like being in this house is causing him discomfort.

"You want to sit on the porch?" I ask. "I brought back some beer last time I went to Wal-Mart."

"Aye, sounds like a nice way to end the day."

I grab two cans and follow him outside.

The glowing has already started in the nooks and crannies of the trees where humidity from the air and dew has collected.

"I wonder where this started?" I motion to the trees.

"The blue light?" Abraham asks as he sips at his drink.

"It was never like this before. You had to go to foreign countries or Florida to find cyanobacteria that glowed like this in lakes and oceans."

"This world is changing." The way Abraham says it, it sounds like an omen.

"It's already changed," I remind him. "So much has changed. It's all so different. Joy will never know the world I grew up in."

We drink in silence and take in the night.

"Thank you, Nova," Abraham says.

"For what?"

"The clothes you left in my room."

I tip my head. "I thought you might like something a bit more normal to wear when you're not traipsing across the planet doing whatever it is that you do. Fresh clothes always make me feel a little more human on the worst days."

"Aye." Abraham sips at his drink. "They do."

"Sorry my kid hit you in the head."

He smiles wide. "It was the best part of my day." He rubs his temple.

"It was?" I laugh.

"Aye, well, besides right now. Being bopped in the head by wee Joy was the best part of coming home."

Home...

"Promise me you'll move on. You'll start a family. You'll do everything we won't get to do."

Abraham referred to this place as home and suddenly this situation seems like a bit more than two people surviving together.

In an effort to escape a tangle of emotions, I ask, "Do you want to listen to some music?"

"Sure." Abraham is calm, unknowing how much his simple mention of home has affected me.

I pull my phone out of my pocket and press a playlist. The battery light is still blinking, and I know this might be the last music I listen to for a while.

CHAPTER FIFTEEN

Abraham

Far to the south Abraham walked a winding road; he was thinking of the chicken in the jar. It reminded him of something dangerous he'd encountered once in a far-away place, a creature with scales and a black beak that smelled like rot. He shivered. At least the soup tasted good. His thoughts rambled to his time with Nova and Joy. Never before had he lived in the home of a live human. It wasn't much different than the homes of his people, except that humans tended to collect things like pictures and trinkets and extra blankets.

Abraham slowed. Not far ahead the decaying bodies of humans were scattered in the leaf-strewn road. He could tell they had died not long ago. He walked closer, inspecting. They wore makeshift armor; a bicycle helmet, kneepads, homemade chainmail from baking pans and cooling racks. Some died tangled in combat; others curled in a lonesome fetal position. There were men and women and the numbers grew greater the further he traveled.

He continued walking toward the village center, passing an elaborate sign announcing,

Welcome to Grovetown
Population 6,002
Established 1998

Abraham thought it was interesting how some towns had signs and others just appeared in the middle of the road with no warning. He passed a brick entrance with a wrought iron gate that was tilted open.

A war had occurred here. Blood smeared the streets and the scent of rotting bodies wafted in the thick air. Baseball bats, hammers, and axes were still gripped in decomposing hands. It could have been the heat that drove them to war, or it could just be that one group had something another group wanted, like a secure town with a gate. He'd seen it on other planets; coveting a neighbor eventually brought war.

Abraham took to the shadows. He stepped over emaciated bodies with sunken skin and crushed skulls.

The street smelled so terrible that he pulled his tunic over his nose as he walked farther. The main road was no more than a strip of four shops and then there were houses with spacious yards and large front porches. Every house looked nearly the same with the exception of the paint colors.

Movement from under a porch caught his attention. Abraham hoped it was an animal or stray dog. He knew bringing back one of these people would be a waste of his time.

He heard a whimper then the sound of something dragging.

"Mister," a young voice called. "Mister, will you help me?"

Abraham crouched and shaded his eyes so he could see under the porch. There was movement, a thin figure reached toward him.

"Don't leave, I need your help." A girl was dragging herself across the dirt. Her lips were pale and cracked, her hair tangled with leaves. Her legs were mangled. As she dragged herself she ripped the skin of her legs on the rough rock. Abraham could smell the fresh blood.

"What can I do for ye?" he asked.

She reached out, her hand clutching a small pistol.

Abraham stepped back.

"Don't go!" The girl cried. "I need you..." Tears were streaming down her face, washing away rivulets of grime.

"What do ye think you need from me?"

"I need..." She groaned as she crawled closer. "I need you to take this gun." She shoved it his way and it scrabbled across the shaded rock and dirt before flipping onto the brown grass of the yard. "And shoot me in the head."

She rolled on to her back, exhausted. "I need you to end this. I don't care what you do with me after. I need you to send me to Jesus. Now. Please. I can't do it. I've tried a hundred times already."

The girl was nothing but jutting bones and pale skin. Abraham could see the lumps on her legs where bones had been broken and healed in odd knots.

"How long have ye been like this?" Abraham asked.

The girl shrugged. "Too long."

"And who did this to ye?"

She pointed at the bodies across the road. "That was one of them, the ones who came to kill us." She pointed to another body. "That's my father, he tried to save us."

"Are ye alone now?" Abraham asked.

She was focused on something far under the porch. "My little brother is there."

He followed her line of vision to a mound in the soil.

"Is he alive?" Abraham asked.

She shook her head. "He's been gone for days." She pointed to the gun. "I'd like to see him again. And my parents. In Heaven. Could you please?"

Abraham kicked the gun away. "Oh, aye, suppose I could if I were a worse kind of man." He reached down and grabbed her wrists, pulling her out from under the porch in one swift movement.

The girl cried out in pain.

"Sorry about that, miss. No good way to do it."

"Don't hurt me!" She screamed. "Please!"

Abraham searched his bag for a blanket. "I don't plan on hurting ye, miss." He laid the blanket out and lifted the girl, placing her in the middle, and then he wrapped her like he'd seen Nova wrap Joy. He set a biscuit in her hand and a thermos of water against her chest before lifting her in his arms.

The girl's eyes were large and round as she watched his every move. "Where are you taking me?" she asked.

"To my people. A safe place. They'll help ye."

"I don't want to go to your people." She flung the biscuit and thermos at his face. She clawed at him, slapped the sides of his head with a strength he didn't expect a broken little girl to possess. Abraham had never seen a reaction like this before when he offered to bring another soul to safety.

"I asked you to end it. I want to go to Heaven. I want to see my family again." She screamed. "I want my brother and mom and dad. I want them, not your people." She was swatting at him and Abraham felt his lip split when her small fist hit his face.

"Stop!" Abraham yelled at the girl. "I am trying to help you."

"I don't want your help!" She screamed in his face. "I want it to end."

"Why do ye want it to end?" he asked.

She whimpered. "It hurts. Everything hurts." She pointed at her legs. "The broken bones." She pressed her hand against her concave stomach. "My belly." She touched her chest. "My heart. It all hurts."

"You must take this pain," Abraham tried his best to choose his words carefully, "take this pain and use it to make yourself stronger. Things can be created from pain. Paintings and poems, books and magic, stars and planets. They all came from pain. This is not the end you think you want."

"How?" She was crying now, even though he was sure the girl didn't have enough moisture in her body to produce tears, they still fell.

"You harness it. Take the pain and envision it rolled into a ball, as hot as the sun. You tuck it deep down in the center of your heart and wait. It will make you strong. And when you need it most, call upon it; the pain will keep you alive." Abraham hoped he'd chosen the right words.

When he looked at the girl again, he noticed she'd stopped crying.

"What's yer name?" he asked.

"Lily." She wiped her face dry with the edge of the blanket.

"Lily." Abraham cleared his throat. "Will ye trust me to help you?"

She nodded. "Okay."

He shifted her to one arm and pulled the burnt Bible from his pocket. He'd packed it when Abigail wasn't looking. "Can ye read?"

"Yes." She turned the small book over in her hands. "My mother used to read this to me and my brother."

"This brings some of yer people comfort."

"Does in bring you comfort?" Lily asked.

"It brings me awareness," he replied.

His people didn't follow the word of a single book, but the thoughts and recommendations of millions from every planet imaginable. Still, it didn't break through the stubbornness of his people at times.

Lily read from the book until she fell asleep in his arms.

Abraham carried her throughout the night. He stopped once to eat and drink and to set food in her hands for when she woke. Lily was so exhausted she slept through his movements. She slept while he followed a deer trail through the forest, avoiding the town and house where Nova slept. He'd made a promise not to return to her house with another soul, even if it was a child.

Abraham stopped twice to check Lily's pulse. It was thready and weak and he suspected the girl wouldn't have survived much longer if she couldn't gain the strength to shoot herself in the head; dehydration or starvation would have taken her.

Abraham walked though his arms were nearly numb and his own stomach growled for food. He walked as fast as he could, carrying Lily, feeling her thin bones press against the muscle of his arms. The girl was near death.

Abraham couldn't help but envision Joy in her place. He tried to push the thought away. What he wouldn't do to prevent pain like this from reaching Joy or Nova.

"Mister, shouldn't you set me down and get some sleep?" she whispered.

"Oh, aye, suppose it would be a smart thing to do but getting you to the safety of the city is more important now. More than once in the night I was sure you'd left me."

"I wish I had gone." She looked above them, to the canopy of the trees and cloudy blue sky beyond. "I'd be able to see them again."

"Yer a very sick girl," Abraham pointed out. "But ye won't be dying on my watch."

Abraham couldn't walk fast enough. Between the need to get Lily to safety and head back to Nova, every step was faster than the previous.

Abraham hadn't felt this feeling before, an urge to return to Nova. He'd left her many times to go searching for people to bring back to the floating city and he always returned to her afterward, but on this trip his legs wouldn't move fast enough.

He was distracted and distraction begets the cautious eye of the weary traveler. Abraham didn't hear the sound of movement in the majestic trees above him, and he barely heard the soft thud of boots landing on the forest floor. It was too late when he finally did hear the hammer of a handgun knock, and the sharp ting of a blade being pulled from its sheath.

Abraham stopped moving. He turned in a slow circle, taking in the nine men surrounding him.

"Hand the girl over," a man ordered. The man was carrying a baseball bat and enough confidence to let Abraham know that he was in charge.

"Do what he says, now," a man missing his front tooth said, nudging a gun in Abraham's direction.

Abraham spoke to the man with the bat. "Seems you have a bone to pick but you'll have to find another traveler. I have to get this girl home."

"Unfortunate for you," the man said as he tapped the end of the bat in his open palm.

Abraham felt those behind him moving closer.

"I'm scared," Lily whispered as she tucked her face against Abraham's chest.

"His clothes are weird," the one with the missing tooth said.

"You're not from around here. My boys here will welcome you to the neighborhood." The man tapped his bat against his boot.

"Aye, prefer they'd let me pass in peace," Abraham said.

"Can't do that for you." The man thumped his bat on the ground. "We're hungry and your clothes look warm and that girl looks sweet. We take what we want."

They laughed.

It was sickening.

Abraham was no longer distracted. He was focused. He knew a crowbar was swinging for the back of his skull. Abraham dropped to the ground, releasing Lily from his arms and swiping his leg to knock down the man behind him.

"Don't move. And close your eyes," he warned Lily as he pulled the three-pronged weapon from where it was secured at his belt.

The man behind him fell, his head hitting the hard ground with a sickening *thwack*. Seven men advanced on Abraham. The one with the bat watched. Abraham was quick to deliver kicks to the center of the chest and sternum-cracking punches, then stabbed two men through their necks. They dropped gurgling. Another was sliced through the ribs and Abraham could hear the whisper of human lungs leaking air. One was stabbed in the lower back; he'd probably live for a few weeks but never walk again. Another didn't take the hint when Abraham stabbed him in the shoulder, the burly man kept coming after him and Abraham was left with no choice but to decapitate him. The burly man's head dropped to the left, but his body dropped to the right, falling on Lily. Another was relieved of his arms, one stabbed up through the soft space under his chin and into his skull.

"Enough!" The man with the bat roared.

Abraham turned; ready to take on the remaining few men who were standing.

The one in charge had both hands on the bat, ready to swing.

"If yer ready for more," Abraham held his arms out.

The man in charge pointed his bat at Abraham.

Abraham flung his weapon, end over end it flew and struck the man in his left eye. He dropped to the ground.

The remaining three men were no bother after that. They turned and ran into the forest.

Lily groaned from under the body of the burly dead man. Abraham went to her side and rolled him off.

"Lily?" he asked. "Are ye okay?"

She was very still but Abraham could see the slight movement of her chest. Abraham lifted her into his arms.

"I can't feel my legs," she whispered.

"Aye," he nodded, "suppose I won't soon either."

Abraham was still a day's walk from the city, maybe two if he were traveling with a particularly slow bunch.

But Abraham didn't have a day or two, he was sure Lily wouldn't make it more than a few hours.

Abraham ran.

He ran over tangled brush and through empty towns, down barren roads and across rocky paths. He ran until he could barely breathe, and his arms ached. He ran until he saw his people's city floating in the sky. When he reached the tentacles he finally stopped.

Lily was pale. Her head lolled to the side, her breath nothing more than a raspy rattle.

"I promised ye my people would fix you," Abraham said as he grabbed a swaying tentacle. "Let's hope I'm not too late."

Abraham wrapped the tentacle around Lily's middle, another around her legs, another he coiled and laid her head on. All the while he could feel the summoning pulse of the city, eager for another child.

When she was secure, Abraham stepped away. The free tentacles moved on their own, wrapping themselves around Lily's nearly lifeless form, supporting her in a cocoon. It lifted her with a speed he'd never seen before, as if the city could tell she didn't have long.

Once she disappeared into the base of the city, Abraham could finally breathe. He collapsed on the ground; taking in the deep breaths he'd deprived himself of when he ran. His legs ached, his arms were numb, something burned behind his eyes. Abraham had never felt so hollow before.

So much had happened in this short day. Abraham had killed men. He hadn't done that in a long time. Even though they were bad men, he hadn't given them a chance. But he'd saved Lily.

Abraham rolled to his side and crawled to his feet. He collected his things and began walking away.

The walk to the mountain road where Nova and Joy lived gave him time to collect his thoughts and center. Abraham was focused. He circled the town, backtracked and tried to hide his path, he had to make sure none of those men had followed him.

Only when he was certain did Abraham start walking down Mulberry Road. His heart beat faster with each step he took. Anticipation was a drug propelling him forward, faster with each step. Except. Just before he reached the break in the trees that once served as a driveway, Abraham stopped.

Someone was standing there waiting for him, and it wasn't Nova.

"How did ye find me, Jacob?" Abraham asked.

"It wasn't hard. I should have asked how is it that you didn't know I would be standing here. It seems you've forgotten a few things about your kind." His brother stepped forward.

"Been down here for many years, away from my people. It wasn't hard to forget."

Jacob shook his finger at Abraham. "I couldn't see it before but I see it now, you're unfocused," Jacob pointed out. "That's dangerous."

Abraham pressed his lips together.

"I saw what happened with those humans and that little girl." Jacob circled Abraham, took in the rips in his clothing, the healing wounds. "Another screw up like that and you'll be dead. Then what use will you be to your people?"

"Aye, suppose I'm not much use if I'm not sacrificing to Mother."

"All of your brothers and sisters have paid their debt. You're the stubborn one who refuses. You're the stubborn one who caused a scene in a sacred place."

Abraham shook his head. "It's an archaic tradition."

"Says the banished one." Jacob's tone was condescending, more than usual.

Abraham began walking again.

"I've seen them. That woman you go to and her child," Jacob pressed on.

Abraham stopped in his tracks and his spine went straight. His people were not a violent race, but Abraham felt a wave surge within him. "Aye, figured you might get wind of that. Best you forget them," he suggested.

"How could I forget them? That woman is a perfect specimen, nearly as good at that blond-haired one you brought us many moons ago." Jacob crowded close to Abraham's face. "You're supposed to bring *everyone*."

"I'm having trouble convincing them to leave." Abraham wasn't one to lie to his people; he'd never lied a day in his life, which was why he was down here working this dreadful job. But he'd lie to protect Nova and Joy.

Jacob laughed. "Bring them to the city. Soon. Or I will."

"Oh brother, I suppose you're still sniffing the Elders' assholes, which is why you walk among the heathens every so often so you can run back and tattle on me." Abraham gripped the blade on his belt. "But I'll promise ye, like I promised Mother before my banishment, I'll kill ye before I turn them over to you."

Jacob smirked. "The Elders will love to hear that. I bet it will get your sentence doubled. You'll be culling planets until your balls shrivel up and fall off."

"All the better then, brother, once I lack my reproductive parts Mother will expect nothing from me." Abraham smiled wide at the thought. "It sounds mighty liberating."

Jacob's face turned red. "Every time I come down here, you're more and more like them. Crude and... filthy."

Abraham spread his arms wide. "Aye, ye sent me to live in the house of the heathens, what did you expect?" He slapped Jacob on the shoulder as he passed. "Now get in yer pitiful little ship and fly on up to the heavens. I'm tired of looking at you."

Jacob twisted to face Abraham. "You have to answer to someone, you can't just keep living out here in the wild with all this," Jacob snapped his arms wide, "freedom!" Jacob's eyes were wild like Abraham had never seen, like the eyes of a beast before it attacked. Perhaps the boundaries of their people were weighing on Jacob, perhaps the Elders were requesting more of him, and perhaps Jacob would never stop competing with his exiled brother.

"Ye gave up yer freedom the moment you sided with the Elders." Abraham stepped close to Jacob, threatening. "There was a time that we agreed. There was a time that you believed in the same thing I did." Abraham tapped two fingers over his breastbone and held them out. "Have ye passed your firstborn on to her yet? Did ye feel the ache in yer heart?" He jabbed a finger against Jacob's chest, over his heart, it was as though he could feel the pain of loss. "You did. Have we grown so far apart that you couldn't tell me ye'd found a partner? And with all the time that has passed she was with child, ye never mentioned a word of it to me. Did she give you a moment to hold the babe before she took it or did she rip the child from your arms like a greedy monster?" Abraham paused for only a moment. "Do you see what I fight for now?"

"It's your turn to hand over something you love," Jacob sneered.

"I gave up my home. I gave up my brothers and sisters. What else would ye like me to give up?"

Jacob quietly pointed at the farmhouse in the distance.

"I may be but a sole man, but I will bring a reign of pain upon you if you touch them." Abraham held his hand out. "Join me, brother. Join the fight for change. There could be a chance that your firstborn could be returned to you. We could win. If only I were not alone in this struggle."

Jacob shook his head. "It's too late for me. It's too late for you. Bring them to the city. I won't keep your secrets for much longer. We can't stay on Earth forever; there are more planets suffering from violence. The Elders complain that you are taking too long already. You've culled larger planets in half this time."

Abraham stood steady and still as he watched Jacob walk away. His heart was thumping like a racehorse. He worried that Jacob had gone to the house and that he might have done something to Nova and Joy. He had to control himself from running up the driveway to check on them. And if his brother touched either of them, Abraham knew he'd make his second visit to the floating city in a day, he'd climb the tentacles himself and enter the city through the emergency hatch and he'd slaughter his brother in front of the Elders.

Abraham stilled and took a breath; he decided to refrain from plotting the murder of his brother, for just a little bit, to check on Nova and Joy.

CHAPTER SIXTEEN

Nova

Abraham is limping. He's passing the low branches of the driveway and not putting his full weight on his left leg. I've never seen him come back wounded before and it worries me. I leave the shucked peas in the pots and the shade of the porch to walk toward him.

He smiles, tight-lipped. While every other time he's come back he's been smiley and relaxed, this time there is a wrinkle across his brow and he's strangely quiet.

"You're injured." I move closer to help him but I'm not sure what to do. Abraham is caked in dirt and smells like a swamp.

"Aye, suppose a bit." He scans the yard as we walk to the house. "Are you and Joy okay? Was anyone here?"

"Why? Did you come alone?" I ask, blocking the steps to the porch. All I can think is that he was attacked, and he led them straight to us.

"Promised ye I would always return alone." He places two fingers over his breastbone.

I glance at the path behind him, waiting for someone to jump out of the shadows.

"What happened?" I ask.

"Same as always happens." He sighs. "You said you wouldn't ask."

He won't look at me. He always looks at me when we're talking, to a point that it makes me slightly uncomfortable.

"Abraham." I reach out, gripping his chin, and force him to look me in the face. There are dark circles under his eyes. "When is the last time you slept?"

"Oh, been a few days. More than five moons at least." His eyes wander and he's looking everywhere but at me.

"Abraham."

"Nova." He finally stares at me and exhales. His shoulders slump as he relaxes.

"Were you violent?" If he's changed, I can't have him here any longer. I can't risk it.

"Aye, but it was in self-defense." He touches my elbow and I let go of his chin. "I promise."

"Okay." I believe him.

"Might I pass ye?"

I step aside and let him finish climbing the steps. I run ahead and open the door. "Set your bag there." I point to a chair in the kitchen. "I'll wash your clothes while you rest."

The way he's dragging his feet I doubt he'll be upright much longer.

He kicks his boots off near the door and makes his way to the stairs.

"Do you have wounds that need cleaning?" I ask.

"Aye." He nods.

"I'll get some water and meet you in the bathroom."

His heavy footsteps echo as he walks up the stairs. I cringe, hoping he doesn't wake Joy from her nap.

I pump water from the well into a bucket, grab some towels and washcloths and bring it all upstairs to the bathroom. I set everything on the countertop, thanking my time spent with the women at the Convent who taught me a few medical things.

"Do you need help?" I ask Abraham.

"Not at this time."

"I didn't have time to warm the water," I warn. It's not ice cold like the well water of my childhood but lukewarm these days.

I leave him alone and return to the kitchen. I dig through his bag, searching and searching, until I find them. Four packs of double A batteries.

"Thank you, Abe," I whisper.

I scramble for my external charger, switch out the batteries, and plug my phone in. I tap my foot, waiting and waiting and waiting for the screen to illuminate. When it finally does, I slide my finger across the screen and make sure the pictures, videos and music library are still there. I release a breath as relief floods me.

There's a thud from upstairs.

I run up the stairs to check on him.

He's not in the hallway or the bathroom. The guest room door is closed. I crack the door open. He's on his side, looking out the window at the afternoon sky, eyes half-lidded in exhaustion. I enter the room, focusing on the wound on his shoulder. There's deep bruising on his ribs, neck, and lower back. It's rare I see him in any state of undress; it makes me wonder if he's embarrassed about something.

"What was that noise?" I ask.

Abraham's eyes focus on me. "Ye shouldn't be looking at me like this."

"Sorry. I heard a noise. I came to check on you." I pause. "I'll go now."

"Wait, Nova." His voice is weak.

I stop.

"Could ye do something for me? Could you touch me?"

"Ah…" I swallow hard. The last time I touched a man I got knocked up. I'm sure the only reason I've survived this long is because I never touched a man again and I never let one touch me.

"Aye, know what yer thinking but not like that. It will help me heal. My spirits at least. Just a little bit of your energy." He taps his fingers on his shoulder. "Right here. Could ye just settle yer hand on my shoulder here? It's the only place that doesn't ache terribly."

I turn to face Abraham. His eyes are closed as he waits for my decision.

"It sounds easy enough." I walk closer and set my hand on his shoulder. He's half-covered by a sheet but under that I can tell there's nothing else.

"You can sit," he says. "Just keep yer hand there for a little while longer, please."

"Okay." I sit on the edge of the bed and lean across the extra pillow.

He makes a low sound in his throat like a cat purring.

I've spent plenty of time with Abraham, but I can't say we've ever touched each other, nothing more than the gentle swipe of our fingers when passing a glass and such. We seem to respect each other's space. Still, laying here with him with my hand on his bare warm skin, it makes me miss John something terrible. I have to exert plenty of control not to run out of the room and scroll through all of those pictures and watch his videos.

"Yer thoughts are racing faster than light speed." He sighs. "Be still, Nova. Be still."

I take a deep breath and do my best to vanquish all thoughts of John and Abraham and everything that's happened since the Heat Wave.

Be still, I repeat in my mind over and over again. I settle my head on my folded arm and close my eyes.

*

"Momom mamma!" Joy shouts from her crib.

My eyes flick open. I'm in Abraham's room, my hand resting against the back of his neck instead of on his shoulder like he asked. He's still sleeping, exhausted. I sit up straight, slide off his bed so not to disturb him, and make my way out of his room.

"Momom!" Joy babbles.

"I'm coming," I whisper as I close the door to the guest room.

I collect my child from her crib, change her and make lunch. We spend time outdoors in the shade of a large willow, hiding from the sun that's breached the other side of the mountain peak.

I pick tomatoes and cucumbers for dinner, then check the chicken coop for eggs.

"Freeloaders," I mutter when I find their nests empty, again.

Dinner is a simple cucumber salad with soft goat cheese and tortillas spread with butter and basil. I open a bottle of wine, needing a drink to numb my brain after all that thinking I did in Abraham's bedroom. I turn on my iPhone and play some music, the volume low so only I can hear it.

Joy falls asleep in her highchair after she's eaten. I bring her to bed and return to the table alone. I light a single candle and wait. I drink a half glass of wine and let it soak in. It's a store brand I've never heard of before that's not too sweet and not too dry.

John always used to bring home the wine; he was the wine connoisseur who knew what to pair with what. I felt like a bit of an idiot scanning the shelves for something to bring back. Luckily, I got a few different types. The one I'm currently drinking has a screw top, which is how it was chosen for dinner. Strangely enough there isn't a corkscrew here and I couldn't get the others open.

It's not long before I hear Abraham's footsteps coming down the stairs.

"Evening," he says as he sits across from me.

"Feeling better?" I ask.

"Aye, a bit." There are still dark circles under his eyes. He drinks from a tall glass of water, but I see him eyeing my wine.

"Want some?" I ask.

"Aye, if it will soothe this ache in my ribs."

I shrug. "It can't hurt to try."

Abraham eats like a man who went away for nearly two weeks and didn't eat a bite. The cucumber salad and goat cheese are gone before the tortillas.

"It seems you didn't eat on your trip," I say.

He motions to my phone. "Aye, was too busy scouring the world for batteries for ye."

"Thank you for that. Even if it led to starvation, I think it was worth it." I tease him with a smile.

"No problem." He raises his hand. "I almost forgot." He stands and walks toward his bag. "There's one other thing." He digs through the bag and pulls out something fluffy and white that I didn't notice when I was rummaging through his belongings.

"What's that?" I ask.

Abraham turns, he's holding out a little chicken stuffed animal with derpy eyes.

"Oh god." I laugh. "She's going to love that."

Abraham smiles. "Aye, thought so myself when I saw it." He sets the chicken on the couch before he returns to the table and starts eating again.

"When is the last time someone touched you?" I ask.

He stops chewing and swallows. He wipes his mouth. "Over seven hundred moons have passed."

"Abraham?" I try to control my facial expressions, completely shocked that a man like him has been abstinent for so long.

"Aye?"

I'm not sure what to say. Not that I'm much different, but men have a way of finding comfort and touch when they need it. And all his talk of his family, I figured his brothers or sisters or parents might give him a hug each time they see him or shake his hand.

"Humans require touch. It's... it's a basic need," I say.

Abraham stares at me intensely.

I think to myself, I'd touch him again. Especially now that he's out of those strange embroidered clothes and wearing something normal; a white T-shirt stretched tight over his biceps and a pair of board shorts. He looks like one of those bodybuilders on the beach. I could touch him like I touched Romeo that night. I couldn't touch him like I did John, that was pure love. But I could touch him like a woman touches a man. It's been a while, but that kind of touch would be easy to remember.

I stand to take care of the dishes.

Abraham grabs my wrist and is looking up at me as I reach for his plate. "Be still, Nova," he suggests.

His breaths are shallow as he licks the corner of his mouth.

I wonder if he can read my thoughts?

"I'm always still," I say.

He releases my arm and pushes his chair back. "You are rarely still."

The screen door slams as he leaves the kitchen and walks out to the porch.

*

In the morning, the hens do not disappoint. I find five eggs and I fry them up on a metal pan I left out on a rock in the middle of the unshaded yard. I find this has been the only benefit of the Heat Wave; I don't need fuel to cook. I can boil water on a rock in the midday sun and bake pumpkin seeds on the hood of a car.

When Joy is done eating her sun-fired eggs, I wash her hands and set her on the floor. She's been crawling and pulling herself up on cupboards and chairs to a standing position. I was worried that she'd never progress this far. But it seems on the good days, when her clubbed foot isn't hurting her, she's reaching her milestones, though a bit later than a child her age should.

Joy is making her way toward the screen door that leads to the porch. She's on a mission, whispering "Chee, Chee, Chee." Joy stands, her chubby fingers gripping the flimsy latch on the screen door.

"Don't open that door, Joy," I warn her.

She looks at me, drool dripping down her chin, her little bottom jaw jutting out and two baby teeth pushing through. "Chee, Chee," she whispers through her teeth.

"The Chees can wait." I scrape leftover egg into a bowl.

Joy rattles the door latch.

"Don't do it, Joy," I warn again. "Don't open that door."

She's been doing this for a few days. Usually she plops down and crawls away. But today she's especially defiant.

She rattles the door again.

I have this fear, similar to the day when Abraham showed up. I'm somewhere else in the house, trusting Joy on her own for a few minutes and when I return to the kitchen where I left her the door is swinging and she's gone. Simply gone. Forever.

Joy rattles the door, looking at me defiantly. If she weren't so adorable—

She rattles the handle harder, opening the door.

"Chee!" She senses freedom and she likes it.

Everyone loves freedom, especially toddlers.

I drop everything and run after her.

"Joy! No!" I slap her hand.

I feel guilty the moment I do it.

Joy starts crying.

I lift her, re-latching the door once I have her settled on my hip.

Abraham is on the porch, watching. His brow wrinkled in concern. No, it's not concern—it's disappointment. He stomps away.

As if I didn't already feel like shit.

Joy cries herself to sleep on my shoulder then I bring her to bed for a nap.

I return to the kitchen to make lunch. I make Joy's and set it by her high chair. I make Abraham's and set his plate at the chair across from mine. Finally, I make mine and sit. I don't eat. I can't eat. It feels like there are a thousand rocks dropping in the pit of my stomach. *Ping ping ping*. I'd rather vomit.

The door swings open.

Abraham walks in and he's staring at me like he has no clue who I am.

"What?" I ask.

"I didn't think you were the type of woman who would hit a child like that."

The guilt I already felt at scolding my child intensifies. "I didn't want to. I have never done it before. But I can't let her hurt herself."

"You should try a different method of teaching," Abraham suggests.

"Like what?" I snap. "You've never been around children before and now you're an expert?"

"Aye, that's the truth, but my people—"

I can't even deal with this shitty conversation right now.

I snap. "How dare you try to tell me how to raise my child? I have to teach her to be safe. I have to teach her these things because the world out there," I point at the very door she was trying to escape through, "will teach her pain and death. I have to teach her how to survive and sometimes there is no other way to teach her. I might have slapped her hand for the first time ever in her life, but it's a hell of a lot less painful than what a horde of violent men would do to her if they found her."

Abraham rubs his chin. "Aye, suppose you might have a point."

"You *suppose*?"

Our interactions have always been mild, but I don't think I've ever been this pissed at him. I have to get out of this house. I have to get away for just one minute—or maybe thirty—before I say something I regret.

"Your lunch is on the table," I say as I weave around him, opening the door and jogging down the porch steps. I walk across the yard to the far end of the pasture, behind the chicken coop and small barn where the chickens and goats are.

I cool down in the creek that's a few hundred yards off the property. The water is warm but it's refreshing, and the trickling sound more soothing than Abraham giving me a hard time for trying to be a decent parent.

At least, I think I was trying to be a good parent. What type of parent lets their toddler just walk out the door at will? Then again, what type of parent runs off after arguing with her roommate, leaving her child? Even if it's only to find a moment of peace 500 yards away.

*

After cooling off, I return to the house. Abraham is standing at the door next to Joy. She's balanced on her foot, her hand on the latch.

Abraham is talking to her in a calm voice.

I rest my arm on the railing to the porch steps and watch.

"Chee," Joy says, rattling the latch.

"Aye, Joy, you want to see the Chees but you have to have your mother with you."

She rattles the latch defiantly, just as she did to me.

"Don't open the door. The world out there isn't safe for a small girl such as yerself."

She rattles the latch, smiling, as any rebellious toddler would do.

"No, Joy. I said ye couldn't go outside right now. You can't go outside alone. It's not safe out there for a little girl all alone." He pauses and swallows hard like he remembered something that didn't settle right. Abraham touches her hand that's on the latch. "No. You can't go outside without yer mother."

"Chee!" Joy pushes as hard as she can against the latch and the screen door pops open. She escapes, crawling across the porch.

I climb the steps and pick her up.

Abraham and I make eye contact.

I raise my eyebrows. No words are needed. Another toddler might listen, but what Abraham doesn't seem to understand is that every child is different; some listen, others need to experience. She was born with free will, something Abraham seems to have forgotten.

I walk Joy across the yard, bringing her to see her chicken friends.

CHAPTER SEVENTEEN

Romeo

I found gas. It only took my last two packs of cigarettes, but we have a full tank and a full backup.

The Sheriff's shirt is soaked in sweat; across his back, under his armpits, and around his neck. His face is as red as a cherry tomato ripe for eating.

"Stop looking at me boy," he snaps as he walks to the driver's side of the truck. He starts coughing and holding his chest like I've seen in the movies every time an overweight man was about to have a heart attack.

"You feeling alright?" I ask.

"Peachy." Duke swallows down his coughing fit and gets behind the wheel of the truck.

I settle our belongings behind the bench seat then get in. "Where are we headed?" I ask.

"New route to Minnesota. Drew it out on this map the past few nights." He tosses a map in my lap.

"Why didn't you mention this before? I could have helped."

"You were too busy floating in that glowing cesspool." His lip rises in disgust.

Ignoring him, I look at the map. "Haven't read one of these in years." I unfold the paper and find his wobbly lines drawn in a crude path. Around the south of Illinois, through Missouri, the edge of Nebraska, South Dakota and then through Minnesota, the wilds of Superior National Forest, with an "X" marking Ely, MN. "We're still trying to make it there?" I ask.

"Never stopped." Duke turns over the engine.

The truck starts with a grumble. After sitting for these few weeks I'm surprised it even started at all.

"I think it might do us good to go back to the Carolinas," I say.

"Can't go back there, son." Duke shifts the truck into reverse and maneuvers out of his parking space.

"This route will take weeks and weeks. We'll be lucky if we're there within a year. Gas is hard to find, and I haven't been able to get the solar panels working again."

Duke slams his palm on the steering wheel. "I don't need to argue with you." He yells, his jowls jiggling, "We are not going back there. I can't go back to see what I did to the missus. I can't!"

He shifts the truck into gear and speeds out of the motel parking lot and onto the highway, two wheels on asphalt, two wheels tilted toward God.

"You should slow down." I grip the door handle as he weaves down the road, the unused solar panels on the roof clanking as all four wheels hit the highway and the suspension bounces.

"I'll very well damn slow down when I'm good and ready," Duke roars.

"Sir," I struggled to decide between the harmonica in my pocket and the gun at my hip, "you're having one of those rage moments," I warn.

He's been getting worse and worse every day. I'll never forget the promise I made to him.

He grips the steering wheel, twisting his hands.

"Calm down," I suggest.

"I am calm!" he screams back. "When, in the history of the world, has a man calmed down when instructed to do so?"

I pull the pistol from my hip and lay it on the map that's spread across my lap. "Pull over."

He glances at me twice, the second time seeing the gun. "Aw, hell." He skids to the side of the road. The driver side door flings open and he barrels out, kicking the overgrown grass on the side of the road. He tears it from the ground and shreds it in his hands. It's something, watching a grown man act like this; sadly I've become accustomed to it over the miles we've driven together. He's like a deranged gorilla.

I should have never agreed to travel to Ely, should've just stayed at my townhouse and burned with the rest of the world. Should've just let my memories of Nova drive me in this slow death.

After his fit, Duke collapses on the ground in the shade of a willow tree.

"Get in the back," I tell him.

"Cursing me to being licked by Satan's breath. I'll die in the heat."

"Better you than me." I motion to the truck bed. "Go on now."

"Aw, you don't trust me anymore, do you, son?"

"Can't say I do, Sheriff." I glance at the map. "And I can't say I'm taking you to Ely. Minnesota is a mighty far drive and we don't have the gas. I've got a stash of supplies back at my old place, enough to keep us going until the end of days. We're going back home." I climb in the driver seat and slam the door.

Duke slides the cab window open. "Don't know why you agreed to this trip if you were going to just make us go back."

I tap the gas gauge. "Barely enough gas to make it back. We might have to walk a ways."

"Fine by me," Duke grumbles. "This truck is about as good as tits on a turtle anyhow."

CHAPTER EIGHTEEN

Nova

Abraham was gone for five days after our fight. He didn't stick around for dinner that night. And while he was gone, I missed the days when you could text someone incessantly after a fight until they responded. But for us it was just silence for days. I guess the lack of communication is actually better because I was sure glad to see him return. I even forgave him for being an asshat.

Abraham is sitting on the couch reading a book. After his travels he always seems to return with a new one. They range from the Bible to magazines; I even caught him reading a romance novel once. Knowing how delicate men are, I don't say anything about the romance novel.

I take inventory on our food stock levels and make a plan for meals for the next few days. Although, whether Abraham is going to be around impacts my planning. Joy and I eat significantly less.

I lean out of the pantry. "Will you be sticking around or do you plan on hitting the road soon?"

Abraham uncrosses his legs and closes the cover of his book, his thumb holding his place. "Oh, guess I should be on my way soon. Maybe in two nights I'll head out."

Well, that's the first time he hasn't referred to the passing of time in moons.

"I only ask because I'm taking inventory on the food situation," I say.

"Do ye need me to go down to that store and collect something for you?" he asks.

A shiver runs up my neck. He just offered to walk down to the store in the middle of the night. I haven't had a soul ask me that since before the Heat Wave struck. Not since John, before he was sick.

"Nova?" Abraham asks.

"Um, no. No, we're good." I'm a little sad now, thinking about John, Jess, and Abraham and how good they've been to me. Who deserves to meet people like this more than once in their life?

I put in my earbuds and zone out as I tinker in the pantry, rearranging and planning. Then I move on to the kitchen to put away the dried dishes from dinner and clean the countertops and table. I pause at the sink, watching the world glow from my kitchen window.

"Low Battery," the voice on my iPhone warns. I pull out my earbuds and check. My phone battery flashes in a worrisome and disappointing wink.

"Do you have any more batteries?" I ask Abraham.

He shakes his head.

"I need some." I turn the brightness of the screen down to try and prolong what little life the battery has left. "Really soon."

"Aye, thought you might say that. Bad news is I brought you every battery between where I've been and where I'm going. Sorry to say I doubt there's one left." He turns a page on his book.

"I need a battery." The ache in my heart starts. I knew the time would come when the iPhone would die for good.

"Aye. Don't think I'll come across any for a while."

"That sucks," I mutter as I sit on the far end of the couch.

There's one thing I've been saving for the end. For when I know I'll never be able to use this phone again. One thing I need to watch.

"I am truly sorry for ye." Abraham turns another page of his book, distracted.

I take a deep breath. I need to do this now. I press my finger to the screen and hit the movie icon, then the image of John. The video starts with us talking, sweet talk like young lovers. Here comes John's smile, his dark hair, his tanned skin. He reaches for me, I swat him away. "Just play it," I hear my voice in the video.

"Okay," he laughs. "Okay. I'll play it."

John has a harmonica. It's wooden, specially made, the reeds inside positioned perfectly. It sounds like a mix between a violin and a cello when he plays. I recognize the notes of "Tears in Heaven." Low and sorrowful. If only he'd known.

I feel a tear slide down my face.

"What's wrong with ye?" Abraham asks. He sets his book down and shifts to face me.

I press my hand over my mouth and shake my head, unable to talk. I should have done this when I was alone, but that damn flashing battery light really kicked my inability to wait into gear.

John keeps playing in the video. He closes his eyes, puts his heart and soul into it. He was always like that when he played.

Abraham scoots to my side and tilts the iPhone so he can see. "Someone special is he?" Abraham asks.

I nod.

The battery light starts blinking. I'm losing power and there's a chance I'll never get to turn this on again.

The screen suddenly goes black. No more John playing.

I pull my knees up and bury my face against my legs.

Abraham touches me, slides his hand up and down my back. "I didn't know ye were keeping this secret from me this whole time, Nova."

I swallow a sob. "I wasn't ready."

"Oh, aye, sometimes we never are." He settles his arm across my shoulders. "Will ye tell me about him?"

"His name was John," I begin. "I lost him before the Heat Wave started."

I tell him about John, about his illness, the suffering. Abraham actively listens, providing nods and encouragement.

My words sound hollowed down a bottomless pit, never to be heard again. I knew deep down I couldn't speak of John beyond this moment. I have to let him go for good. I have to move on. And when my soul is emptied of his memories, I pass the phone to Abraham.

"When you leave again, throw it in a river or a lake or the ocean, if you travel that far," I say.

Abraham rubs his thumb over the smooth screen. Then his hand is on mine, comforting, stroking my skin. His hand moves up my arm to my shoulder. He stops there, squeezing for a moment before pulling me close in an embrace.

"What are you doing?" I ask.

"You yourself said humans require touch. When was the last time?"

"Years," I whisper. His arms tighten around me. "Tell me something else about you," I beg. "I don't want to focus on my past. I'm trying to move on. Tell me something, anything about your family or your travels."

"Aye, well, I can tell you I've been north to the hills of Virginia. It's pretty country up there. Green and lush. Plenty of horses left in their fences."

"Did you set them free?" I ask.

"Aye. I did. A creature so big and beautiful shouldn't be locked up like that." He crosses his leg, shifting closer. "I'll never forget how the beasts looked in my eyes as they galloped out."

"Where else have you been?"

"Down to South Carolina. There's plenty of sand and pine forest. I think that's what sticks out the most, the hint of pine in the air. It's just like the Adirondack Mountains. Have you been there?"

"The Adirondacks? In New York?" I shake my head. "It was always too cold up there for me."

"Plenty warm there now." His fingers rub on my skin in lazy circles. "Oh and then there's Georgia and Florida." He lifts his arm to demonstrate. "The sun is directly over your head. Just shining down on ye."

I nod. "It used to be nice weather around these parts before the Heat Wave, it was just a little bit warm and a little bit cool, never too extreme."

Thunder rumbles and lightning cracks. A fast rain begins pounding the roof. I can sense the change in pressure and within moments Joy begins crying.

I stand and run for the stairs.

"Nova?" Abraham asks. I hear the confusion in his voice, and I don't want him to think I'm running away from him.

"I'm worried someone will hear her," I say. Tension twists tight in my gut. I run up the stairs and pick Joy from her bed, doing my best to soothe her.

I hear the creak of the stairs and the floorboards outside Joy's door.

"Can I help?" Abraham asks in the dim light.

"You can try." I pass him my child.

Abraham holds her close, like her father might, her head settles on his shoulder as he strokes her hair.

"My Mother used to say pain brings strength and great power. You must learn to harness this pain you feel, it can propel you great lengths," he says.

Joy lifts her head and stares at him as though he were speaking another language.

"She's too young to understand when you talk to her like that," I inform him.

"How do you talk to her then?" Abraham asks.

"I just talk to her like normal, not like she's a theology student in college."

Abraham asks, "A theology student?"

"Actually, that's how you talk," I realize.

"Oh, aye, knew I spoke strange, didn't know there was a name for it." He tips his head to eye level with Joy. "Let me simplify for you, wee one. Use the pain to make yourself stronger."

Joy giggles as drool drips down her chin. "Chee, chee, chee!" She waves her hand toward the door.

I move closer, passing her the stuffed chicken Abraham brought her. "The chees are sleeping now, sweetheart. It's bedtime."

The storm passes overhead and the tiny hairs on my arms stand on end with the change in pressure. My ears pop. Joy screams loudly for one dangerous second.

Abraham and I make eye contact.

And then the storm is gone; just like that the rumbles only quake in the distance and the lightning ceases.

Joy head-butts Abraham's chest and wipes her face on his shirt.

I study him as he watches Joy curiously. "You want to help put her to bed?" I ask.

"Aye, suppose I could try."

I motion to her crib. "You just lay her down on her back, tell her goodnight, and walk away slowly."

Abraham sets her in the crib with gentle motion. "Goodnight, wee Joy." He picks up the stuffed chicken he brought her and tucks it under her arm.

*

By morning the storm has left ninety-nine percent humidity in its wake.

I twist my hair up in a bun and dress as light as I can without being half naked in a tank top and thin shorts before heading outside to release the chickens and goats.

The morning starts out the same as it usually does with me talking to plants and animals, stopping every few minutes to listen if Joy has woken up.

The goats are happy to be fed and free of their barn, the female happy to have her udders relieved of milk. I return to the house to set the container of milk on the counter for breakfast then return to release the chickens and feed them. The hens cluck eagerly, pecking at the bugs in the ground. I search their nests, finding three eggs.

"Well at least you're not freeloading today," I chuckle as I pocket the eggs.

"It's funny you mention that," a strange voice says.

I turn.

There is a stranger standing in the doorway of the hen house.

I hold my breath, searching for a way out, but I'm trapped in the small shed. The only way out is a two-foot door meant for the chickens, and I won't fit out that.

The tall man backs away. "Why don't you step out of there," he says, sensing my unease in the small, enclosed space.

I step down out of the henhouse and scan the yard. It seems he's alone.

"What do you want?" I ask.

"Hm." He paces around me in a circle. "It's easy to see why he's kept you from us."

"Who?" I ask.

The man smiles. I recognize his embroidered and layered clothing as similar to what Abraham usually wears, but this man's is unfrayed and vibrant blue and purple.

"My brother." The man circles me.

He looks like no one I know.

"I don't know what you're talking about." I swallow hard, thankful that Joy hasn't woken up yet. And now I'm wishing that I'd take up Abraham on his offer to learn how to hunt. I've got nothing to protect myself from this man, except three chicken eggs, which I don't think will be much help at all. Yolk slime doesn't exactly scare away unwelcome visitors

"He hasn't told you?" the man asks. "I'm surprised, usually our kind are completely truthful."

The screen door to the house slams.

"Look, here he comes now," the man says.

Abraham is making his way across the yard toward us, faster than ever.

The man stands there, smiling proudly, watching.

"If you're talking about Abraham, there's plenty I don't know about him," I confess.

The man looks confused as though he didn't expect me to say that.

"Why are ye here, Jacob?" Abraham asks. His strong hands grip my shoulders and he pulls me away from the man he's called Jacob.

Abraham steps in front of me, shielding me.

"Brother, is this how we greet one another?" Jacob asks.

"At this moment it is," Abraham's voice is calm.

"You haven't introduced us." Jacob steps to the side to get a better look at me. "It's nice to meet you," he pauses, waiting for someone to fill in a name.

"Nova," I offer.

"Nova," Jacob repeats. "So different. Not the usual Abigail or Michelle or April or Lily." Jacob is staring at Abraham with a knowing expression. "Nova," he repeats my name again, slowly this time. "Oh, forgive me. Your kind likes to greet with a handshake."

Jacob holds his hand out, and I am reminded of the first day I met Abraham in that diner—he held his hand out to me just as awkwardly.

I shake. "Nice to meet you."

Abraham scowls at our hands touching. He grabs my wrist and separates my hand from Jacob's before a second passes.

Jacob turns to Abraham. "Your job is to bring *everyone*."

"Aye," Abraham nods, "I am quite aware of this."

"Them." Jacob motions to the house and me.

He must know about Joy too. Unease fills my chest.

"Eventually," Abraham replies.

"What is he talking about?" I ask.

"Go back to the house," Abraham orders.

"What? Why?" I ask.

Jacob is smirking.

"Go, now." Abraham has never yelled at me or spoken sternly, he's expressed how he's felt always in a calm manner, but in this moment I know something is wrong. I turn tail and run for the house.

My mind is reeling and all I can think about is what happened back at the Convent and Jess protecting me from the violence. I thought I'd escaped violence like that. Now I'm not sure. Jacob doesn't seem like he is going to turn violent. He actually seems quite calm.

I take the porch steps two at a time, push open the door, and lock it behind me. I wonder if I should go get Joy and hit the road while the men are distracted? I know I wouldn't get very far. Even if I made it to the Wal-Mart I never found gas for the Hummer. We'd be sitting ducks.

I watch them from the window.

Abraham stands tall, nodding while Jacob speaks. It's the calmest argument I've ever witnessed. Jacob motions to Abraham's clothing. Abraham looks away, ashamed. Something protective comes over me, I have to hold myself back from running out there again and giving Jacob a piece of my mind. Before I can, the conversation ends. Jacob points at the house again. Abraham nods. They part ways, Jacob heading for the trees and Abraham heading for the house.

I leave the safety of the kitchen and walk out onto the porch to meet him.

"I told you to never bring anyone back here," I say once Abraham is within hearing distance.

"I did not bring him here. He came on his own." Abraham looks pissed.

"Who is he?"

"My brother."

I pause. "What does he want?"

Abraham stops at the base of the steps. "He wants me to bring you and Joy to my people."

"Well he is quite rude," I say. "Sneaking up on me like that and acting so high and mighty. I should have throat punched him."

"Aye, he doesn't mean to be so foul. He's just doing what he thinks is best. He's trying to impress the Elders of our people. There are times when forced performance only emphasizes our flaws."

A long time ago, Abraham tried his darndest to get me to travel past the Blue Ridge Mountains to his people. He told me it was safe there and that his family could help. Now I have Joy and her little twisted foot that causes her so much pain at times.

Abraham is watching me closely.

"Your people?" I whisper, remembering there was a time when I was traveling alone with a baby trying to find them. I only stopped because I couldn't go any further. And then things got comfortable. And then Abraham found us.

Memories of last night haunt me. Joy's cries of pain.

"Can they help Joy?" I ask.

"Aye, they can," Abraham says.

"Maybe... maybe we should go?"

Abraham steps up on the stairs until we are eye to eye. "If that's what ye want, Nova. Do ye want me to bring you there?"

"Is it safe?" I ask.

"Aye, safest place left on this planet." He's searching my eyes. "For now."

"Okay." I bite my lip in thought. "Then we should go. If they can help Joy and it's safe there, we should go. How far is it from here?"

"Day or so walk." He looks worried.

"We're that close?" I feel like an idiot for giving up searching, all of those months ago.

"Aye." He steps closer. "Nova—"

"What?"

"If I take ye both to my people, they'll fix Joy's foot; they'll keep her safe and give her a long life. Possibly you as well. But if I take you there, I'll never see you again."

He's looking at me. He's looking at me like we've shared more than a few dinners at a table and my hand on his shoulder while he slept and a warm embrace when I cried for John. He's looking at me like there's much more he's not telling me. Like there's much more he's feeling.

"Whatever your decision. It's no longer safe here," Abraham warns.

"It is safe here. We have everything we could ever need to survive. The only unsafe thing is Jacob. I really like this place."

"Aye, it's mighty peaceful. But it's time to move on regardless." Abraham frowns. "Jacob will be back for ye."

Since the Heat Wave struck, I've been left with nothing but tough decisions. Before it was just me, now I have Joy and I have to protect her. How long before Jacob finds us again, or a violent group of men or women? What if the heat gets worse? What if Joy's foot twists the more she grows? What if I never see Abraham again?

This is not just about Abraham and me.

"I guess you can take us to your people," I finally say.

Abraham looks away, his expression changes worrisome. "Is that where ye want to go?"

I nod. "You said they'd fix Joy."

"That they will."

"I had a hard time traveling alone, but if you're here to help us, I guess we can go now. Plus, what kind of parent would I be to deny my child healing?"

Abraham nods. "We should prepare then. I'll pack my belongings."

He walks by me without another word. The stairs creak as he climbs them. His back is straight and his shoulders tense. As I watch him, I think about how different he looks from his brother. I guess if he were

wearing that strange clothing he would look like he
might belong with them, but right now he looks very
different from his own people.

Abraham

Abraham watched from the kitchen window as Nova opened the pens for the goats and chickens, releasing them into the wild.

He went to his room, cleaned and groomed himself, and dressed in the clothing of his people—the least frayed set. He relocated his bag downstairs and then went to town to collect a list of things that Nova had given him. In his hand he gripped a folded piece of paper with her handwriting on it.

He found baby food, clothing, a backpack that one could carry a growing child in. Abraham checked every aisle for batteries, but the store had been cleaned out of them and he already knew that. Still, he was hoping that he might find some for Nova. Since she'd decided to leave this place a gloom had come over her. Nova had given him the iPhone to dispose of, but he couldn't bring himself to do it. Instead he'd packed the thing in his bag with the hopes that maybe he could find some batteries and bring her happiness again.

On his way out, Abraham passed glass cabinets displaying jewelry. He stopped to look. He knew that the people of this planet showed their joining with rings on their fingers. Abraham had seen similar and different methods on other planets. Some male species shared their women, some women shared their men, but there was always something a ring, bracelets, tattoos, implants. Abraham thought of selecting a ring for Nova, it was the human thing to do if he wanted to keep her in his life. Or, he could follow the way of his people.

Abraham stood, thinking. He was worried that if she touched the tentacles that hung from the city, she might not survive. He didn't know everything about the woman, although he was usually a good judge of character and could tell what the city would take and what it wouldn't. There could be something in her past he didn't know about. There could be something hidden deep inside her that the city would deem unfit and Abraham didn't want to risk losing her.

He returned to the house.

"This is perfect," Nova said as she opened the child carrier. She adjusted the backpack and had Abraham help with strapping Joy into it.

"Ready?" Nova asked as she turned. She seemed hesitant.

"Aye," he replied.

Nova twisted the door handle to ensure it wasn't locked. "Just in case," she said, biting her lip.

They walked across the yard. "Chee chee," Joy reached for the hens.

"Say bye to the Chees," Nova told Joy.

"Chee!" Joy kicked her legs as she waved her stuffed chicken at the real ones.

Abraham led Nova away. They walked along the canopied driveway, headed for the road.

Joy was still beckoning the hens.

Nova turned and laughed when she saw a row of six hens following them, bopping from side to side on their short legs as they did their best to keep up.

"At least we might have eggs," Nova said.

"Aye," Abraham nodded, "eggs would be a nice change on the road."

*

Abraham led Nova down Mulberry road. They took to the shadows so the sun wouldn't beat down so badly on them. They walked through the valley and over small hills, the Blue Ridge Mountains looming before them.

Hours had passed. Abraham and Nova barely spoke.

They stopped to eat and drink. Nova changed Joy and the hens caught up. Then they were back on the trail that only Abraham knew. Eventually they left the road for good and Nova followed Abraham's footsteps through the rough terrain that led up the mountain. Nova was out of breath within a few hours, her clothing soaking up sweat from the heat of the day. The heat hadn't bothered her in a long time, but then again she hadn't been hiking in the woods with a twenty-five-pound toddler on her back. Nova tried her best to bury her fears of eventually turning violent like the others and attributed the sweating to the exertion of the hike and nothing more.

"Want me to carry Joy?" Abraham asked.

Nova seemed hesitant, but she unclipped the child carrier and helped Abraham put it on. Their arms tangled. Abraham's hand brushed Nova's bare shoulder as he fumbled with a clip. When the pack was finally secure, Nova stepped away.

Joy slept, their pace slowed.

The mountains were cooler than anywhere Nova had visited since the Heat Wave, especially so once the sun started setting. She shivered in the evening cool, wishing she'd brought something heavier to wear. Abraham noticed and passed her his cloak. Nova spread it over her shoulders, but she was much shorter than Abraham and the back of it dragged on the ground. Nova draped a blanket over Joy even though she was sure the heat radiating off Abraham was enough to keep the child warm.

While they were stopped, the hens caught up and plopped down on the back of the cloak Nova was wearing. When they started walking again, the hens didn't move, instead they were happy to let Nova drag them through the forest. They walked through the night, their footsteps illuminated by the cyanobacteria glowing softly in the damp grass.

By morning they were descending the lowest peak. Nova found it easier to wrap the lower portion of the cloak around her waist and carry the hens in a sling. "How much further?" she asked.

"Not far now," Abraham said as he pointed in the distance.

When the forest ended and the plain spread out before them, Nova could see where the tall grass ended and the ground turned to burnt dirt. Something in the distance shimmered.

"What is that?" Nova asked.

"Oh, that's the city. Won't see it very well until we're nearly underneath it." Abraham made an arc with his hand. "It's shielded to the common eye in the distance. It reflects the sky."

"Okay." The hens started stirring. Nova stopped to untie the cloak and release them. No eggs rolled out. "Freeloaders," Nova muttered as the chickens began pecking the ground.

"Are ye ready?" Abraham asked. "Won't be long now."

"Yes." Nova nodded. "I think so."

They walked, Joy continued to sleep, and the hens followed at their own slow pace.

"Do you think they'll take the chickens?" Nova asked.

"No." Abraham frowned. "There's not much need for chickens up there. My people are happy to leave the gentle creatures of this planet on the land."

"Why do you keep saying 'up there'?" Nova asked.

Abraham kept walking. "You'll see soon enough."

Within the hour they'd breached the plot of dark red soil. A giant shadow loomed overhead.

Nova looked up. She grabbed Abraham's arm in panic. "What is that?"

"It's the city," Abraham said. "Where my people live."

Nova remembered the story of the floating city when she was staying with the women in Charlotte. They joked about it being a morphine dream from an injured man, but now that Nova was standing underneath it, she couldn't deny that it was real.

"A floating city," she said.

"Aye, it is." Abraham kept walking until he stopped at a section of tentacles hanging down from the base of the city.

"What are those?" Nova asked.

"A way to bring ye up."

Abraham started unclipping the straps that kept the child carrier in place. Nova pulled Joy out and held her close, kissing her soft curls.

Abraham was quiet, deep in thought.

"What's wrong?" Nova asked.

He shook his head. "Nothing." Abraham hadn't been a liar for long, but this was too much to explain in the few short minutes they had left.

"Okay," Nova shook her arm in anticipation. "How do we do this? Before I chicken out."

Abraham cleared his throat. "Ye grab hold of a tentacle and it will bring you up." He demonstrated.

Nova nodded, determined. "That sounds easy enough." She stepped forward.

In that instant, Abraham felt as though the world stopped spinning. It felt like the pit of his stomach was going to come flying out of his mouth. He'd felt this before, during his trial and his banishment. He'd felt this way last time he wasn't sure of himself and danger was near.

Nova reached out to the swaying tentacles as they pulsed with greed.

"Wait!" Abraham pushed her hand out of the way at the last second. "Just, you don't touch it."

"Why?" Nova's eyes were wide with disbelief. "You told me to." Her forehead creased in confusion.

"Aye, but I was wrong." He shoved her further away. "I don't want ye to touch it."

"I don't understand." Nova slapped at his hands as she tried to get closer. "Stop pushing me!" she yelled at him, waking Joy.

Abraham held her away from the tentacles, which swayed and pulsed with anticipation. "Most people, I can judge them quite well of whether they're good or bad. But I can't with you. I can't let you touch that with the chance that you might die, and I'd never see ye again when they let me back in."

Nova glanced at Joy. "Die? You said you were taking us to a safe place."

"Aye, this is it. A whole city is up there, safer than the heaven mentioned in that Bible I read. But there's a chance... if you didn't tell me everything... if there's some terrible secret ye've been keeping... there's a chance you could die right as soon as you touch it. There are certain rules to enter."

Nova pulled Joy away from the tentacles. "And her?" Joy was shaking her head as the adults argued.

He said. "She is young. It will always accept the children. The Mothers and my sisters will fix her foot and take care of her."

"You didn't tell me this." Nova was trying her best not to yell and upset Joy, but she was losing her composure. "You told me none of this!"

"There's plenty you don't know about me and my people." He tipped his head as his tone turned grim.

"Well start explaining." Nova shifted Joy on her hip. "Now. Right now. This instant. Tell me!"

"There's not time now. We have to send her up." He glanced to the side. "Before Jacob comes back and forces ye both."

Nova stepped away from Abraham. "I'm no longer sure this is a good idea." She was ready to run for the mountains.

"Nova, there is no time to waste. Bring her to me." He beckoned her with his hands.

"I—I can't." Nova squeezed her daughter tight.

Abraham held his hand out. "Ye must."

"I think I'll go back to the house and just wait. I'll wait until she's stronger."

"It's no longer safe there. Jacob will be waiting for you. He'll bring you himself." Abraham rubbed his face, distraught with the thought of Jacob bringing Nova here. "Please, Nova."

Nova looked behind her at the treed mountains in the distance. Her eyes dragged across the valley, the burnt dirt at her feet, the swaying tentacles, and then the sparkling city above. "She'll be safe?" she asked, swallowing down a hiccup of fear.

"Aye." Abraham stepped forward.

"And I'll see her again?" Nova fidgeted with Joy's clothing and stroked her soft cheek.

"My hope is that we both will." The inflection in his voice was truth.

"Okay," she whispered. Nova stepped forward and passed Joy into Abraham's arms.

Abraham took a tentacle in his hand. "Now don't be scared a bit. My brothers and sisters will help make you better; the Mothers will care for you. And your mother and I will return to you one day soon."

"Momom momma." The little girl reached for Nova.

"I can't come with you, sweetie," Nova hugged her tight and kissed her on her full, cherub cheeks. "But soon, I hope." Nova glanced at Abraham, her eyes watery.

"Just hold tight," Abraham said as he coiled the tentacle around Joy's palm and down her arm. "It will lift ye high in the air."

Nova reached too close to the tentacle for Abraham's comfort and he shoved her away, his heart beating fast at the thought of losing her.

Abraham kept coiling the tentacle around Joy's middle and her thighs until she was secure. And then, he let go.

"Momom momma," Joy babbled as the tentacles pulsed, more moved to secure her as they lifted, cradling her in a cocoon of writhing arms.

It was disturbing to witness. "Oh God." Tears were streaming down Nova's face. "I can't." She reached for the tentacles. "I can't let her go."

Abraham tackled Nova. He held her away from the tentacles with his arms secured around hers, lifting her off her feet as she kicked. "Don't touch it," he warned as he dragged her back.

"But you did," she argued. "You did and you're fine."

"I'm not like *you*."

Nova stopped moving. "What does that mean?"

Abraham was at a loss for words, or else he didn't want to reveal the truth.

"You're not like me? What *are* you?" Nova asked.

"Come with me," he changed the subject. "You can help me. Your people are more trustworthy with a couple than a lone man."

"Help you?" Nova was confused; her head was spinning with all that was happening.

Abraham pressed his lips together, afraid to reveal to her what his true task on this planet was. "Trust me," he said. "Come with me. I don't want to lose ye, Nova."

Nova looked up to the space where the tentacles had lifted her child. "I've got no one else." Her chin wrinkled and trembled.

"We must move now. Before Jacob comes back." Abraham collected their bags. He adjusted his cloak and settled the small backpack on Nova's shoulders.

"Help you what?" Nova asked.

"I'll explain later." Abraham took Nova's hand and led her away.

He headed north, to territory he had yet explore, hoping that Jacob would stay away long enough for them to hide. And maybe, just maybe Abraham could bring enough humans to sacrifice to his city that they'd leave Nova alone.

Abraham had never done anything like this in his entire life, but right now all he knew was he had to get Nova as far away as he could from his people.

She was crying as he led her back to the mountains. She sucked in deep breaths and hiccupped.

Abraham had seen similar situations where women had lost their children, the reaction was always mournful. But this was the first time that Abraham had felt sadness as well. He should know better but he was invested. He'd spent enough time with Joy to be affected by her loss. It wasn't his first-born, but Abraham couldn't help but feel that he'd just made his first true sacrifice to his Mother. And he hated himself for it.

CHAPTER TWENTY

Romeo

I drive a similar route home to the one we took when we
started our trip to Illinois. I think I'll drive all night to
keep the sun off Duke. If nothing exciting happens we
could get back to the Carolinas by the middle of the
night. I could sleep in my old bed. Smoke the last of my
cigarettes, and play harmonica with the creatures of the
night. It's a promising plan, one that causes a hum to rise
from my throat as I anticipate returning to my creature
comforts. At least I might die in peace instead of
searching for something I'll never find.

Hours on the road make a mind weary.

My eyelids feel heavy. I blink. It's hard to sleep in
the heat, nothing more than catnaps, only to wake
dripping with sweat. Lack of sleep does something to

your mind, and combined with driving it's a dangerous mix.

I flick on the radio button, and search the stations only to hear static as I press each button. On the second to last, I think I hear something, a familiar voice through the white noise, *"Play one more... Oh, Romeo."*

"Nova?" I slow the truck.

Duke pounds on the cab window. "Did you fall asleep, son? You want me to drive?"

I shake my head and slap my cheeks. "I'm fine."

"Don't sound fine. Heard you talking nonsense. Don't much feel like dying in a car accident."

I accelerate and check the gas gauge. There was a time when a truck like this would only get fifteen miles to the gallon. I thank the engineers of my time for changing that or we'd be on the side of the road, siphoning every last drop out of each gas tank we come across.

The luminescent eyes of a deer glow from the side of the road, watching us as we pass. Bats flutter in the moonlight. It seems the animals have thrived in humans' lack of presence.

The night is a blur. I barely remember the landscapes we pass as I fill the urge to go home. The night cools as we drive into Appalachia. On the highest peak, Duke shouts, "What's that there? Hey, son, did you see it?"

I pull over and glance out the back window to see him pointing.

"I don't see anything." I squint. I can see the glowing blue and green coastline of the rising ocean waters in the distance.

"No, not there." Duke raps on the window. "Wait for the clouds to pass. It shines."

I get out of the truck and climb in the back to get a better view.

The peak we are parked at isn't the highest in Appalachia, but it's high enough to see a few hundred miles, and when the moon shines clear and the wind blows the evergreens so they sway lazily, the glinting in the distance becomes visible to me.

"There!" Duke says. "Did you see it?"

"I did."

"What do you think it is?" he asks. "It looked like a city lit up in the night, covered in glass like a snowglobe."

"Looks like a city." I jump down from the truck bed. "Or a mirage. Lord knows we're dehydrated and tired. It's probably nothing more than a lake filled with glowing algae."

He starts coughing, uncontrollably, coughing and coughing and coughing. He holds his hand up for me to see, it's speckled with blood and a glowing blue.

"I told you that glowing stuff would kill us all." Duke wipes his hand on his pantleg. "Now it's inside me. Rotting me from the core." The smear of blue fades as his pants dry. "We should have gone to the desert. Probably the last place on the planet with dry air. I bet this crap doesn't grow there."

"The desert might not be what you remember."

"Nothing seems to be," he grumbles.

I should leave Duke, leave him to deal with the violent outbursts until some stranger comes along and puts him out of his misery. Even though I promised him, it's hard to think of putting a bullet in the old man's brain. I wasn't bred to be violent, never experienced a moment of outburst like I've seen others do. But there is something about this heat, this thick air, this tension wrapped around the earth like a giant rubber band stretched to its snapping point. Deep inside there is a dark primal urge. I can sense it, and I've done my damndest to control it.

CHAPTER TWENTY-ONE

Abraham

Abraham didn't stop walking until they were at another peak, far from the floating city. He hoped they were far enough away that Jacob wouldn't find them anytime soon.

Nova was shivering. She'd finally stopped crying and Abraham could tell the day had left her exhausted.

"Here," he draped his cloak on the ground. "Sit," he told Nova. "I'll get us something to eat."

Nova sat cross-legged and rubbed her hands over her face.

"Oh God. Oh God. What did I just do?" Nova ran her hands through her tangled hair. "I just sent my baby up and away. I sent her to strangers."

"My people will take care of her." Abraham took out a bag of biscuits. He dug through Nova's bag and took out a container of water. "Here. You should eat."

"I can't eat." Nova waved him away as she pulled her knees against her chest.

Abraham set the meal down in front of her. "Ye must eat something."

Nova was fidgeting with the edge of the cloak, her fingers tracing the detailed embroidery. "Your clothing is strange."

"Aye, to you it is."

She pulled at the layers and felt the cloak trying to figure out how it was sewed. "And you talk strange. But not like Jacob. You said you knew a thousand languages."

"Aye, I do."

"Tell me something." Nova was staring at him. "Tell me something true right now."

Abraham began collecting twigs and settled them in a pile in front of Nova, building a fire.

"I can tell ye some things, but much you won't understand. It is the way of my people"

"Tell me *something*!" Nova was standing now and shouting at him. "This, everything with you, I know nothing! Nothing about you and that floating city. You're so vague that it kills me. But you want me to give you everything, everything! I gave your people my daughter with a hope and a dream that they can help her—"

Abraham stopped what he was doing. "They will cure her ailment. I promise ye."

"I sure hope so. Because you," she poked him in the center of his chest, "give me *nothing*." Her eyes glimmered on the verge of tears. "You want me to divulge my entire life to you, so you can judge if your people might find me worthy. Well what about you? What about you Abraham? Tell me something, because I'm this close," she held her fingertips less than a millimeter apart, "to running back there and grabbing those strange ropes hanging from that floating city so I can see my daughter again. It's only been a few hours and I am heartbroken without her."

Silence.

Not a bird chirped in a tree.

Not a fish jumped in the nearby stream.

No leaves rustled in the mountain breeze.

The glowing bacteria dimmed in fear.

Abraham had never felt dread like this before, not even the day his sentence was handed down. Banished to Earth to hunt, his kind would kill themselves over such a punishment. But that was nothing compared to this feeling of losing Nova.

"My name is Abraham," he started, his mouth dry with fear.

"No shit, Sherlock." Nova paced.

"Not Sherlock, Abraham." He was completely serious at this moment.

Nova stopped moving and turned to face him.

He cleared his throat. "My name is Abraham, and I am..."

... falling." His eyes searched her face, settling on the tip of her nose, then the subtle brown flecks that were speckled in her blue iris. "I am falling. I think your kind call it something..." He pressed a finger to his head, recalling memories of all the languages he'd learned. "Laska, Liebe, Ast... Amor."

"Love?"

"My name is Abraham and I am falling in love with you." He pressed a hand to his chest. "My people call it something different, but it is love. I know this. It's the only thing."

Nova crossed her arms. "And how would your people feel to know that you love me?"

"Why bring my people into this?" Abraham frowned. "Ye feel nothing for me?"

Now it was Nova's turn to be uncomfortable. The last time she gave her heart and soul to someone, he was taken away. She was taken away. Ripped from her heart. "I feel something for you," she finally said. "I'm just not ready."

"You are what?" Nova asked, clearly annoyed with him.

The fantasy was over, reality struck him full force. "I am not from this planet," Abraham finally said.

*

The truth did not bring more questions. Instead, Nova had turned away from Abraham without another word.

She settled on the cloak and curled on her side. When he thought she might be asleep, Abraham draped a blanket over her and sat close, not quite touching, but he wanted to. He wanted to offer her comfort and keep her warm. She was so different from the women of his kind, so blessedly different. Strong and kind, she raised a child alone in the worst of situations.

It had been a terrible day, and while Abraham knew better than to force Nova to interact with him, he remembered her words. *Humans need touch.* He settled his hand on her shoulder, nothing more but a firm presence to let her know that he was there. She'd done the same for him not so long ago.

"I am sorry for the pain I've caused," Abraham whispered as he settled next to her on the cloak.

Nova didn't move.

CHAPTER TWENTY-TWO

Nova

I wake to the sound of soft clucking. Opening my eyes, I find the hens nested on the cloak around me. Somehow in the night they caught up to us. But one is missing. Chickens aren't really travel companions and I doubt they'll survive in the wild much longer. They'll be eaten by wildlife or get lost.

Abraham is awake. He's trying to be still but I can tell it's a struggle for him right now. I stand and walk away from camp, feeling Abraham's gaze on my back. I can't face him. I still need more time to process what he told me last night and what I did to my child.

I relieve myself in privacy and wash in a nearby stream. I haven't felt water this cool in ages. I haven't had a desire to climb this far up into the mountains either. It's much cooler than anywhere else I've been these past few years. And I didn't notice any blue glowing in the trees, it seems to stay on the grass. Maybe it's too cool up here for it to spread?

I return to camp.

Abraham is sitting up. There are two biscuits and two canteens of water set out.

I sit across from him.

"You're not from this planet," I say, gathering the courage I'd seen in others, like John and Jess.

"Aye." He nods.

"What planet are you from?"

Abraham leans back and tilts his face to the sky. He raises an arm and points. "My home planet is in that direction. Several hundred thousand light years away from here." He gazes a bit longer before facing me again.

"And what are your people doing here?" I ask.

Abraham tapped his fingertips on his knee. "Trying to rid your planet of violence so peace can prosper."

"Did you bring the Heat Wave?"

"No." Abraham shakes his head. "Your people brought the heat upon yourselves. We arrived after. To help when the violence got out of control." He motions to the biscuit. "You should eat. Please."

"Don't tell me what to do." I take a bite of the biscuit. The texture and taste are reminiscent of the first time I met Abraham in that diner. All that time ago, if I had gone with him, I wonder what would have happened? Would he have let me touch those tentacles and rise to the floating city? Or would they have taken Joy and kicked me out after? One thing I can surmise is that her birth might have been a bit more peaceful in the floating city than at The Convent.

"Are there more of you?" I ask.

"In the floating city there are many. And we are scattered over the Seven Sacred Galaxies."

Abraham is patient as he explains the galaxies. He tells me about the humanoid creatures he's met, and how his people have helped planets such as ours recover and flourish.

"Why are the galaxies sacred?" I ask.

"The Seven Sacred Galaxies are the first which sustained life. To my people, they are sacrosanct."

"So you're telling me there is more life out there," I wave at the sky, "beyond this galaxy?"

"Yes."

"Why have we never known this before?" I ask.

"I cannot answer that for ye," Abraham replies. "The technology was there. Humans should have discovered this long ago."

The information is overwhelming.

"You should drink something," he encourages.

I finish the water in my canteen and then we head to the stream to refill our containers.

"Are there more, doing what you're doing? More of your people culling?" I ask.

"No. I am the only one." He looks away when he says it, like he's ashamed.

"And how did you get that job?" I ask.

Abraham sighs. "It is my punishment."

"What did you do to deserve a punishment like this?"

"I challenged the archaic ways of my people. The Elders determined this was an appropriate sentence." He scratches his cheek. "Others of my kind would rather kill themselves than do this."

"But not you?" I ask.

"Aye." Abraham secures his canteen and bag. "It seems I am different."

"Why?" I ask.

"It is my fight for change. For the Elders to finally realize change is necessary."

"Is this your nonviolent resistance?"

"Oh, there has been violence involved." Abraham begins walking. "My hand did not initiate it, but there has been violence. On the soil of this planet and the soil of others."

"I want you to tell me everything, from this point on." I point with an accusing finger. "Everything."

"Aye, never deceived a soul until I met ye," Abraham said. "Never saw the reason to." He stops walking for a moment, and looks at me. "Never met a soul I wanted to keep to myself so badly."

Normally I'd be offended, but now I know that his awkward moments aren't meant to be insulting. He just doesn't know how to communicate effectively.

"I guess I'll be telling ye, I must bring others back to the city. Or Jacob will come looking for me. The Elders send him to spy and keep me in line. They don't like having their ways challenged."

"And you want me to help you?" I ask.

"Aye. Or at least stay with me. It's a dangerous job and life on the road is lonesome."

"How long will you do this for? How long before I see Joy again?"

"I expect that soon the city will move west, and I'll search those parts. When I am done, we can return to the city. If it will have you."

"North America is huge, not to mention the rest of Earth. You'll be at this for eons." His plan just doesn't sound believable.

"I think ye underestimate how many humans have actually survived the Heat Wave."

Now this is my choice; follow around Abraham like an indentured servant biding my time or go my own way, which would be straight back to that floating city and Joy. I pause and take a deep breath. My instincts haven't led me completely wrong in my life. I've survived this long and something is telling me that staying with Abraham is the right thing to do, for now.

Still, I warn him, "I'll help you for as long as I can, but I can't guarantee you I won't go back to the city and beg to enter. Mothers don't just give up their children to strangers."

"Aye," Abrahams nods, "I can understand that."

CHAPTER TWENTY-THREE

Romeo

The truck dies as we are crossing the eastern pass of the Blue Ridge range. The gas gauge wasn't completely on empty and the cooling system seemed to be working. I'm not a mechanic but my best guess is the old truck got tired of running nonstop in this heat for all these miles. Lord knows I am.

"I guess we're walking the rest of the way," I say as I get out of the truck and slam the door closed.

"At night, like this?" Duke looks around. "We'll be eaten by mountain lions, or worse."

"What's worse than being eaten by mountain lions?" I ask.

"Being eaten by an atheist yuppie from the city." His upper lip twitches in revulsion.

I collect my bags from behind the bench. "There's always that." I pass the Sheriff and start heading down the road.

"Or the missus, coming back from the dead to slit my throat." Duke swallows hard. "Can't say I don't deserve it right now." He rubs his neck.

"Those are your words." And I completely agree with them.

During our long walk descending the mountain, a hundred zombie movies flood my mind. That's what it feels like out here in the wilderness, the angst of nearby danger tethered with the emptiness and death. A zombie movie, essentially.

The Sheriff is quiet and no doubt wallowing in the regret of having killed his beloved wife.

Me, I'm thinking about the girl who got away. Nova. Still. I'd never seen her before and never seen her since, but there was something about her that I can't forget.

"What are you thinking about, son?" Duke asks as he itches his arms in agitation.

"I was thinking about zombies." I twist my head at the sound of a stick snapping in the woods.

"Zombies?" Duke replies with disgust. "Stupid creatures. Why waste your thoughts on them? They're not real. You watched too much damn television."

"Maybe so." I shrug. Maybe talking will keep him calm. Lord knows I don't want to endure one of his outbursts out here. "If you must know, I was thinking about a girl I once met."

Duke grunts with disbelief, "Never knew you had a girlfriend."

"She wasn't really." One-night stands are rarely girlfriend material.

"Was she beautiful?"

Nova was more than beauty; she was an enigma, a puzzle. "Yes," I reply. "Gorgeous in every way."

"So was the missus, back in the day before time took her height and the color from her hair. She aged as beautiful as a redwood tree. Have you ever been to the North Pacific? Those trees touch the sky." His arm rises as he talks, demonstrating. "Hundreds and hundreds of years old."

"Never been that far." I wonder if those ancient trees still stand or if they burned to dust and flame during the Heatwave?

Duke itches and jerks. At least in the night he's not sweating profusely and looking like he's ready to go into cardiac arrest.

"At least there are no gators here," Duke says.

"I'll second that." I push one hand in my pocket and check my waistband for the pistol I took from Duke. It's there, ready and waiting. "Couldn't be nothing worse than a gator in the night."

"Well," Duke replies, "maybe one of those yuppies. I'd take a gator over them any day."

"I'll second that."

My hope is that we'll find another car that's not melted to the pavement, something with a partial tank of gas. That's all I need to get home. I'll walk if I have to, but the thought of finding something with air conditioning is hard not to dream about. Maybe I can find a patrol car with a caged backseat and I'll make Duke sit back there. I know it's dangerous to keep him around, but I can't bring myself to put an end to him. He's my last friend at the end of the world. I'm sure I might come across someone else, but with violence running rampant I wouldn't trust another soul. And what would it say about me if I just ended him when he didn't deserve it? I can't do that.

"Why don't you play something, son?" Duke asks. "To help pass the time."

I pull my harmonica from my pocket and play. There are night creatures that join in, the hollow hoot of a nearby owl, the fluttering wings of the bats, the chirping of songbirds as the sun begins to brighten the morning sky.

The air is becoming tense with daylight, molecules vibrating around us, straining the creatures of Earth, and making Duke restless. I do my best to hold it in myself, but I can feel it on my periphery. If I must be honest with myself, the urge to let go completely and embrace the animal like Duke has is disturbingly close.

The music makes it worse. Too much vibrato, too much hum. What was once soothing is now setting us on edge. I stop and pocket the harmonica.

"Here comes the heat again," Duke's voice sounds defeated, he sounds like Annie Lenox's haunted voice singing, "Here Comes the Rain Again."

CHAPTER TWENTY-FOUR

Nova

"What's that sound?" I stop and step away from the hens and focus on the sound in the distance.

"Oh, was wondering when ye'd hear that." Abraham twirls a stick in the air. "It's been playing for a while now."

"How could you hear it?" I ask.

He taps his earlobe. "I've very good hearing."

The sound stops.

I ask, "What was it?"

"Music playing," Abraham says. "Sounded a bit familiar. Something ye've played before."

Well, that would be a coincidence since not everyone holds the appreciation for nineties tunes that I do. I'm sure less than half the people left alive know who John Popper was.

"Have you been through these parts before?" I ask since he doesn't seem concerned that there might be people nearby.

"Aye, over yonder to the east. Down in the valleys." He starts walking away from the area he just motioned to. "We'll go elsewhere this time. They weren't very friendly, and I was hoping they'd be gone by now. Either to heaven or high water."

I pick up my pace and walk closer to him, afraid of the others finding us. At the same time I am slightly relieved that Joy isn't here with us. She'd most certainly draw attention and be in danger. The void in my chest fills with grief and my eyes burn with unshed tears. I swallow it down and keep walking.

"So let me get this straight," I say. "You want me to help you coerce people into going back to that floating city?"

"Aye, but I don't think coerce is the correct word." Abraham holds a tree branch from smacking me in the face.

I walk past him. "This feels wrong," I complain as I turn and stop to face him. "I feel like we're tricking them. I don't like that."

"I've never tricked anyone. I offer them safety. That's the truth."

His logic isn't working on me. "Withholding information then."

"What information do ye think I'm withholding?" he asks.

"Um, the fact that they might be pulled up to that city to safety or burn to a crisp the moment they touch those tentacles." I open my eyes wide and hold in a "duh" comment.

"Aye, ye have a bit of a point there." Abraham rubs his chin. "Are ye trying to tell me that ye won't help?"

"I just…" I shake my head. "I don't know what to do."

"I must do this." Abraham turns to face me. "I've no choice in the matter. "Ye can stand by and watch, ye can help me, or—"

He's giving me choices, this is interesting considering he didn't give me many choices when it came to sending my daughter up to a weird floating alien city alone.

"Or what?" I ask, crossing my arms.

"Or ye can go on and leave me be. Go elsewhere and live your peace."

I could punch him in his stupid face. "You are aware that I would go straight back to her." I stare him down and Abraham looks a little uncomfortable under my gaze. "If you gave me the option to leave, to 'go elsewhere and live my peace,'" I add air quotes. "I'll never be at peace without her."

"Please don't do that, Nova." He steps closer. "Just give me a chance to figure it all out."

My fingertips tingle with anger and anticipation as my heart beats with fury at this man. "The clock is ticking my friend."

He nods with understanding. "Come then."

We walk for a few miles, Abraham drawn by some unknown force to find the last humans in these parts. But me, I am drawn by nothing now. I've lost everything and the hollowness in my chest overrides any other feeling I've ever had in my life. I hope Abraham enjoys dragging around an empty shell.

The hens cluck behind us, pecking the ground and hopping over fallen branches.

Bang!

One of the chickens explodes in a puff of feathers.

"Abraham!" I run toward him. "Someone is shooting at us."

"Aye, appears they are."

Bang!

Another chicken explodes mid-cluck.

"What's yer name and what's yer complaint?" Abraham shouts.

"The name is Silas," a short man with dark hair steps out from behind a tree, "and you took something that belongs to us. Two things actually."

Abraham clears his throat.

I look between the men and him.

Abraham holds his hands up. "How is it ye think I stole something from you?"

"You fit the description." Silas motions to Abraham's height with the tip of his gun. "The height, the clothing. You talk like some weird jerk-wad from overseas."

"There's plenty of strange men walking around these parts," I shout. "It's not him."

Silas steps closer and shoots another one of the chickens. *Bang!*

"Leave the chickens alone!" I shout. "They didn't do anything to you."

"No," Silas smiles, "they didn't. But they're good eating and we have mouths to feed." He focuses on Abraham again. "You took our women. Two sisters named Susan and April."

I step back. Abraham took women from these people? I didn't think he was the kidnapping type. He's very persuasive which makes him easy to trust. But kidnapping? There is that saying that you never truly know a person, but I can't see Abraham as the Ted Bundy type.

"I rescued them," he whispers to me, sensing my uncertainty. Then he says to Silas and his men, "I rescued April from that roasting shed you were keeping her in. Susan came on her own free will."

"We want them back. Those are our women." Silas nods to his men. "Take us to them."

Abraham shakes his head. "I cannot do that. April has been relocated. And Susan is dead."

I suck in a breath. Did Abraham kill her? There is no way. But then, there are those tentacles, their knowing pulse, their greed, and Abraham's fear. I wonder if that's what happened to Susan?

Silas's face twists. "And now you owe us two women."

"I'm not in the trade of trafficking women." Abraham settles his hand on his hip.

"Then where did you take them?" one of Silas's men asks as he sneers in disbelief.

"I took them to safety. From what I could see yer settlement was anything but safe. It takes a certain type of human to whip a young woman who's tied to a post. I could not let her suffer." I notice Abraham pulls a blade of some sort from his belt loop. "Yer men are getting mighty close. I suggest you tell them to back away."

I look around, noticing that there are at least seven men surrounding us.

"Should I run?" I ask Abraham, thinking that if I could run for it I might avoid these terrible men. Abraham can take care of himself, he travels alone all of the time. I'm sure he's run into more than one group like this.

"Not unless you see a clear opening," he whispers back.

I nod and back away.

Pop. Pop! Bullets fly.

"Don't hit the woman!" Silas shouts.

Someone grabs me from behind and strong arms immobilize me. I curse myself for thinking it could be as easy as ducking out of a fight. Well, I did take karate as a kid and while I didn't learn the Crane Kick, I do remember a few things. Like one punch to the balls might knock out a man.

I lift my feet and drop to the ground, twist and punch the guy in his groin. He doubles over and moans in agony. The guy is distracted enough for me to scramble away.

Abraham glances in my direction as he takes on the other three. Thankfully they've decided to save their bullets and deal with him by hand. I crouch behind a tree and watch. Abraham makes swift methodical movements, taking his opponents out without killing them.

As they roll on the ground in the fetal position, Abraham turns to Silas. "Leave us now and I will allow you to live." He pulls a three-pronged weapon from his belt, holding it in defense.

"Sure, we'll leave. But we're taking your woman." Silas points at me.

"No you're not," I say.

I feel something sharp in the small of my back. "But we are, sweetheart." A man whispers in my ear.

He starts dragging me away.

My eyes meet Abraham's.

I've never seen this intense look on his face before like he could kill somebody. He raises his arm and throws something. There is a strange sound in my ear and I turn. The man holding me has a knife sticking out of his face. He drops to the ground.

Things happen fast after that.

Silas points his gun at Abraham. "Kill him," he says.

Silas points his gun at me. "Come here, now."

I hesitate. Silas runs toward me as his men fire at Abraham. I don't know much about Silas but when you see someone running at you, it's hard to avoid the instinct to run the other way. I should run. I need to run. But I see Abraham go down.

Oh no, they shot him!

Hands grab my arms with sharp pinches.

"Abraham!" I shout as Silas pulls me away.

*

There is always violence at the end of the world. It's never simple. There's always danger. I've seen it in every movie and read it in every book. There are always bad men and a few good men. A world without the bad ones sounds pretty nice right now. Maybe Abraham's people are on point. I was on the fence about him collecting the human race, but right now, I think it might be the perfect plan. I like the sound of living in peace, without the worry of some creep like Silas stealing you out of the forest by gunpoint. I think a world with fewer people like him is a good plan.

"Don't be thinking of escaping," Silas warns. "We know these woods like the back of our hands. We'll find you in an instant."

"He'll find me," I say in a moment of bravery. "Abraham will come and find me."

Silas backhands me. Pain explodes across my face. I drop to my knees and taste blood in my mouth. I've never been hit before. Somehow, I've made it all this time without ever feeling the pain of physical punishment like this. A good smack in the face, it smarts like a bitch, and I quickly add Silas to the list of people I hate in this world.

"He's good as dead in that forest at night. Satan will find him." Silas tugs me up and drags me along. "And if there is one thing you must learn, it's that women are to be seen and not heard." He gives me a warning.

We spend hours walking through the forest at a pace I can barely keep up with. I try to take in my surroundings, but every tree looks the same, every pile of leaves the same shape, every stone jutting from the ground the same point. One thing I'm sure of is that we are heading down the mountain.

The men grow antsy as it gets warmer and warmer. Finally, when the ground levels, we walk into a clearing where a settlement of houses and a church in the middle appears. Perfect. These are just the type of Bible-thumping Blue Ridge mountain folk I was trying to avoid when I was making my way to Charlotte. I hope they don't worship snakes here.

"Welcome home," Silas says as he releases my arm.

This is not my home. This will never be the house I had with John or the farmhouse on Mulberry road. If there's one thing I know, it's that I can't stay here. Who would have thought that Abraham would have led me straight to them?

I turn and run as fast as I can.

"You can't run away," Silas shouts. "We'll find you. My men will smell you from a mile away."

Someone tackles me from behind. My chin hits the ground as I fall, and I bite my tongue.

"I got her, boss." The man who tackled me shouts as he pulls me to my feet and shoves me forward.

I twist and thrust the palm of my hand into this guy's neck. He bends and gags.

I run.

Someone whistles.

Three men step out of the surrounding forest and tall grass. They won't kill me, I'm sure of it, so I keep running.

There's a man behind me, one who starts running at my side, and another ahead, simply waiting for me.

The one behind me tackles me. He grabs at my legs as he drops to the ground. I stumble but get away, just in time for the guy at my side to make a move. I make mine first. I bust an old school karate move, it's not quite what

I was hoping but I manage to connect my foot to someone's gut, scramble and run.

The last one left is the one who is waiting ahead. His arms are crossed, and he's got a frown plastered on his grim face. I weave from side to side, hoping he's not faster than me.

He's faster than me.

He takes me down in a heartbeat; with his arms around my shoulders he drops like a sack of shit, and I do too.

"Abraham!" I scream over and over again, hoping that he'll hear me, hoping that he's still alive. Please be alive.

"That man won't be coming for you." Silas is standing over me. "Best you get that notion through your thick skull. We left his carcass in the forest to rot. Look." He grabs my chin and forces my gaze, he points at the steeple of the church. "You're one of us now. Deliverance to heaven is the only thing that saves you from this heat. You can thank me later."

He hauls me to my feet, but unlike his men, Silas has the foresight to grasp my wrists together behind my back.

As I am led to the settlement I realize that my life has become a series of perfect moments followed by dreadful fragmentation. It's a vicious cycle and I wonder if it will ever stop repeating.

CHAPTER TWENTY-FIVE

Abraham

Abraham's eyes fluttered open. He was on the ground, staring up at the night sky. There was nearly unbearable pain in his left shoulder. Abraham moved his right hand to the spot that hurt the worst and felt something wet. The strap of his pack was in the way. He rolled to his side and sat up, pulling on the strap. A bullet fell out and rolled onto the ground. Abraham inspected the wound in his shoulder. It wasn't deep but it had damaged him. He pressed his hand over the injury to try and get it to stop bleeding. His head throbbed as he gingerly touched the goose egg near his temple with his free hand. It had been a long time since Abraham was outnumbered by so many and lost.

The forest around him was glowing, providing enough light for him to see that he was alone.

Abraham searched for his weapons, but it seemed those he'd used were taken with the bodies. Silas took his dead and did not leave them in the forest to fester and corrupt.

Nova was gone.

Emotions were a freight train rumbling through his chest. How could he let this happen? He'd lost them both, Joy and Nova.

Abraham wasn't sure what to do. He wanted to run to Silas's settlement and kill every one of his people. He wanted to run back to the floating city and request the help of his people. The only problems with these plans were that the first one might get him killed and the second one would get him laughed at. Jacob wouldn't lift a finger to help and there was no way Abraham was going to beg the Elders to help him find Nova. They wouldn't see the sense in it.

He removed his pack and rummaged through it, searching for food and water. He ate three biscuits and drank his canteen dry. He knew he had to keep up his energy and the biscuits would do that while his body healed itself.

Abraham stood, but the head injury made him dizzy and he held onto a tree for support. He reflected on the events of the afternoon, what he'd done wrong, what he could have done better. Abraham began to realize that everything he'd been trying to avoid had happened and there was no stopping it. He'd sacrificed a child he cared about to his Mother, he'd lost a battle against the rogue humans, he'd lost Nova. It was all turning to shit and Abraham was losing control.

He gripped a nearby tree to steady himself. The bark cracked and chipped off in large chunks.

"Nova..." he whispered to the night. "What have I done?"

The glowing around him pulsed as though answering in Morse code. He'd done plenty wrong. He loved one of them, one different from his own.

Abraham was beginning to wonder if it was worth it to save these humans. If the entire race burned to a crisp on this evolving planet it might be a good thing. They were brutal to their own kind, many physically violent with their young. But Abraham didn't want to let go of Nova. He didn't want to leave her to succumb to the darkness of her home planet.

Abraham rubbed his face and his vision blurred. "Aye, I am a fool." He grabbed ahold of a tentacle to steady himself. The pulsing warmth reminding him of somewhere else, the only home he'd known his whole life, the only home he'd remembered. He focused and as he leaned, the tentacle of the floating city snapped loose and fell. He wasn't at the floating city and the tentacle that had snapped off in his hand was nothing more than a thick forest vine.

"You're only a fool if you stand here and do nothing," a soft voice said.

Abraham turned to find a woman standing behind him. He recognized her robes, glittering white with light blue overlays at the neck and sleeves. The embroidery was not geometric designs as he and his brothers wore, but whimsical swirls and whorls in sparkling threads that designated her status. It wasn't just any woman; it was his Mother.

"What are ye doing here?" Abraham asked.

As she smiled warmth ran through him, flooding his veins as though a dam were opened. It brought forth memories of her smiling throughout his childhood, when he'd hurt himself, when he'd had a nightmare, when he first realized he didn't quite fit in amongst his people. "I come when I sense my children are in distress," she said.

"Aye, sure ye do. Never came when I was on trial, never helped me slay beasts but now in this moment is when you arrive." Abraham did his best to stand steady but his head hurt and the dizziness had not fully passed.

"I was there, even if you did not see me."

"Aye, and so was the sun," he dismissed her.

"Why, Abraham, you are the only child of mine that has worked so hard against me. The only one who defies me. The only one who refuses to do what his own people have done for eons." She folded her hands patiently.

"Aye, but I'm not your true child," Abraham said.

"But you are." She nodded with a soft smile. "Our people have practiced this for centuries. I know you want change, but change does not happen with the passing of a single moon." Her expression was always that of pride and contentment, but it wavered. "Nothing is perfect within the Seven Sacred Galaxies. No matter how strongly the Elders feel it is. Our people will not change for this moment, but there is more time. You should know that we try to do what is best."

"Aye, what is best is not what comes to mind when I think about ye."

His Mother looked away, a tear glistening in her eye. There was an uncomfortable silence that passed between them.

"How is wee Joy?" Abraham finally asked.

His Mother smiled. "She is well, very happy now that her foot is fixed. She misses her mother." She made eye contact with him. "She misses you also."

"And Lily?" The small broken girl he'd come across had never fully left his mind, and he wasn't absolutely sure he'd gotten her to the city in time.

"She is quite healthy. All healed. However she carries a sadness in her soul that we cannot cure." She looked to the ground for a moment. "I'm afraid she won't be going with us when we leave." An uneasy silence passed between them. "I know the plans I have for you, they are for good and not for misfortune, to give you a future and hope." She looked directly at him. "You were always mine," she said gently. "You were destined for much more than this." She waved across the glowing night forest. "One day. I had hopes that you'd be an Elder one day. But I get this feeling that your path is very different than what I want for you."

He shook his head. "That is a lie."

"I did not come here to argue your plight." She was starting to look worried. "I am here to tell you that you need to save Nova. She doesn't have much time. You need to get her away from those creatures before it's too late." She glanced through the forest. "The heat is getting to them. Violence will ensue. It will become worse. It always does."

"And how do ye know this?" he tipped his head in question.

"We've seen it before."

He paused for a long moment before he sighed, feeling defeated. "The problem is that I am lost, being away from the way I was raised for this long. I thought I could make a change, a difference. I'm not so sure any longer."

"You've made a difference." She waved her hand across the night forest. "You have saved so many humans who would have otherwise perished. This is a good thing."

"Aye." Abraham nodded.

"This is not the first time our people have been here." She paused and let her words sink in.

"I haven't been here before." Abraham was studying her now, trying to catch her angle. It was hard though because Mothers were majestic and calm and had a manipulative way about them that made any child of theirs bow to their wishes.

"Oh, but you have." His Mother waved her hand again and her sleeve billowed. "Go."

There was a time when Abraham would find comfort wrapping himself in her sleeves when he was small. Her fluttering sleeve was a flag of victory, or defeat. Different for each of them but a sign nonetheless.

She was gone.

Abraham heard music playing again, the same music he heard earlier when Nova was with him. This wasn't from Silas and his people. This came from elsewhere.

Abraham followed the sound of the harmonica.

Nova said that the father of her child would never come for her. He'd seen the video of her and John, and she'd told him about Joy's father. Things happened on this planet that were more than luck. Some energy brought people together again; he'd read about it in books, he'd seen it with his own eyes, he was sure it was how he found those most in need of his people's city. Now Abraham was sure that he was about to be reunited with someone he needed as much as they needed him.

CHAPTER TWENTY-SIX

Nova

I never wanted to see this violence again. I had enough of it at the Convent. I watched enough of it on television before they stopped broadcasting. I hid away, survived with avoidance instinct.

Silas and his men tell me to stay. But I run. Every single time. I run as hard and as fast as I can. I become acquainted with the whipping post that Abraham mentioned. Two lashes were all it took for my legs to collapse from underneath me.

Silas laughed. Everyone laughed. It seems the world has hardened with the Heat Wave, but I have stayed the same sensitive Nova. My instincts tell me this place feels wrong, this place is evil and I am not meant to stay here.

I am thankful that Joy is not here for this. My heart aches in her absence and I am sure I will never recover from losing her to the floating city, to strangers. I want to hurt Abraham just as badly as he's hurt me. Whatever he is, whatever planet he's from, I'll burn it to the ground before I trust him again.

"It's not that bad," a young woman named Felicity says as she tends to the cuts on my shoulders. "It could be worse," she continues. "We could be out there, without Silas's protection." She shakes her head. "Lord knows what would happen to us out there."

"I was fine out there without Silas." I turn away from her and stare at the rough-hewn wall of the cottage. I should have never left the little farm on Mulberry road. I should have killed Jacob, or locked him in the basement, or… something. Anything besides this.

"Plenty thought they were fine without Silas," Felicity continues. "It wasn't until they'd been here for a while that they all learned better."

"Sure," I mutter.

Felicity presses gauze over my shoulder and secures it with tape. "These will heal up just fine but only if you stop trying to run away and don't meet the lash again." She stands and moves away. "If you're lucky, they won't even scar. Lucas was gentle enough to spare you the deep lash. The deep lash never truly heals. It scars the skin, the soul, and for some even the bone."

I couldn't imagine anything digging deeper into my skin. "It used to be illegal to lash women," I say. "And to treat them as property. Silas and these men have done nothing but dip humanity back in the Middle Ages."

Felicity's face flexes in disappointment. "Murder was illegal too. But that didn't stop anyone once the Heat Wave came. It would be better for you if you just stay," she says as she walks out of the room, giving me privacy to change. She leaves clothes on the bed, a simple black and white dress with buttons to the neck and sleeves to my wrists. I'll overheat in this ridiculous outfit in a heartbeat.

"Do you need help with the buttons?" Felicity asks from the other room.

"No. I've got it." I put on the stupid clothes.

"Silas will be happy to see you dressed like the rest of the women. He doesn't like too much skin showing. He says it leads to temptation."

"Uh-huh." I close the five buttons that stretch to my neck.

"We should get to dinner soon." Felicity enters the room again. "Oh, Nova, you look very nice."

I stretch out the neck of the dress, feeling claustrophobic. "It's a bit much for this heat."

"You'll get used to it." She heads for the door. "Come on. Silas is waiting."

I follow Felicity out of the small house and down a set of rickety steps.

In the far distance I hear the echo of something that sounds like music. It could be a harmonica, or an angry bird. My heart wants it to be a harmonica's song.

"You look well fed, considering," Felicity says.

"We had plenty of food."

"Must have been nice." We turn and head toward a plain house that people are filtering into. "Sometimes we run out here. The seeds haven't been growing well and the forests have been hunted dry."

"There's plenty at most stores," I tell her. "Canned goods that are good for ten years and grains that have been vacuum sealed. You just have to know what to look for."

Felicity shakes her head. "Silas won't venture that far. He says this is God's land and God will provide for us between the peaks of the Blue Ridge." She turns to me, looking a bit confused. "Who were we? You weren't alone out there?"

"I just meant I had plenty of food. I misspoke." I look away from her.

When we step onto a dirt path, I ask, "How did you meet Silas?" I am wondering if she came here on her own or if they brought her.

"Oh," Felicity turns to me and smiles. "Silas is my daddy and uncle."

Wait. What? I wrap my head around that explanation.

"I know what you're thinking." Felicity smiles softly and tips her head as though she were speaking to a child. "But our people have been living like this for a long time, ain't nothing wrong with it." She quiets her voice as we near the building that's designated as a dining hall. "Remember, women are to be seen and not heard," she reminds me.

"Sure," I reply as she opens the door.

I follow her, keeping a safe distance.

Felicity whispers, "You'll stay with me for the time being. I'll teach you everything you need to know." She smiles, seeming so sweet and daft. She escorts me to a large open room filled with tables. "They're serving chicken stew tonight."

I'm sure it's not made from an old canned chicken like the one I found in my pantry. It's probably a fresh one. It's probably one of my chickens. Bastards.

Felicity waves across the room. Silas tips his head in acknowledgment.

"He wants you to sit at his table," she whispers to me. "It's an honor."

"I'd prefer not to." I try to veer away but Felicity grips my upper arm and pushes me toward the table on the opposite side of the room, her brittle fingers pinching my flesh.

Everyone is watching, schoolmarmy women and bodily-odor smelling men. There are children too. Newborns and toddlers and teenagers, most who are too young to realize that the world outside this setting might be scary, but it's better than this.

Lucas, the one who handles the lash, is watching under dark hooded eyes. I think he likes his job a little too much.

"You should smile at him," Felicity whispers. "Or next time he won't be so gentle when you're receiving your punishment."

"Who says there will be a next time?" I smile and tip my head, I pretend I'm saying thank you, *thank you for marking up my back, dickhead.*

Felicity's eyes narrow on me. "There will be a next time. You've yet to learn your lesson. That's plenty clear." She pulls a chair out and motions for me to sit. I do and settle my hands in my lap.

Felicity sets a bowl and a glass of water in front of me.

"You should eat," Silas says. "Tomorrow is Sunday, a day of rest. You'll need your energy for worship. It gets mighty hot in that church. Women have been known to tip over from heat stroke."

I swallow, my throat dry and scratchy from yelling the past few days.

"Ain't that right, dear?" Silas asks Felicity as he reaches out and takes her hand.

"Yes, sir." She tips her head and a pink blush colors her cheeks. Makes me wonder about their real relationship.

"Now, you go sit over there and leave the new one to me for supper." He waves his hand to an empty seat at a nearby table.

"Yes, sir." Felicity stoops before she walks away.

"Good, girl." Silas scoops a spoonful of stew into his mouth. After he swallows, he nudges me, "Eat."

I try the chicken stew. It's warm, seasoned well with onion and parsley and basil. It could be their chicken, but I can't be sure.

CHAPTER TWENTY-SEVEN

Romeo

If I had known the mountains would stay this cool, I would have packed up my stash of cigarettes and beer and snack food and lived here in a tent instead of taking that ridiculous trip to Minnesota with Duke. Since I can't go back in time, I do my best to live in the now.

"That glint we saw across the mountains," Duke is excited about whatever it was, "it's in this direction."

He seems to have forgotten his general hate for the bioluminescent algae that grows on everything for the moment. This hunt for what looked like a floating city has overcome him, consumed him, it's eating him from the inside like a maggot in a bratwurst.

"How do you even know what it was?" I ask.

He's shaking his head. "It has to be what we saw. There's no other explanation."

He's hauling it through the woods, walking faster than I've ever seen him move.

"A mirage maybe?" I suggest.

Duke's neck twitches and he itches his arm. He pauses to cough.

My spine goes straight. "Is there blood again?" I ask.

"Nope." He wipes his palm on his pants. "Maybe I'm cured."

There's a fresh streak of blood on his pants.

"Has it occurred to you that you might be dying?" I ask.

"Sure as shit." Duke nods. "Something's eating me from the inside, be it guilt or that glowing shit. Or maybe my insides are just boiling slowly." He taps his belly. "I'd say I'm about medium rare right now."

I shudder at the thought of a grown man cooking upright while he's walking through this world. I'm sure it's happened in the deserts and the blacktopped cities.

"Did you hear that?" Duke stops walking.

I hope he's not hearing Nancy's voice threatening to tear him apart in his sleep again.

"Someone's coming at us." Duke grips his belt, where his gun should be, but his hand comes away empty. I have it. "Hope you're ready to use that, Romeo."

I am.

We brace ourselves, hiding behind overgrown shrubs on the edge of the clearing.

A man steps out into the clearing.

He looks around before zeroing in on us, like a hunter to his prey. Like he's always known we were standing here, waiting just for him.

"I need yer help," the man says as he holds his hands up. "I'm of no harm to ye."

"What kind of help?" Duke asks.

"My friend has been taken. I need help retrieving her." The man seems unnaturally calm. "Please?" he asks. "You see, I have to get her back home, to my people. She has a baby waiting for her. A child needs her mother."

Duke shakes his head. "Nothing worse than a mother missing her child. That's truer than rain. Seen it plenty of times in my life. Family takes the baby, God takes the baby, the state takes the baby. Doesn't matter who it is, the mother is never the same afterward. Let's get this woman back to her child."

I glance at Duke with a questioning shrug.

"Do we have anything better to do?" he asks me.

Well, I'd like to be on my back porch with a shot of whiskey and a fat Cuban cigar. Instead of mentioning that, I shake my head. It's the end of the world and surviving sounds boring at the moment. What kind of a human am I if I'm not helping the last of my people? I'd be no better than those animals tearing each other apart.

Duke nods in agreement.

"Okay," I say. "We'll help."

Duke steps forward first. "You talk strange, son." He holds his hand out to shake. "Name's Duke. What's yours?"

"Aye, it's the curse of my many travels. My name is Abraham."

They shake.

"Where are you from?" Duke asks.

"Oh, here and there," Abraham replies.

Duke eyes the man before he calls over his shoulder. "Think it's safe to come out now, Romeo."

I step out of the forest and make my way to the two men.

"Nice to meet you," I greet the man. "I'm sure you understand our hesitation. There's not many strangers who can be trusted these days."

"Aye. Thank ye both."

"You need help finding your friend?" I ask.

"Aye." Abraham nods. "She was taken by a man named Silas and his men. There's about six or more of them."

"And what kind of man is Silas?" Duke asks.

"Oh, he's not a very good one. I rescued two women from him a while back and he took my friend in revenge," Abraham says. "Will ye help me?"

"What do you think?" I ask. "Are you sure you want to do this?"

"I reckon I've got a multitude of sins to atone for and if rescuing this man's friend brings redemption, I'd like to help." Duke nods. "I'd be more than happy to spend these last few days of my life helping someone less fortunate. This sounds like my last hope for redemption."

Abraham's face is flexed in confusion.

"It's the heat," I point out, "he's having trouble controlling himself, among other things."

"Aye," Abraham shakes his head, knowing. "I see what yer saying. I've seen men do terrible things due to the heat."

Duke breaks into a coughing fit. There's blood, it splatters on his knee as he bends over to catch his breath.

Our new friend watches Duke's fit with a placid face. He's either not concerned, or maybe he's seen this before, or maybe he knows there's no helping Duke.

"I am grateful for your assistance." Abraham pats his pockets.

"Our pleasure." Duke nods like he's been working at Chick-Fil-A and eager to please strangers.

"But, before we get moving too far, do either of ye have any batteries?"

I packed batteries for flashlights and what not. "Sure do." I open my pack. "What size?"

"Double A's," Abraham says as he pulls an iPhone with an external charger.

I dig through my bag and find the batteries. "Two?"

"Aye."

I pass him the batteries and Abraham clips them into the charger.

"You won't be making any calls, son," Duke says as he watches the man. "No matter how charged that phone is. The lines are down, have been down for over a year or more."

Abraham nods in understanding. "I don't plan on making a call, but to use this as a distraction."

"Okay, son." Duke claps his hands. "What direction are we going in and what kind of a mess did me and Romeo just sign up for?"

Abraham tells us his plan. "I'm going to use this to play music as a distraction." He touches the screen, bringing the phone to life. "My friend will know the music. She'll know I've come for her. I will place this elsewhere. Silas and his men will go for the sound and then we'll sneak in from the other direction and get her."

Abraham presses the screen and a song starts playing. A bluesy harmonica tune I've heard before.

Duke slaps a heavy hand on my shoulder. "Well ain't that lucky. Romeo here plays music just like this."

"You do?" Abraham asks.

"Yes. Yes, he does. Why don't you show him?" Duke encourages.

I pull the Fender harmonica from my pocket and Abraham watches with what I only recognize as disbelief. I play a little John Popper, identical to the song he just played on the iPhone for a few seconds. Then I shred with a backwoods southern pace; heavy on the blues, the space between the notes just as important as the notes themselves, and if there were crickets or peepers nearby I'm sure they'd help fill the space between. The south has a way of doing that; turning the night into a symphony.

I have to stop myself.

Abraham is watching with rapt attention. "That was mighty impressive."

I pocket the Fender and nod. "Thank you."

"Don't let him fool you," Duke shakes his finger at me. "That boy's got plenty more talent with that harp than he's letting on. He used to travel all over the United States playing in bars and festivals. Making the ladies swoon."

"Aye," Abraham scratches his head. "I believe ye."

"Which way do we start walking to find this Silas person?" I ask.

"His people have a settlement not far from here." Abraham points to where the mountain slopes.

Abraham leads us through the forest.

CHAPTER TWENTY-EIGHT

Nova

Silas is standing on the pulpit. He raises a Bible. Since he seems to be high on the Holy Spirit and I half expect him to raise a snake like one of those Pentecostal pastors in Kentucky and Tennessee. Watching Silas now, I'm beginning to think that Appalachia's serpent-handling pastors have nothing on this guy. I suffer through his sermon, bored to death and only able to focus on another mode of escape. One that doesn't get me flogged again.

"… as it says in Revelations, as for the cowardly, the faithless, the detestable, as for murderers, the sexually immoral, sorcerers, idolaters, and all liars, their portion will be in the lake which burns with fire and brimstone: which is the second death. This. Is. The second death." Silas meanders through the crowd until he is standing next to me. "Who will be standing with me at the ascension? Who?" He pauses and his parishioners nod and raise their hands. "You must accept Jesus into your soul. You. Must!"

Silas settles his hand on my shoulder quite firmly.

"Repent and Jesus shall save your soul." Silas is looking at me. "Repent. Repent! REPENT!"

He grips my arm and pulls up until I stand.

"This woman, our newest member, Nova." With his free arm he does a sweeping motion. "Greet her."

"Welcome, Nova," the room full of crazy god-fearing rednecks echoes.

"Nova must repent to ascend with us. Nova! Tell us of your sins."

My face flames red. I don't want to tell these people anything. But I'd also like to avoid the whipping post and the shed where they lock up disobedient women. So I say, "I—ah—I... had a baby out of wedlock."

"A child!" Silas roars. "The birth of the child is not the sin, but the act between the unwed man and woman is. And what does the Bible tell us? We could turn the pages, but I know. I know! Deuteronomy 23:2, a bastard shall not enter into the congregation of the Lord. They shall not enter!" Silas's head tips to the side. "And what have you done to this baby?"

"She's... um." I bite my lip. I don't want to tell them.

"Where has your bastard child gone?" he asks, venomous in his tone. "Tell us."

"She's not here." I try to lean away from Silas, but he has a crushing grip on my arm.

"Clearly we can see that she is not here, woman. What have you done to her?" Silas's eyes look a little crazy.

I have to tell him something, so I tell him, "Abraham took her."

Silas stomps his foot. "Abraham took her. The same man who took Susan and April." Silas raises his hand, his index finger pointed at the ceiling. "It seems we have a sinner, one who likes to steal. A kidnapper." His open hand spans across the room of parishioners. "What does Exodus tell us about those who stealeth a man?" He doesn't give anyone else time to answer before his voice booms, "They are to be put to death! And he that stealeth a man, and selleth him, or if he be found in his hand, he shall surely be put to death." Silas slams his fist on the back of the pew. "This man called Abraham must be put to death for the kidnapping of our Susan and April, and for Nova's child!"

The church erupts in commotion.

"Gather yourselves," Silas says. "For tomorrow we will hunt down this man called Abraham and put him to death just as God has asked us to." He raises both of his hands. "Go forth!"

The people stand and begin leaving.

I step away but Silas takes my arm and jerks me back to him. "You stay."

Everyone is gone and it's just Silas and I in the empty church.

"I thought Abraham was dead?" I ask. Silas and his men seemed so sure of it and he didn't come when I called for him. The last I saw was him lying on the ground after bullets were fired. "You told me that you left his carcass in the forest to rot."

Silas smiles. "It's not that easy to kill a man such as he. One with purpose, one with fight. Those men never die easily."

He watches me now; I'm guessing he's trying to gauge my reaction. I do my best to keep my face placid.

"Where did he take your child?" Silas asks.

I fidget with the hem of my dress. "I'm not sure you'll believe me."

"Many did not believe the word of God." He narrows his eyes on me. "Try me."

"Ah, okay. There is this floating city out there." I wave toward the mountains. "And there are these..."

Lord I sound like an idiot, but I barely believed what I saw.

"Go on," Silas urges.

"Tentacle things that extend from the bottom of it. And, um, they'll bring you up to the city. To Abraham's people. So... that's where my daughter is. She's with Abraham's people."

"A floating city?" Silas asks.

I nod.

"And ascension." He paces before me and pounds his fist into his open hand. "I knew it! I knew the Lord would provide." He turns to me, his eyes wide. "You will bring us there."

"I don't know exactly where it is. Abraham brought me from another direction and through the forests, there were no roads." Although, I lost a few chickens on the way; maybe there's a path of feathers left behind.

He backhands me. Silas preaches about infidels and cowards, but he has no problem hitting a woman. "You will bring us there!"

"Okay! Okay!" I shield myself from him and press my hand to my sore cheek. "I'll bring you there."

"Good." He adjusts his shirt. "Now." He heads for the door. "Come with me."

I'm not sure who April and Susan were, but if anything, Abraham did them a favor getting them out of this Hell hole.

I follow Silas against my better judgment.

CHAPTER TWENTY-NINE

Abraham

Abraham led his new companions through the forest until they were close to the settlement. He stopped and crouched, gripping a tree to steady himself, the movement causing his injured shoulder to pinch. "There." He pointed to the dusty road in the clearing. "These are only the first few buildings, there's more. Follow me." He led them deeper, stopping frequently when he heard a noise or the voices of Silas's people.

"How many are there?" Romeo asked.

"A good dozen or more," Abraham replied.

"When do we make a move?" Romeo was nervous choosing sides in a stranger's war. He nervously tapped his finger on the harmonica in his pocket as he walked.

"I say we wait until after dinner, when they're full as ticks and groggy from a day in this heat. They'll move slow." Duke covered his mouth with his whole hand and stifled a cough.

Abraham nodded as he walked closer to the settlement. "Aye, perhaps that is a good idea."

"Do you have a real plan?" Romeo asked.

"Not much of one." Abraham crouched, settled on his knee and studied the settlement before him.

It hadn't changed since the last time he was here. He focused on the shed where he'd found April, wondering if that was where Nova was being held. He wanted to run in and check, without restraint, without uncertainty. But he knew better, he'd made mistakes when he let his guard down and that had cost him. Most recently it had cost him Nova. There was fresh blood on the post near the shed he hoped wasn't hers.

Thunder rumbled in the distance.

"It's comin' up a cloud," Duke said as he searched for a break in the canopy. He wiped his sleeve across his forehead. "These mountains are starting to heat up worse than the lowlands."

Two men walking along the dusty road stopped and quieted.

Romeo shushed Duke as the ochre dust swirling in the men's footsteps clung to the humidity and fell to the road in lazy descent.

There was shouting coming from one of the buildings with a cross nailed over the front door.

Romeo pointed. Duke shifted and focused.

"Stinks to high heaven," Duke muttered.

The door opened and people flooded out. Men, women, and children left the building and dispersed to their own homes. The men in the road turned and headed back to the settlement.

"Do you see your friend?" Romeo asked Abraham.

Abraham was studying the group of people. "Aye, she's not there." But through the front windows there were shadows moving in the church building. "But she could be."

Romeo turned to keep an eye on Duke and as he did the door opened again and out stepped Nova with Silas close behind her.

"Aye, there she is." Abraham stood and pulled the iPhone from his pocket. He opened the music program like he'd seen Nova do so many times and chose one of her favorite songs. Abraham held the screen up so Romeo could see. "Can ye play this on that mouth harp in yer pocket?"

Romeo moved closer. "Yeah," he nodded.

"You," he motioned to Duke, "take this and set it on as high as it will go, over there," Abraham pointed to where the trees broke. "I need you to play," he pointed in the opposite direction, closer to the settlement, "to create confusion."

Duke made a noise of contention.

"What?" Abraham asked.

"That dog won't hunt." Duke shook his heat.

Abraham scowled. "Aye?"

Romeo shook his head. "He thinks it's a bad idea."

Abraham glanced back at Nova; she was getting further away from them, deeper into the settlement, closer to more of Silas's men. "Aye, that's too bad, you see." He hit play on the phone and slapped it in Duke's hand, then he shoved Romeo in the direction he needed to be. "I suggest ye boys get on with the plan." Abraham dropped his bag and stripped his cloak off, taking just the three-pronged weapon with him.

As the high pitch of the harmonica crescendoed, Abraham ran in Nova's direction.

CHAPTER THIRTY

Nova

"What is that noise?" Silas asks.

I turn my head and focus on a sound in the distance. It's a harmonica, someone belting out Blues Traveler as loud as their lungs will let them, the peaks and valleys and pitches of "Run-Around" are the sweetest music to my ears. My heart starts beating faster; hope thumps hard in my chest.

Three men appear, hovering behind us as though they'd been hiding in the shadows all along, watching and waiting. "Go," Silas directs them toward the sound. "Find whoever is making that noise and bring them here." He turns to me. "I'll kill him myself this time. The Lord loves a good sacrifice."

Silas grabs my upper arm and turns, headed for the shed near the whipping post. I've been there before. I've seen the blood on the floor that's never dried.

"No. No. No." I struggle to break his hold on me; he squeezes tighter. "Don't want you escaping tonight." I dig my heels into the ground and wait for him to take a few steps ahead of me, then I kick him in the back of the knee as hard as I can. Silas drops to the ground and I make a run for it.

Between the sweet notes of the harmonica I hear a strange sound, a war cry, the thundering of footsteps, and then a large man runs out from the tree line. I stumble when I recognize Abraham dashing toward me with a killer look planted on his face. He looks like he's in a scene out of "Braveheart," Mel Gibson rushing in with a war-painted face. He's scary looking and for a moment I wonder if the Heat Wave has affected him, if he's raging just as hard as everyone else. He promised me he never would.

Silas is swearing. One of his men wraps an arm around my waist and lifts, transporting me away. I struggle, clawing at his hands and twisting. Sweat is running down my back and making my hands slippery and I can't pry his fingers off me.

I hear the sounds of shouting, the music getting louder, someone losing their pace as they play. It takes me a moment to realize that the music is coming from two directions. Between the notes, the sound of fists thumping hard against bodies resonates.

Silas's friend drops me and rushes in to help his people.

I scramble to my feet and watch as Abraham knocks Silas's head against another man's, just like smashing two melons together, dense thud and all. They both drop to the ground. Lightning strikes in the roadway, followed by a loud rumble of thunder and the remaining two men decide to drag away their friends and run from Abraham.

In a matter of minutes the fight is over.

Abraham comes at me, wide-eyed and bloody-knuckled. I've seen this before, I've done my best to avoid it, but I've still seen it. Joy's birth comes to mind and the way those women changed. I can see it now, in Abraham.

"Stay away," I shout, motioning for him to stop, palms up and ready to run.

"This place is not safe," Abraham says, advancing. "I can't leave ye here."

"Those men," I point in the direction that Silas and his people went. "You… you…"

"Aye," Abraham says. "I came to rescue ye from Silas."

I look in his eyes and see that he is not like the others were. I'm wrong. He is calm, the violence I've seen in others is not there.

"Okay." I nod. "Okay. Thank you." I walk toward him. "Don't forget, I still hate you. Now get me the heck out of here."

"I thought ye'd never ask." Abraham takes my hand and we run for the tree line.

The music suddenly stops. There's shouting coming from the forest.

"Abraham," a man shouts. "We need some help over here."

"Come now, Nova." His grip tightens.

He doesn't have to tell me twice. I'm outta this place. The rain starts, wind howling through the valley. I'm not sure where Abraham plans on heading next but I hope to hell it's away from the Blue Ridge Mountains.

CHAPTER THIRTY-ONE

Romeo

I've never been one for fighting but I'm holding my own. Abraham is running to our rescue dragging a woman behind him but he's not going to make it in time. The brute facing me isn't much different than a drunken townie unhappy with the show. He shoots two fists at my face, but I duck and cover, then roll and do my best Kung Fu, slipping my leg out to knock him off balance. It doesn't work; the guy jumps then kicks me in the knee. I roll, my ribs cracking against a tree trunk.

I get a good look at Duke while I'm rolling pathetically on the ground. He's got two men on him but he's holding back. I saw him fight better with two beers in his hand when the Heat Wave started.

"Duke!" I shout. "You know all this time I've been telling you to control yourself?"

Duke nods.

"Don't."

In that moment it was as if a light switch were flicked, everything Duke had been holding in was released and I get to see everything I've been missing by threatening to take his life. It wasn't just violence he's been containing all this time, it was pure unadulterated rage. My last friend in the world turns into a monster before my eyes.

My breath is knocked out of me as Silas's guy gives me two kicks to the back. Before I can move, I hear Abraham growl as he bowls the man over and pummels him to the ground.

Chaos ensues. Thunder booms and the sky opens up. Torrential rain pours down. I move to my feet, barely able to see my hand in front of my face. Lightning strikes a tree a few hundred yards away.

"Git yer feet to the ground and run, boy," Abraham shouts. A hand on my shoulder points me in the right direction, up. I hear the thundering footsteps of Duke and since I'm not sure if he's running from the rain or ready to kill everyone in sight, I run faster.

I hear a woman's voice arguing. I turn to see Abraham picking his belongings up and throwing the cloak over the woman to protect her from the rain. "Go!" He shouts at us as he lifts the woman and runs uphill.

The sky darkens and the rain pounds harder, soaking me to the skin. I slip and fall more than once, the undergrowth of the forest is worse than a Slip and Slide. I find myself grabbing on to branches and trees to steady myself. Duke is nearby, breathing heavy and coughing.

"Have you calmed down?" I check my waistband for the gun.

Duke's response is a growl, followed by, "Fixin' to."

The ground begins to level, and we come to the peak. The sun sets and it's darker than I've ever seen the night, no doubt from the heavy storm clouds that rolled in just before our crash and grab. I check my pockets out of habit. Damn, I lost my harmonica in the fight.

"Abraham?" Duke asks. "Which way?"

"Aye, it's hard to get my bearings in this mess."

Duke pulls up, hunches over, and hacks. "That glowing shit... It's coming for us."

"What's that?" the woman asks. "Look." She cups her hand to collect the rain and it takes me a moment to notice, but then it always takes a moment for it to start. The glowing doesn't come on strong and abrupt; it's always a leisurely lyrical pirouette. Specks within the collection of rainwater in her hand begin to luminate, and it's not just the puddle, it's the rain-soaked grass, the trees, the rain falling out of the sky, the clouds. The whole world is lit up and glowing a dampened seafoam. It's rolling down our cheeks, collecting on our shoulders, and hanging from our eyelashes.

"It's so strange," the woman says. "I can see clear as day now."

Everything damp is glowing, everything hit by a drop of rain glows brighter as it disrupts the bioluminescent bacteria. The glowing illuminates her chin, but with the drooping hood of the cloak I can't get a good look at her face. There's something familiar about her.

Duke coughs hard and I notice the blood splatter on his hand is glowing too. He wipes it off and stands, pretending that there's nothing wrong but the swipe mark is clear as day.

"I suggest we get moving," Abraham says as he settles his hand on the woman's back and directs her to walk, headed south. "There's a cave not far from here. It will offer protection and cover until the storm clears," Abraham says.

"How do you know?" I ask.

"Aye, I've been through this area a time or two."

As we walk, our shoes sink into the saturated mountainside. The rain finally stops but the glowing never does.

The woman with Abraham pulls the hood of the cloak down and removes it from her shoulders. "It's too hot for this thing," she complains.

I stumble. I'd recognize that face in a heartbeat. I blink a few times, search my pocket for my harmonica—like I often do when I'm nervous, but come up empty. It was years ago but this has to be her. It looks just like her; her hair a bit longer and tiredness around her eyes. "Nova, is that you?" I ask.

She turns toward me, her face twisted in confusion as she walks closer. Soon we are standing across from each other with an abyss of blue lamination lighting the moment. I have searched for her, dreamt of her, prayed for her. I have seen Nova in everything, everyone, every moment. I'd hoped to see her. Now she's here. But this world has changed and I'm not sure if I can trust my eyesight.

Her complexion pales. "Romeo?" she asks. "Romeo, is that you?"

Abraham is looking between us.

"Is this the woman you've been pining over for years?" Duke asks.

"It's her." I walk closer. "You remember me?"

"I remember." Nova nods. "But that was so long ago."

"It was." I reach out, wanting to touch her.

"That was you playing in the woods? Back at the settlement?" she asks.

"Yes."

"I remember—" she starts.

"Aye, we must be moving," Abraham interrupts.

"Come on," she takes my hand and drags me as she follows Abraham, "we'll catch up later."

My mind is in a whirl. Nova survived the Heat Wave. She doesn't look worse for the wear, maybe she's avoided the violence. Then I take in her long skirt and rain-soaked top, the material molding to her body, revealing long strips of scabbed skin.

Thoughts of someone hurting her makes me angry. After all this time I shouldn't care. I didn't really know her. Just that she liked my music and tasted like peaches and rocked my world for all of two hours of my life. I tamper down the anger, afraid that it could boil out of control.

Duke's footsteps become heavy behind me. He coughs more frequently than before, the humidity saturating his airway.

"We're here," Abraham announces. He pushes a few branches to the side and reveals a narrow path to a westward facing cave. "I left some supplies here last time. If the creatures haven't helped themselves."

Nova lets go of my hand and steadies herself on the jutting rock.

We form a single line, following the narrow walk to the opening. The cave has more than enough room for all of us. There are two containers stacked in the back and a rock circle with black soot from the last fire that burned. Abraham grabs the containers and opens them. He hands us blankets, canteens of water and bags of small, circular biscuits.

He makes a fire with dry wood from the back of the cave, stopping only to speak quietly to Nova. It seems like they might be arguing. It seems like they have more of a history than I do. I control my jealousy and focus on the good fortune of seeing her again before I live my last day.

There is some small talk, a plan for tomorrow, silence as the fire dies down. Then our tired bones take comfort in the rocky ground.

Duke rolls to his back, his hands folded over his stomach. I notice through the thin skin of his temples and the back of Duke's hands, the blood pulsing through his veins is glowing a gentle sapphire. It pulses up his arms and into his chest. If Duke noticed this before he never said a word. As he lay there with his eyes closed, I realize that I may never have to put a bullet in his skull.

Duke is dying.

Nova and Abraham are quiet for a while as they too watch the progression and eventually the songs of the mountain forest breaks through. There are peepers peeping and crickets humming, but it is a slow, sad song of the night, nothing as fast paced as what I'm used to further south.

CHAPTER THIRTY-TWO

Abraham

Abraham was eager to have Nova at his side once again. Their time alone had been short, but she was here and alive. The gleam in her eyes had dulled since Joy had gone to his people. He was glad that Silas and his men hadn't broken her.

Abraham touched her shoulder and Nova flinched away. Without a word he spun her and laid his eyes on the damaged skin of her shoulder.

"I'm fine," Nova stepped away from him. "It's fine. One of the women there treated me. It might scar but I'll live. Others have had worse."

"Don't move." Abraham left her side to dig through his pack, pulling out a small metal tin. He moved her shirt and pulled off the sopping wet bandages before rubbing the salve from the tin on her injuries. "This will heal ye quickly."

Nova tipped her head down as his fingertips gently spread the salve.

When he was done, she adjusted her top and as she focused on Abraham again, he pulled her close, not giving her time to push him away again. "I thought I'd lost you," he whispered as his large hands gripped the uninjured skin of her arms.

"Well you didn't." Nova's voice was flat, and he knew that she was still upset.

"I have something for you." Abraham pulled her iPhone from his pocket. "I'm afraid it got mighty wet. But it still works. Romeo had batteries."

Nova's face was blank. "I asked you to get rid of that."

"Aye, ye did, but you spent so much time with the music and the pictures. I wasn't sure if ye were serious."

Nova took the phone, walked to the edge of the cave and chucked it over the side of the mountain as far as she could. She turned to him, pressing her index finger into his chest. "I am still really, really, *really* pissed at you."

"We could have listened to the music," Romeo said with disappointment.

"Or you could whistle a tune," Nova snapped back. "You could play something." She paused and held her hand up in calming apology. "I'm sorry, Romeo. It's been a rough few weeks."

"Lost my harmonica back there in the scuffle," Romeo said as he tapped his fingers together.

Nova and Abraham settled near the fire. Abraham wanted to move closer, he wanted to sleep with her touching him like that time back at the farmhouse, but he knew she wouldn't have it.

*

Nova woke early in the morning, as the sun was streaming through the valley. The peaks and ridges of the mountains were wrapped in a soft blue haze. The mountain maple and swamp birch were draped in morning mist and the sky was pale blue, without a cloud and as serene as the calm ocean. Nova had the feeling that she could sit here forever, wake to this sight each morning and die happy. She'd die lonely though, without her child, the last sane woman on earth.

There was commotion inside. Romeo was shaking Duke, slapping his face and pumping on his chest.

"I think he's passed on," Abraham was saying, only to be interrupted by a giant gasping sound from Duke.

Duke coughed and sat up, unaware that he had been completely unconscious and that Romeo was attempting CPR on him.

"I think he needs a doctor," Romeo said. "Do you know of one?" he asked Nova and Abraham.

Nova shook her head. "The last doctors I knew lost their minds and tried to kill me. They are all dead now."

Abraham paced for a moment. He was only ever supposed to bring back two. Never three. Perhaps Jacob wouldn't count Nova since she was off limits?

"Is there anyone?" Romeo pressed. "He's dying."

Duke rolled to his side and moved to his feet. The action took much effort and was followed by a string of coughing and deep breathing.

Abraham nodded as he watched Duke uneasily. "Aye, there is a place."

Nova nervously turned away.

"There is a floating city we can take him to. There's medical help there," Abraham said.

"See, boy," Duke slapped Romeo. "I told you there was a city floating past those mountains the other day."

"Yeah," Romeo nodded. "Yeah you did."

"He thought I was crazy." Duke slapped Romeo on the shoulder again, this time harder. "Crazier than a shithouse rat most days but I know what I saw." He pointed to the nearby valley. "Out there, past the highest ridge, nestled in the holler. I could see the sun glinting off its dome."

"Nova?" Romeo asked. "Have you heard of this floating city before?"

"My daughter is there," Nova whispered as she walked to the mouth of the cave and wrapped her arms around herself.

"Okay, okay," Romeo nodded as he inspected Duke closely. The man's vasculature wasn't glowing any longer.

They collected their things and Abraham resealed the containers and replaced them in the back of the cave. Abraham steered the group away from his normal path, having a sense that someone was following them. He couldn't be sure who it was, it could be the last of Silas's men, or Jacob, or a wayward squirrel. Either way, Abraham was on high alert. The group was quiet, hyperaware of their surroundings.

The day was hot and then the night glowed brightly. Romeo had difficulty igniting the wood for a fire. Every stick and twig he set together glowed intensely where his fingers touched and refused to ignite, instead the flame from his lighter danced around the wood.

"Why couldn't the world turn hot and dry?" Romeo complained. "This humidity is killer."

"Could burn something else," Duke recommended, pointing to their bags.

Romeo threw the lighter into the fire pit he'd dug. "No. We don't really need the fire. It's more for comfort than warmth."

"How much further?" Nova asked Abraham.

"Tomorrow." Abraham scanned the forest, uneasy about the noises he'd been hearing as they traveled. He didn't mention this to the others, instead he observed and planned. He didn't want to be caught off guard like he had before.

"I just have to survive one more night." Duke chuckled to himself as he settled on the ground for the night. "Did you hear that, sweetheart? Your revenge is soon." He rolled to his side and held in a cough that made his body twitch. "Talking to the dead never helped a soul."

The others settled down for the night. None of them spoke as Duke's veins lit up with the rest of the world. Nova and Romeo held their hands up in front of their faces to inspect if the same phenomenon was happening to them.

"Aye, don't think it's a natural event," Abraham said to Nova. "Wouldn't worry much about it in a healthy person."

What Abraham didn't say was that he thought this was Earth's way of cleaning out the last of the human race that didn't belong. First it was the unbearable heat, the violence, and now the internal glow. Duke was the first he'd seen with the affliction and he was hoping it was the last. While the glow of the earth at night was spectacular, this man luminated unnaturally.

Abraham couldn't help but think that this planet was doing his job for him and ridding itself of violence from the inside out.

*

Rustling in the nearby brush woke Abraham just as the sun was rising. He sat up, moved to a crouch and repositioned himself closer to Nova.

"What's that noise?" Nova asked as her eyes snapped open.

There was a deep hum, scratching, the sound of a heavy weight releasing the thin branches of the shrub.

They waited, Abraham's hand over his weapon, ready to fight.

A chicken clucked loudly and sprinted out of the bushes headed for Nova. "Oh my god." Nova moved to her knees and scooped up the chicken. "Oh my god, how did you survive?" She was smiling like Abraham had never seen before, like he'd hoped she would when he found more batteries for her iPhone.

"Uh, do you know this chicken?" Romeo asked.

Nova pets the hen and rubbed her face on its soft feathers. "It's from our farm. I thought we'd lost them or Silas had killed them all."

Abraham stood and glanced at Duke. The man looked dead, again.

"Let's get moving, Sheriff," Romeo said as he shoved Duke's shoulder to wake him.

Duke didn't move, and upon closer inspection they could see clear tendrils stretching from his skin to the ground. They wove away in vein-like fashion toward the forest. Using a stick, Romeo cut the thin-as-hair tendrils. With each separation there was a burst of light as the cyanobacteria were disturbed. Romeo shoved Duke harder and slapped his chest, it was only when the last tendril was cut, the one connected to his earlobe, did Duke open his eyes.

"We'll be walking 'til the cows come home." Duke rolled to his side. "Why don't you hush your mouth and give me another five minutes?"

Romeo stood and looked at Nova and Abraham.

"Aye, five minutes is plenty time to break down camp," Abraham said as he went about his business.

Romeo scattered the fire that never was and then his eyes settled on Nova as she chewed.

"Do you want one?" she offered.

Romeo nodded and sat next to her as she handed him a biscuit.

Romeo cleared his throat. "You said you had a daughter?" he rocked as he waited, unable to quell the need for motion that was coiling inside of him.

"I do." Nova nodded.

"And she's at this floating city?" Romeo asked as he ate.

Nova nodded again.

"What's it like?" he stood again as he glanced in Abraham's direction.

Abraham was studying the tendrils on the ground and the strings that were still connected to Duke's face.

"Well," Nova cleared her throat, "it floats." She forced a light laugh.

Romeo waited.

"I'm not sure what you want to know about it. Maybe if you had a specific question." Nova didn't want to talk about sending her daughter to live with strangers; she didn't want to focus on the hole it left in her soul. She just wanted to figure out how to get her daughter back. She really knew nothing about the floating city.

Duke coughed loudly, rolled to his knees and stood. The remaining tendrils underneath him stretched and snapped. Duke looked around the camp for a moment, seeming lost. Abraham walked by and set a biscuit in his one hand and a canteen of water in the other.

"Now that you've rejoined the living, we should head out," Abraham picked up his belongings and motioned for Nova to follow.

They left the camp and followed Abraham as he traveled a new path through the Blue Ridge. He couldn't help but feel as though they were being followed. It could be Jacob, since his brother had a habit of sneaking up on him and keeping tabs.

Nova carried the hen and it cooed happily as tears collected in the corners of her eyes. She wiped them away with the hope that no one would notice how happy she was to have one of Joy's beloved chickens again.

Romeo was humming a song, and the culmination of it all bloomed a spec of hope in her chest.

The closer they came to the base of the mountain, the hotter it got. The previous night's rain still saturated the land and soon the travelers' shoes were thick with mud. Abraham moved them to the paved road.

"Don't think this is a good idea," Duke argued. "We're mighty visible to all."

"Aye," Abraham nodded. "It's unfortunate but the land is soaked through, soon we'd be up to our knees in muck."

"I guess you have a point," Duke said.

"It won't be long now." Abraham pointed to a field, and near the edge there was a shimmer of camouflage meant to hide the floating city from others. What Abraham didn't bring up was the way Duke stuck to the ground as he walked, his knees pulled away slower and slower. Tendrils rose up from the grass and clung to his boots. His face was turning a pallid blue and Abraham wasn't sure if it was because of the lack of oxygen in his body or the overgrowth of the glowing bacteria.

Eventually, they stopped at the edge of the road, before them was a field spotted with trees.

"It looks like a marsh," Nova pointed out. "We were just here days ago and the land was dusty and dry."

"Aye," Abraham nodded. "It seems the rain was heavy."

They started walking and just as Abraham feared, the mud was thick and slowed their pace considerably. Nova picked up the hen and set it in the large pocket of Abraham's pack.

Duke was barely moving.

"Come on, Sheriff." Romeo took Duke's elbow and dragged him along. There were tendrils clinging to Duke, they grew in serpentine motion and attached to his boots and ankles. Nova moved to help, she brushed the tendrils away with a stick she'd picked up. But more grew back.

They were barely moving, and Abraham definitely sensed someone was nearby. He heard voices now. The urge to get out of the field was overwhelming.

Romeo tugged at Duke's arm.

"It's the missus," Duke said, barely making sense. "She's dragging me down to Hell where I belong." He was shaking his head. "She's sucking me through this mud, she's waiting below."

"Come on," Romeo said. "We're almost there. Abraham's people can help you."

"Don't need no help." Duke had stopped lifting his feet. His temples pulsed with blue light. "I told you, boy. I told you that glowing crap was going to eat us from the inside out."

Nova was trying to lift Duke's leg at the knee to get him to move.

"Just lay me down to sleep, little lady." Duke's eyelids fluttered and his eyes rolled until the whites showed.

"We must go." Abraham moved closer to the trio.

"We have to save him," Romeo urged. "You said your people would help him. He doesn't deserve to die in the mud."

Abraham frowned. "Aye, I did." He took in the size of Duke, he passed his pack to Nova then leaned his shoulder into Duke's gut and lifted him.

The sudden movement caused Duke to pass out and then he was simply a few hundred pounds of dead weight. Abraham turned and resumed his walk toward the floating city. He knew if he got there, then his people would protect them from whoever was following.

The mud became thicker and glowed with each step he took, even in the daylight now.

Romeo helped Nova through the mud, and as he held her arm, the suction of the swamp took her boots right off her feet. "Wait!" She reached down to retrieve them.

"Leave them," Abraham urged. "We must get to the city."

The edge of the swamp was near and Romeo was the first to reach it. He tugged Nova from the edge, and the thick mud didn't want to release her. Nova let the hen down to wander as she helped Romeo pull Abraham. The mud was up to his knees and he was sinking deeper.

"Give Duke to us," Romeo said as he held his hands out.

Abraham shifted Duke and half tossed, half rolled him to the edge. Romeo and Nova grabbed onto Duke's arms and the back of his shirt and pulled him out. When they'd rolled him far enough away, they turned to help Abraham.

"Come on," Romeo swore as his feet slid.

Nova pulled with every ounce of strength she had left, her bare feet skidding across the ground, tearing her skin.

Finally, Abraham reached the edge. He crawled as the others kept pulling and got him as far away from the swamp as they could.

"Maybe we should have gone around." Nova pointed to what looked like a field, but as she stood she recognized that there was only standing water reflecting the plants. "It's changed so much since we were here last."

"Aye," Abraham agreed. "They'll have to move it now."

"Move the city?" she asked, her heart in her throat with the thought of Joy going further away from her.

"To the other side of the continent. It's the only land I've left to cull." Abraham wiped mud on his pants to clean his hands. "If there's anyone left over there."

"I think he's dead." Romeo interrupted them. He held his fingers over Duke's carotid. "I can't feel a pulse."

Nova ran to Duke's side. "But his chest is rising. It looks like he's breathing real shallow."

"Best get him help then." Abraham lifted Duke again. The motion wasn't as smooth as the first time, as Abraham ached from carrying the large man's body just a few moments ago. He pushed through and as he shifted, Duke's extra pounds jiggled and repositioned like a beached whale lolling onto the sand dunes. Abraham began walking.

As they stepped under the shadow of the floating city, Romeo's gaze rose as he took in the massive object and the long tentacles that dangled nearby.

Soon they were at the base. Abraham set Duke down on the rusty dirt.

Romeo studied the base of the city. He walked to the edge and examined the perimeter.

Nova looked nervous. She glanced between Romeo and the tendrils. "What will it do to them?" she asked Abraham.

Abraham stood with his back to the others. "The city will decide."

"But will it... will they... burn up like you worried it would do to me?" she whispered.

"I have no way of knowing that."

"But you said you did. You wouldn't let me—"

"They are not you." Abraham shook his head.

"They should know," Nova argued. "They should know the risks. They should have a choice. It's only fair. It's only human."

Abraham ran his hand through his hair in frustration. "Duke is quite likely dead. And the other one—"

355

"Is Joy's father," Nova spat out, interrupting him.

The hen clucked around Nova's feet.

Abraham turned to look at the man. "All this time and ye didn't tell me it was him?"

"All this time and I didn't tell *him* it is him." Nova crossed her arms. "Plus, there's plenty you didn't tell me." Nova wasn't sure she wanted to tell Romeo; it would just make things more difficult. There would be questions and judgment and Romeo might want to see Joy. Joy was Nova's, all hers, and she didn't think she could share her child with a one-night stand.

"Aye, I'll give you that. But they need to go. They need to try. Someone's been following us and I need to get you to safety." Abraham continued to wipe his mud-caked hands on his pants.

Nova picked up the hen and stepped toward the sweeping cilia. "I'll just go up."

Abraham grabbed her hand away. "No."

"What do these do?" Romeo asked.

Nova and Abraham turned just as Romeo was reaching out and a tendril was beckoning. Before they could say a thing, Romeo touched it.

Nova held her breath.

Abraham sighed.

The tendril wrapped itself around Romeo's wrist, pulsed with judgment and tore his feet off the ground, propelling him upwards hungrily. Romeo disappeared into the base of the floating city.

Nova's eyes dropped to Abraham. "Now what about him?" She pointed to Duke.

"Aye, we should get the dirty work over with." Abraham moved toward the near-corpse on the ground, grabbed Duke by the wrists, and dragged him closer to the tentacles.

"Will it take him?" Nova asked. She didn't want to see the man die. He'd helped save her from Silas, after all.

"Aye, doubt it but I must try." Abraham moved a tentacle to Duke's hand and stepped back.

Duke's hand stayed raised, as though the last spec of life left in him was begging. "Take me home, sweetheart," he muttered as his fingertips swiped the tentacle, and he turned to dust in an instant, the grains hovering in the thick, humid air before settling in a man-shaped pile.

"Oh my god," Nova gasped. "Oh my god. Where'd he go?"

"Be still, Nova," Abraham hushed. "He went where he needed to go."

CHAPTER THIRTY-THREE

Abraham

Abraham was right to worry that they were being followed. Before the dust that was Duke had time to settle completely, Silas and four of his men made themselves visible. They weren't caked with mud like Abraham and Nova were; they'd found a way around the swamp and water, or a clever way over.

"Ha!" Silas shouted as he pointed to the floating city. "She tells the truth!" He approached Nova and embraced her as though she were an old friend. "And yet she runs from her duties." Silas slapped Nova on the cheek like an Italian grandmother would, a bit of warning, a bit of love, a bit of punishment.

"Aye, that is enough." Abraham intervened and pulled Nova away from the men. He shoved her behind him, toward an outcropping of rocks.

Since Nova had nothing left to lose, she didn't follow Abraham's suggestions; she lingered behind him, ready.

"Nova said these are your people," Silas pointed to the base of the floating city.

"Aye, they are." Abraham nodded.

Silas rubbed his chin as he paced. "So that makes you, what? A disciple? What are you?"

The four men Silas brought formed a line behind him.

"I am just myself." Abraham spread his arms. "Nothing more."

"A bit more than a man. We saw you taking people through the mountains and returning alone," she said.

Abraham shook his head. "I am no one. I do as my Elders have told me."

"We seek ascension," Silas said. "We are the few who have survived, it is our time." He turned to his men. "Jonah, go home and bring the others here." He clapped as one of the men turned and ran back to the settlement in the valley. "This is our day." Silas smiled. "This is the moment we've been waiting for." He stepped closer to the tentacles. "How does this work? Do we pray? Chant?" His eyes flicked to Nova. "Sacrifice?"

Abraham stepped to the side to guard Nova and reveal the sweeping tentacles. "You simply grasp and it pulls you up."

"Why don't you touch it?" Silas asked.

"I can." Abraham grabbed the tentacle but nothing happened. "See. Easy."

Silas eyed the red dirt that speckled the land under the floating city. "What about her?" Silas pointed to Nova.

Abraham smiled lopsidedly. "Aye, this isn't about her. She's helping me."

"And if she touched it?" Silas asked.

"She will not touch it." Abraham was becoming edgy and it showed.

Silas lurched forward, kicking Abraham in the knee and grabbing Nova by the neck. "What if she touches it?"

"She can't touch it!" Abraham spat like a madman. "She will not. Just leave her be."

Silas smiled as he steered Nova close to the tentacles, his grip digging into her throat. They swayed close, nearly brushing her cheek as though they sensed her presence.

"Okay! Okay! I'll do it," she shouted.

"No," Abraham whispered. "Please don't. Don't do it."

"You are no longer in control." Silas motioned to his men.

Abraham went after the three men, but just as he pulled his weapon from his belt a shot rang out.

Blood bloomed across his shoulder. One of the men had shot Abraham in the shoulder.

"Stop hurting him!" Nova shouted. "Just, leave him alone."

"Do it then." Silas shoved her closer to the curtain of tentacles. "You touch it first and prove it's safe."

"Nova, don't touch it!" Abraham groaned.

Silas shouted, "Put him to death! And he that stealeth a man, and selleth him, or if he be found in his hand, he shall surely be put to death."

They shot him again, this time in the stomach.

"This is for April and Susan and Nova's child. You stole them all," Silas seethed.

Whatever he was; alien, human, god-like or god-fearing, Nova doubted he'd recover from this. They needed help and they weren't going to get it on the ground. The rest of Silas' people were coming and she had to do something. It couldn't be so bad? Nova thought to herself. She'd watched Duke disappear in an instant that was more humane than the many other ways to die. But if she didn't burn up then she'd see Joy again. And that thought was enough to invoke bravery. If she couldn't see Joy at least she'd see John.

She grabbed the tentacle, closed her eyes and prayed she didn't burn to a crisp like Abraham feared.

She didn't sizzle. Instead, the tentacle cinched tight around her arm and hauled her up. Nova twisted her arm, afraid when she felt the tingle that resembled sticking your tongue to the prongs of a 9-volt battery, or the zap of an electric fence on the back while sneaking into the cow pastures. It was a zing; static, cleansing, and fresh.

"My God," one of the men said.

"We do it now," Silas commanded. "On the count of three. One, two, three!" Silas and his two remaining men grabbed a tentacle. They all turned to ash.

"Abraham!" Nova screamed as she reached for him. But she was high in the sky now, over a hundred feet and climbing.

He was watching and blood was pooling on the sand underneath his middle. He watched, and she soared.

CHAPTER THIRTY-FOUR

Abraham

Abraham stared at the clouds and he could feel the rotation of the planet under his spine. It was exhilarating. His skin rippled with a sensation he'd not felt since he realized the wonders this planet held, a sensation he'd not felt since he found Nova that second time. It seems this planet held a bit of magic; perhaps some pull that always brought people to where they needed to be, a balance that couldn't be fought or avoided. He tried to trick it but he'd lost.

"Brother?" a familiar voice asked.

Abraham was very still, lying on the ground, his blood leaking from the bullet holes. "Brother," he whispered, the vibration of his voice erupting a white-hot pain in his chest.

"I told you never to bring three." Jacob was crouched and examining. "Definitely never six."

"Aye," Abraham blinked long and slow. "That wasn't the plan."

"It seems your plans often run askew since you've been here. That's unlike you. We've reaped many planets within the Seven Sacred Galaxies and never have you been like this. What is it about this place?" Jacob reached out and poked at Abraham's chest. "You brought a grassroots gang to our door. The Elders won't like to hear about this."

"Aye," Abraham groaned. "The Elders can bite me."

Jacob frowned. "You are so different from what you once were." He stood, his pristine robes swaying.

"She wasn't supposed to go," Abraham's voice was weak. "She was supposed to wait and go with me at the end. I wanted more time with her. Here."

"Ah," Jacob nodded. "Your pet human."

Abraham pressed his lips in a tight line as pain swept through his stomach.

"Her first words were of her daughter and then to beg us to help you. And now I am here." Jacob tilted his head. "You are only second in her book," Jacob said.

"Why should I help you now? The Elders might rejoice knowing they're done dealing with you."

"The child has always come first for both of us." Abraham attempted to take a full breath but the pain was too great. "Do not see it as a negative. We have always known where we stand with each other."

"It is so odd that you have become just like them in such a short period of time." This was the thread that held them apart, the simple knowledge that poked a cavern in their relationship. It hadn't become a problem until Jacob learned of their difference and then Abraham and Jacob were no longer the same brothers. Perhaps it was the years of betrayal, the shock, the anger that Jacob had to endure when he learned that they were of different blood.

"I did not conform to the standards of our people. For years I have traveled this planet and many others. I have counted the stars and called them by name in my loneliest moments. I have waited patiently and taken my punishment. I did not give full vent to my anger." He paused to take shallow breaths. "Remember, *brother*, there have been moments during our life in which you were no better than a heathen. Should I remind you of them? Still, I did not shun you as you have shunned me."

"We have both changed over the years." Jacob took a new tone now as he began to evoke the compassion instilled in him by their Mother.

"All of the physical pain the humans lay on each other," Abraham was gritting his teeth and attempting to sit up, using his elbow for support. "It barely compares to the way you've lorded over me these years. You are no better than I. This world did not corrupt me but you have come close."

Jacob was scowling. Mulling over Abraham's every word. "We have some things to discuss. I'll have to go ask the Elders and tell them of your current situation."

"Bring me home. Bring me Nova. Or let me die here and now." His eyes fluttered and his head fell back. "Brother," escaped his lips in a hushed plea.

*

Abraham woke to bright light. He blinked and took a deep breath that didn't ache terribly. He knew that he was healed. He was in the city again, he could tell by the clean taste of the air. There was no wisp of evergreen or the tang of fresh soil when he breathed. While Abraham had visited many planets, he never missed the aroma like he missed Earth's right now. Abraham sat up and swung his legs over the side of the bed.

The room was just like any other in the floating city; pristine white, panoramic windows and simple furniture.

This is home. This was home. The home of his childhood. But he'd changed and he wasn't sure he belonged in this place any longer. It felt foreign. It brought sadness, longing, a void from childhood that would never be the same. Everything had changed.

"Home is not a place, it's a feeling." Mother settled her hand on Abraham's shoulder.

"Are ye telling me I am no longer welcome amongst my people? I am no longer allowed to return to my home?"

She smiled softly. "I can tell you that although this place looks like home, that it reminds you of your childhood and safety. it has not been your home for some time now, son."

Abraham knew she was right. He'd come to the conclusion only moments before and he was sure she'd been watching him from the shadows. Just as she'd always done. Just as every mother does. They watch and provide comfort and direction when needed. It is their way. And he'd loved her for that comfort as a child but now was different. Now he wasn't a baby or a toddler, he was a grown man who'd learned many things over the years. He had been without her for so many years since his banishment. Yet, he was still unsure of where he was meant to be within the Seven Sacred Galaxies.

"Be still," Mother spoke with a soft tone. "Your mind races just as it always has." She offered him warm tea from the nearby countertop.

"Aye," Abraham took the mug. "To be still is a challenge these days. I've been on the run for so long." Abraham shook his head to clear his mind. "What became of Silas's people in the settlement?"

"They came to us. Few were chosen. Others weren't." She looked away, her eyes watery with emotion. "There were many children."

Abraham remembered she'd always been like this. Never one to relish the loss of life, wishing she could spare them all, even though her people traveled the Seven Sacred Galaxies to bring peace and cleanse evil and violence away. Abraham began to realize that while he disagreed with certain ways of their people, so did his Mother. Life was precious to her, even if it wasn't to the Elders.

"We are more alike than you think, but you had the courage to fight the Elders. To fight me." She turned to him and wiped her face with a piece of cloth that she always kept in her sleeve, for her tears or the tears of her children. "And all this time I couldn't turn away from the one thing that brought me happiness: to be a Mother. To protect our ways. I'm sorry I couldn't give up the way of my people for you. But then you've known you were different from us for a long time. I couldn't change that. If you want peace in any world you have to learn to say nothing, the same goes for families and our people."

"Where are Nova and Joy?" Abraham asked.

"They're resting. You'll see them soon."

She offered him food and Abraham ate dishes that brought forth memories of his childhood here. Crispy animal fats and baked vegetables from the far reaches of the galaxies, harvested from lands he was sure he'd never see again.

Mother spoke of her other children. The ones Abraham remembered and new ones. He wanted to hate her but found that he couldn't, he found the sound of her voice too soothing and the smell of her far too reminiscent of fond memories.

She cleaned the dishes—soap and water bubbling over her long fingers. Mother made such a mundane task look majestic. After, she offered him a change of clothes; formal robes with stiff pleats and angular stitching. The fabric was dark gray and purple, and the thread contrasting white. The last soul to offer him clean clothing was Nova. It had been so long.

"Go change," Mother urged. "They're waiting to meet you."

Abraham went to the bathroom where he showered and shaved. He trimmed the long pieces of his hair until he began to recognize the man in the mirror. It was when he dressed, that he was different again. He swung the door open and walked the bright hallway to the main living space where she was waiting.

"After everything, I still gave ye a child. So many children even if they were not of my loins." He wanted to make sure she knew that this didn't change anything, he would still never offer up his firstborn to her. It didn't matter if she fed him, or soothed him, or dressed him in clean clothing, he wouldn't do it. Just like he'd promised the Elders.

Mother turned with a placid expression. "They weren't yours to give."

"Ye've had them here. And wee Joy, she may not be mine but I have loved her as though she were." Abraham held his hand over his chest. It wasn't just Joy, it was Nova too. "I once wanted so badly to return to this city, to live amongst my people, to walk proudly amongst the streets I'd changed."

His Mother stood still and placed a hand on his arm. "Hush now, son." She spread her arm toward the window and Abraham could see the farmhouse he'd shared with Nova and the blue haziness of the mountain range behind it.

"You moved the city?" he asked.

"Just for a little bit. Just until you decide what you really want." She winked at him and it brought back a flood of memories of her gentle mannerisms that brought him comfort as a child. "I think I already know. This is your home."

"Aye." His eyes were burning with emotion. She'd known, all this time.

"Come now," she beckoned. "The others are waiting for you."

She took Abraham out of the apartment. They walked down an open hallway until they reached a glass elevator. Once inside she pressed a button and they descended to the streets of the floating city. The sidewalks were decorated with etchings. Ornamental grasses and flowering plants from hundreds of planets flourished all around them. Abraham recognized the faces of species whose planets he'd culled, those who were too young or too damaged to return. They'd been offered asylum in the floating city. Some acknowledged him as they passed, others whispered in excitement at seeing him. His Mother smiled proudly.

They came to a silver building coated with sheens of blue and purple. They went inside.

April was standing near the door with a group of teenagers. She ran to him when he entered the building.

"Abraham!" She embraced him. "I've been waiting so long to see you."

He patted her back and held her at arms-length. "Aye, it's good to see you. Yer looking much better."

"I am. I just love it here." Her face was flushed and full. "I never got to say thank you." She hugged him again.

"You're welcome," he whispered.

April smiled as she stepped away. "The others want to see you."

Abraham walked further into the room. He recognized Abigail in the corner of the room, wrapped around a young lieutenant. She waved and smiled at him.

The room parted and Abraham recognized Jacob standing at the edge of the crowd, waiting for him.

"Brother," he took Abraham's hand. "I must introduce you." Jacob swept his arm to a woman standing at his side, someone he recognized from their childhood. "This is my partner, Shirilee."

"Aye," Abraham greeted her. "I recognized ye from our schooling. Congratulations."

Shirilee smiled wide. "Congratulations to yourself as well."

Before Abraham could ask what the congratulations were for he heard a familiar voice call his name.

"Abraham? Is that finally you?" Nova's voice broke through.

He turned.

She looked the same; dark hair and almond-shaped eyes, her skin a bit pale since she hadn't been out in the sun for a few days. She was holding Joy.

"Aye," he said with a broad smile. Abraham had never been happier in his life to see two people. He gripped them both tight and when he finally released them he noticed Joy's foot was no longer twisted. Nova set her down and she walked until she reached his shin then held on tight. Abraham bent to lift her.

"Mister," Lily approached him standing on her own two legs and no longer skin and bones. Her eyes were still hallowed though and he remembered his Mother said she suffered from great sadness. "I was told I could go back with you."

"Go where?" Abraham asked.

"Home," Nova smiled. "They're going to let us go home."

"Chee Chee!" Joy shouted as she reached for Abraham to hold her.

CHAPTER THIRTY-FIVE

Abraham

The farmhouse was the same. The goats had never left and Jacob helped them wrangle up a flock of chickens from abandoned farms across the Blue Ridge.

"Promise you'll visit," Abraham asked of his brother.

Jacob nodded. "I promise," he said as he tapped his two fingers to his chest. Jacob had changed, his brother was his brother again. Abraham wasn't sure what caused it, maybe his confessions, maybe Jacob saw that deep down they really weren't that different after all. Abraham didn't know for sure but he was happy for it.

*

Lily was reading an old Seventeen magazine she'd gotten from the Wal-Mart. She kept glancing in a pocket mirror.

"Stop that," Nova warned. "These days are different than those days were."

"Do you think I'm pretty?" Lily asked as Abraham rocked Joy.

The chair came to an abrupt stop with a squeak. "Aye, well they say humans don't get to be as beautiful as you are without a story. So I'd think ye are a bit more than pretty."

Joy made a face as she looked at Abraham.

Lily's nose wrinkled. "But you are human."

Nova was there. Her hand on his shoulder. She bent and whispered in his ear, "All this time, you've always been human. You forget so easily."

Abraham nodded. "Aye. I guess I am."

"We all are," Lily said. "All those people and creatures in the floating city left. It's just humans now."

"Aye." Abraham nodded.

"Ayeeee!" Joy shouted as she kicked her feet. "Chee Chee," she huffed as a hen approached the porch. She rose up on her tip-toes.

The sun had set moments ago and the land around them began to glimmer and luminated soft hues of blue and green. This was everyone's favorite part of the evening, when it was absolutely clear that their world was more different than ever before.

The gentle hum of a harmonica broke through the night. It was a tune Romeo played often.

"Did ye tell him?" Abraham asked.

"Yes, I did." Nova was still for the first time since he'd met her, a calm had taken over her now that she knew all was well. "He needed to know. She needed to know." Nova nodded.

"Aye," Abraham agreed as his hand settled on Nova's stomach.

CHAPTER THIRTY-SIX

Romeo

I wish someone had told me the planet was going to glow after the Heat Wave. So few survive and none of us knew. I guess some of us were simply born with one foot in another world. A world where violence was truth and pain was life. A world where deception was the key to survival.

I pull out my harmonica, a lovely SEYDEL that Abraham picked up two towns over to replace the Fender I lost in Nova's rescue. There are no whirrs of A/C units here in the mountains, no peepers or crickets to sing along with me. There is just silence except when I play. The simple vibration is enough to light up the bioluminescent algae surrounding me. I play a light tune knowing that Nova and Abraham will hear since they are just down the road.

It seems my search for her was the only thing that kept me sane even when I was sure it was driving me crazy. Deep down I must've known about the baby, somehow it had to be the drive that kept me searching for her. I think I'll teach her to play, but something new like Billy Joel or Zeppelin or Bob Dylan.

Until then, I play to a silent night where there are no screams, no rapid gunfire, and no one is killing each other. There is simply peace.

Special Thanks

███████████████████████

Thank you for reading The Man Who Fell to
Earth. This book was a lot of fun to write. It was
an idea that started out one way and-two years
later-wound up going in a completely different
direction. This novel is based on my short story
The Safest City on Earth (which is free on Kindle
and many other platforms). If you loved this
book please leave a review on Amazon.com, tell
a friend, or lend your Book to someone who
might enjoy it as well.

ABOUT THE AUTHOR

M. R. Pritchard is a two-time Kindle Scout winning
author and her short story "Glitch" has been featured in
the 2017 winter edition of THE FIRST LINE literary
journal. She holds degrees in Biochemistry and Nursing.
She is a northern New Yorker transplanted to the Gulf
Coast of Florida who enjoys coffee, cloudy days, and
reading on the lanai.

To receive updates on new releases sign up for her
newsletter at http://eepurl.com/TXnkL

Visit her website MRPritchard.com or her blog
http://secretlifeofatownie.blogspot.com/ where she
writes about all things books.

★ Connect with me ★

amazon.com/author/mrpritchard

http://mrpritchard.com/

secretlifeofatownie.blogspot.com

facebook.com/MRPritchard

pinterest.com/mp30/boards/

@M_R_Pritchard

OTHER BOOKS BY
M. R. PRITCHARD

The Sparrow Man Series:
Sparrow Man
Nightingale Girl (2016 Kindle Scout winning Title)
Scarecrow (2017)

Let Her Go (2015 Kindle Scout winning title)

Forgotten Princess (Forgotten Princess Series)
Treasured Princess (Forgotten Princess Series)

Collector of Space Junk and Rebellious Dreams

The Complete Phoenix Project Series:
The Phoenix Project
The Reformation
Revelation
Inception
Origins
Resurrection

Other stand-alone works:
Asteroid Riders: Breaking Hearts and Making Moons
MUSE
The Safest City on Earth

CPSIA information can be obtained
at www.ICGtesting.com
Printed in the USA
FSHW010503030221
78295FS

9 781099 599866